TO LUMINOUS

A KINDRED

MULTI-DIMENSIONAL ANGEL

Blue Sun, Red Sun

A Story of Ancient Prophecy Unfolding in the Modern World

As Told By
Jack Allis

LOVE + BLESSINGS,

ISBN:
ISBN-13: 978-1548712822
ISBN-10: 1548712825

TABLE OF CONTENTS

Jack Allis

INTRODUCTION

Why read *Blue Sun, Red Sun?* Who would want to read a book written by me? That is with the exception of those who are familiar with my other books and DVD's, and who know what they're in for. Every author should ask themselves that question every time they write something, and know the answer. And hopefully the answer changes each time because the author is learning and evolving, as we all must if we choose the spiritual path. If an author isn't marveling at the process of their own ongoing personal change, then perhaps they shouldn't be trusted. I write to both teach and entertain. Learning can be fun. What is it exactly I bring to the table, or to the circle, to use the vernacular of my world? And if I could invent the perfect reader for *Blue Sun, Red Sun,* who would that be? Could it be you?

I am an old man now. Though I'm a white man, it would be fair to call me an elder. An elder is an old man or woman who has followed the spiritual path, and learned much. For over five years now, I have lived in the woods in remote mountains, far from the tentacles of our old paradigm civilization. I am off the grid, with spring water running from the tap and solar power. I have a garden in the summer and I split a lot of wood for the wood stove in the winter. I live at the top of one mile long dirt road, and you cannot make it to my house in the winter without four-wheel drive and lots of clearance. The closest small town is over an hour away by car. I chose not to have TV up here, and I don't even have a phone that works up here. I do have a satellite dish and get an Internet signal, with an online telephone connection. That's really my last connection with the world out there.

My mission is to live sustainably in harmony with nature, and to learn as much about this as possible. This is one of the primary things humanity has forgotten, which is responsible for its demise. When the collapse of our old paradigm civilization arrives in full, which I believe is inevitable, I am as prepared as I know how to be. If one is prepared, the chances to survive up here are far greater. In that event, circumstances will force me to figure out what I haven't already. That's always how it's worked for me on the spiritual path. Even in hard times, spirit always seems to take good care of me, particularly in hard times I should say. I am limited in how much I can do because my body is breaking down. I need a crutch to walk. But I am dedicated to doing as much as I possibly can. I have decided this is the proper way to live, the only way to live. There is no turning back.

In fact, it is accurate to say I have become a character from my books. And my current life is a manifestation or crystallization of the vision that was presented in those books. My life and my art are overlapping so much that I can't tell the difference between them anymore. And that is an achievement that I am extremely proud of. My books weren't just a lot of hot air. They were brought to life. They weren't just a head trip.

This too is my goal with *Blue Sun, Red Sun,* which takes place in the not so distant future. The setting is a small sustainable community of 15 people, Rainbow Village, in the remote mountains of the fictional state of Coronado in the United States of Columbia. My goal is to present a vision of what such a community would look like. This is a community that is achieving its mission. It is entirely self-sustaining. The people are healthy and happy and they love each other. And they're not just pretending. And they see themselves as a base from which a new world can be created from the ashes of the old. Seem too good to be true? Maybe it is. This achievement could not be done by just any group of 15 people. Rainbow Village is the convergence of extraordinary people, drawn together by incredible forces and circumstances, forces and circumstances that could only be described as supernatural, much of which is portrayed and described in my earlier books. *Blue Sun, Red Sun* tells the story of how all this comes about and how such a thing can actually work. We must pray that this vision too manifests into reality.

And before I go any farther, I must be very clear about a few other things. Rainbow Village is a fiction. It does not exist. It is not to be confused with my current situation or anything I am currently involved in. It is a vision of something that could be and how it comes to be. It is something to strive for, both personally and collectively, if we are to survive these challenging times. I also made the decision to fictionalize the entire setting of the book, rather than have it take place in some known location in the United States of America. I simply did this to avoid any possible trouble or lawsuit or some such thing. The vast majority of people in the old paradigm world would probably see *Blue Sun, Red Sun* as seditious, all of my work for that matter, and they might not want to be associated with it. But make no mistake about it. The United States of Columbia is the United States of America – enough said.

Yes, much of what I say in this book could be considered seditious. And I don't have a problem with that. I am not a big fan of the current system, which is simply an illusion, covertly created by a small elite group of people or beings at the top of the pyramid of power, for the purpose of keeping the people of the world brainwashed and enslaved. This is *The Matrix*. I am actually of the belief that the existence of the current system is one of the biggest obstacles to creating a new world to replace it. It's too decadent and sinister to try to reform. The whole thing's got to go, and the sooner it topples the better. This gives fresh uncontaminated turf from which to build. I realize this means pain and misfortune for most of those who remained loyal or sold out, depending on how you see it. But there's nothing that can be done about this. This is a problem with free will. Bad choices lead to unfortunate consequences, even if you didn't know what you were doing because you were tricked. And that's a good reason to read this book. I fell for the trick early in my life, and about 20 years ago I woke up to how the world really worked. The characters in *Blue Sun, Red Sun* don't fall for the trick, and they show how.

The only sin I'm guilty of is free speech. I don't advocate blowing up buildings or killing people. The old paradigm system will fall of its own weight. It doesn't need my help. It must because it is so energetically imbalanced and contrary to the laws of nature. Such systems cannot survive. And the best way to contribute to the downfall of this system is to simply pull out, stop playing the game, stop allowing yourself to be tricked into believing that you need them to take care of you and start taking care of yourself again, stop giving it your energy. If enough people did this, it would work like a magic charm.

My last two books and DVD's dealt with the topic of Winter Solstice 2012 and the shift of the ages, and what humanity is called upon to do at this momentous time of transformation. It's important I comment on this, and where it fits into everything else here. 2012 and the shift continues to be a very poorly understood subject. Since December 21 2012 has come and gone, and we're all still here, there are those who believe it was just another in a long line of false hysterical prophesies and a lot of excitement over nothing. I can assure you that for many of us that was hardly the case. I also think sharing my personal experience of 2012 and the shift is a beautiful illustration of how these kinds of forces work.

Like I said, I wrote two books and created two DVD's on the shift. I interviewed Gregg Braden on this topic for a tele-seminar in 2004. He was a foremost pioneer in this area, at least in the white New Age culture. That was my first exposure to the topic, and it instantly resonated with my spirit. I started doing my own research, and it was during this time that I discovered *Last Cry – Native American Prophesies & Tales of the End Times* (Trafford Press; 2004) by Robert Ghost Wolf, which was also hugely influential. I will say more about Ghost Wolf in a little bit. In 2005 I started writing *Infinity's Flower – A Tale of 2012 & the Great Shift of the Ages.* This was released in 2007. Then, for the next five years, in addition to another book and the two DVD's, I traveled the country and did radio and TV interviews on 2012 and the shift. What is its true meaning? And what are we humans called upon to do, if anything?

In 2009 I met Tat Erick Gonzalez, an Aj Q'ij, or wisdom keeper in the tradition of the ancient Maya. I attended many of the ceremonial events that he led, and listened to many of the verbal teachings he passed along. Other than books, this was my first direct experience of any indigenous tradition. I had been teetering on the brink of this world for several years anyway. My own spiritual journey had brought me to the essential importance of prayer, ceremony and ceremonial fires. I already had an altar, with my power objects from this journey, and I had already become a singer of ceremonial songs. In both my novels there were indigenous elders and wisdom keepers, who were heroic figures. Erick's teachings embellished all this and helped to kick it, and me, to higher levels. To the ancient Maya Winter Solstice 2012, or

Oxlajuj B'aqtun as they called it, was also a date of the highest cosmic significance. As I understand it from Tat Erick's teachings, at sunrise on 12/21/12 a beam of light shot through the alignment of the Sun, the Earth and Galactic Center, and this marked the birth of the world of the Sixth Sun, which is an age spanning 26,000 years.

I say all this to point out that if anybody was prepped and aligned for the energies of 12/21/12, it was me. I was living in Mount Shasta at the time. I was in ceremony for three full days. Two ceremonial candles burned the entire time. On the evening of the Solstice I led a candlelight ceremonial event in the town of Mount Shasta. I had a good turnout, in spite of the fact that Mount Shasta was in the midst of a storm dropping about five feet of snow over three days. That was over five years ago now, and that was also the last public appearance I made.

The message I transmitted about the shift was very simple and to the point. I never suggested that there would be an Earth shattering big-bang event on 12/21/12 that was going to be the end of the world as we know it. I advised that people not concern themselves with specific dates, but rather recognize that we are in age of potentially profound transformation, which is more of a process, taking place over time. There will most certainly be big-bang events along the way, some of which might be big enough to speed up the process. There already have been. And when we talk about worlds coming to an end as part of this process of change, one of the worlds we're talking about is our old paradigm civilized world, based as it is on destroying the very environment that is humankind's lifeblood. It's time is up. We don't know when exactly, only that it will be during this age. It could be tomorrow. It could be 50 years from now. But we're getting close.

And what is it humanity's called upon to do? Well, that depends upon whether humanity wants to participate in this process of transformation or not. For those who don't, they are entitled to their choices, but they are making the decision to go down with a sinking ship. For those who do want to connect with the transformative energies of these times, the answer here again is very simple. There is only one way to do this, and that is with the power of our spirituality. Spirituality is defined here as living in such a way that you are connected with the world of the spirit.

And the emphasis here is on living, where spirituality becomes our lifestyle. It is what we do. Spirit can be found outside this material world in higher dimensions, and it can also be found in the world of nature, which includes the world of our physical bodies. It is our duty as multi-dimensional spiritual beings to live in harmony with spirit and to live in harmony with nature. If we are to create a new world, this must be its foundation. There is no other way. We must learn how to live sustainably again. That is the most spiritual thing we can do.

But that's not all. There is another essential part to this. In order for us to make these changes it's necessary for us to change the nature of our relationship with the old paradigm civilized world. As I've alluded to a few times, this relationship is nothing more than a clever pact with the devil, which we are tricked into giving our consent to at a very young age, before we know any better, and before we have any awareness of what we are dealing with. We barter away our freedom and our spirit in return for being taken care of from cradle to grave by government institutions. We consent to being paid off. This is not the path of the spirit. It is actually detrimental to that. A cornerstone of our spirituality is our declaration that we are free children of the universe. That is where our allegiance lies, not some human institution that is not of our making.

The old paradigm civilized world is a conspiracy. And in moral terms it is evil. I know those are strong words, but if you look up the definitions, you'll see that they fit. The foundation of the old paradigm is deceit and manipulation that's been going on since the beginning of our recorded history, and far longer when you begin to uncover the real history of planet Earth. This has gone on entirely behind the scenes, and in the modern world with the help of its primary propaganda arm, the mainstream electronic media. The purpose is to deceive the people of the world into believing they are free, when in fact they are slaves. This is carried out by a tiny group of people or beings at the top of the pyramid of power, who operate behind this curtain of secrecy. It is reasonable to assume that this elite is also connected with extraterrestrials, quite possibly through interbreeding, which has also been going on since the beginning.

There is only one way to change our relationship with this old paradigm world. This is to detach ourselves from it. We must pull out of this world and begin to strive to take back responsibility for own lives again, both individually and collectively. We must revoke the pact we made, and reassume the sovereignty of our lives. I realize this is very difficult for most, and this is a point where so many get stuck. Yet even for those who believe they are hopelessly stuck in the old paradigm, there are steps you can take to begin to prepare.

Probably the most important step is to become aware of how the world really works. Even if the truth is ugly and dark, as it is here, truth is never a bad thing, and it is so true that the truth can set us free. It is an essential first step. Once we are awake, we can always start to do the little things to begin reassuming responsibility. We can change our diets and begin to eat natural food, rather than the highly toxic, genetically engineered food the old paradigm foists upon us. We can start to go to alternative and natural healers, instead of the medical doctors who are in the pockets of the pharmaceutical cartel. We can pull our kids out of public school and school them at home, which is our god-given right. There are so many little things we can do to prepare. And if you make a commitment to this, the old paradigm will become increasingly repugnant, and when that day comes to make that leap into the unknown, it won't be so hard.

If you still have a soft spot in your heart for the old paradigm, then this book probably is not for you. If you struggle with the idea of a deep and sinister conspiracy, then this book probably isn't for you. If you want to learn more about these things, then this book might be for you. In fact, the deeper you go down this rabbit hole of truth the more nefarious it becomes. Again, many people struggle with this. They just don't want to hear it. This is particularly true of many of the well-intended folks in the New Age scene, and I'm talking about extremely intelligent people, at least in a book sense. This was a hard lesson for me personally to learn because when I started writing books, I thought this would be my best market. But many of the New Agers don't care for this aspect of the message in my books because they see it as negative. And this is something they resist, even if it's a fact, the truth. Their number one priority seems to be reframing everything into a positive. I hear them say things like there is no such thing as evil, and the evil people perceive is a projection of their own dark side, and when we talk about evil we empower it, things like that, makes me nuts.

Positive thinking is a wonderful thing, and I believe in it. I use it in my own life. As I understand it, positive thinking does not include being blind to the truth. There is a lot of evil in the world, and we all should have a plan for how we intend to overcome it. If a person's positive reframing prevents them from seeing this, then they are blind. Chemtrails are a perfect example. When I discuss chemtrails with many of the New Agers, I can see their eyes start to spin around in their heads because they really don't want to deal with it. If what I'm saying is true, there's no way it can be positively reframed. An evil is being perpetrated upon humanity, without their consent, and there's no way this can be turned into something else. And it's not going to go away as a function of not talking about it, thinking about it, seeing it, or spinning it into something it isn't.

So, what does the shift and these transformative times call upon us to do? Simply stated, we are called upon to work on our spirituality and place it as the top priority in our life. And we are called upon to wake up to the truth about how our world really works, and how we've been jerked around, disconnecting us from our spiritual path. In order to fit everything together here, there is one other important aspect to 2012 and the shift that needs to mentioned. At the time of this writing, it's been over five years since 12/21/12. There was no big-bang event. The old paradigm continues to slog along, doing its death march. But this doesn't mean nothing happened, and it doesn't mean nothing is currently happening. It doesn't mean nothing is going to happen. Nothing has changed. That beam of light shot through that portal, and the world of the Fifth Sun (or Sixth Sun in the Mayan system) was born. We are still in the midst of the process of the transformative energies of this shift from one world to the next. The spiritual opportunity continues to be great, to connect with these transformative energies, to transform ourselves, and thus to play our part in transforming the world.

For some of you this still might seem mysterious. It's a lot of pretty words, but how does all this happen in the real world?

What does it look like? There's a reason to read on, to read this book. Rainbow Village is a vision of how to get this done, both spiritually and practically. *Blue Sun, Red Sun* is also a vision of how we can prevail in a challenge against apparently insurmountable odds, David against the mighty Goliath. This is a story of one possible scenario and the diabolical scheme of the existing power elite to keep control of this sinking ship. They seem to hold all the cards, but they have an Achilles heel. Can it be exposed?

I also want to take this opportunity to use my own life as an illustration of how these forces work. For those who say nothing happened with 2012 and the shift, here is an illustration of something monumentally huge that did happen to one person, me, and similar things happened to countless others around the world. Like I said earlier, if anybody was aligned to the energies of 12/21/12, it was me. This had become my life. And there's more that I haven't talked about yet. Over Summer Solstice 2012, I participated in a 13-day ceremonial event led by Tat Erick. We camped on the same sacred land to which I have since moved. It was called the *9-Fires,* and it was a very ancient, sacred and closely guarded Mayan ceremonial teaching. It required six months of extensive preparations, which included gathering herbs and the other ceremonial materials for the fires, making our own personal pipe for smoking, obtaining flints and strikers and learning how to start fires naturally, and much more. It was like having a full-time six month job.

Then in August 2012 I was invited to live on this sacred land. I gave myself one month to make this life-altering decision, from which there would be no turning back. I had just enough money saved to make the move, with all of the preparations, and with a little left over to subsist for a few years. It was definitely a leap into the unknown, but my life has been a series of these, so I'm getting used to it. If I was going to live longer than another five years, I was going to need another miracle or two. But I've had a series of those along the way too. The Divine Spirit always seems to come through for me. And that's because I've kept my part of the deal, staying true to the path.

The decision made itself. It was effortless. This was a huge risk that I simply had to take. The universe was inviting me to become a character in one of my own books. The vision I had presented was crystallizing into physical form before my eyes. When the Divine Spirit guides this clearly, you simply must follow. There is no saying no. This is what it means to always trust the spiritual path you are on, even if it gets a little treacherous. In October the decision was made to move up the mountain, and for the next three plus months I made the preparations and did the work. In mid-January 2013 I kissed the old paradigm goodbye and made the move.

This was a paradigm shift for me. It was a dimensional shift, from a lower frequency world to a higher frequency world. During the entire process of making the decision I was fully aware of the correlation between what I was experiencing and the transformational energies of 2012 and the shift. That was one of reasons I couldn't say no to it. This was precisely what I had been writing and talking about in my books, DVD's and public appearances. It was the precise meaning of the shift, moving from an old world that is dying to a new world that is being born. And all of this was happening to somebody, me, who had totally absorbed themselves in the transformational energies of 12/21/12 for over seven years. Hardly an accident, wouldn't you agree? And though all this happened over several months, it was a big-bang in my life.

I owe a huge debt of gratitude to Robert Ghost Wolf for the inspiration for the backdrop of *Blue Sun, Red Sun.* Ghost Wolf was an emissary in the 1980's and 90's to a group of traditional Hopi Elders as well as elders and members from many other indigenous traditions. After the Gregg Braden interview in 2004, I was reaching out to the universe for more information on the shift, and somebody emailed me an inspiring and prophetic story that Ghost Wolf printed in his book *Last Cry – Native American Prophesies & Tales of the End Times* (page 78). It was an ancient story from Hopi Prophesy, which told of the coming of the Blue Star Kachina and the Red Star Kachina as signs that the time of the great transformation was upon us. It was verbally passed down to Ghost Wolf by Chief Dan Evehema, a Traditional Hopi Caretaker, probably during a ceremony of some kind. This is how much of the knowledge is shared in all the indigenous traditions and saved for the generations to come.

This story is reprinted in the Appendix to this book. Before you read *Blue Sun, Red Sun,* you must read this story. And please note as you read the two fundamental aspects of this story. One is the complete devastation of Planet Earth that is foretold, both by the human forces of the western civilized world, as well as by the natural forces of Mother Nature, who will strike back to rebalance her energies. But this is also a positive story that tells us repeatedly how humanity can prevail, both as individuals and as communities. Remember that the Hopi believed that we are currently at the end of the Fourth World, with the world already having been destroyed three times. On each occasion it was the result of the same thing, the vast majority of humanity having lost their connection with spirit and their connection with nature's ways. And on each occasion a tiny core of humanity, in this case Hopi, survived to build the next world. These were the ones who followed the original teachings, and who served Mother Nature and the web of life. Please refer to *Book of the Hopi* by Frank Waters (Penguin Press: 1963) for more on ancient Hopi history as passed down by the elders. Strikingly similar creation stories can be found in indigenous traditions around the Earth. And precisely the same recipe applies today. It's the message of the story of the Blue and Red Kachinas. It's the message of *Blue Sun, Red Sun.*

Last Cry was a profound influence on me and still is. Ghost Wolf has been gone for years now, and I never had an opportunity to meet him in person, but I feel as though he was one of the most important teachers in my life. I knew little about him, other than what was in the book. I knew he had gained some notoriety for appearing several times on the Art Bell Radio Show (Coast to Coast AM) in the 90's, with a group of the Hopi Elders he had befriended. I know if you do an Internet search on him, you will probably find some dirt, accusations that he was a fraud, things like that. I don't care about any of that. I don't pay any attention to it. It's so easy for complete idiots to post total crap on the Internet, and then it stays there forever. I'd rather trust my heart. The indigenous teachings in *Last Cry* feel totally authentic to me. They touched my mind, heart and spirit, and they made a difference in my life. The influence of these teachings is an important reason why I'm living where I'm living, doing what I'm doing.

This is what I want your experience of *Blue Sun, Red Sun* to be. I want it to touch you in such a way that you make changes in your life for the betterment of our Mother Earth. And then if I can touch enough of you in this way, an energetic critical mass will be reached that can actually make a difference in the world. That's my dream as a writer. That's my purpose. That's what I pray for every time I sit down to write. Even if it doesn't work, even if nobody reads the book, I still have to do this. I must transmit this message and put it out there. That's my sacred duty.

So, that is what I bring to the circle. And I invite you to join me on this journey.

July 2017

CHAPTER ONE - *The Coming of the Blue Sun*

In the not so distant future….

It all started with the coming of the Blue Sun.

The world changed forever on that day. That too was the day they were waiting for, so many in so many different pockets of the world. For most of them it seemed long overdue. It seemed like they had been waiting forever.

David and Kelly first saw it very early in the morning, probably around 4 AM. It was a cool, hazy winter night. The newish crescent moon had disappeared a long time ago. They were sleeping in the loft of their small cabin, beneath a skylight. It was not unusual for them to wake up at this time in the winter, even earlier. They spent a lot of time watching the moon and the stars in the skylight.

David's eyes popped open first. He was expecting to see a few stars framed in hazy darkness. Instead there was a dim blue light coming from the left side of the window, in the northwest part of the sky. And the whole cabin was filled with this dim blue hue. They lived in the middle of nowhere, and there was no logical explanation for this light coming from where it was.

"Holy Shit!"

He threw the covers off, and crawled over Kelly to get a better look. He rose up on his knees, and looked up through the skylight.

There it was: a huge pale blue orb in the nighttime sky. It was about the size of our yellow sun, maybe slightly smaller.

Kelly was up instantly, mirroring his actions. She was on her knees next to him. They were both naked.

They had both seen and experienced many supernatural and other worldly things in their lives, inter-dimensional journeys, ET's, UFO's. They were not inexperienced in this area.

They watched in silence for a moment. It looked different from the other lights they were accustomed to seeing in the sky, the Sun, the Moon and the stars. It did not shine like the sun or sparkle like a star. The dull light of its blue surface was not solid, but had a speckled quality. It did not look like solid matter, but more fluid, like a cell membrane. It gave the impression of transparency. It looked like the orbs you so commonly see captured in photographs. And its blue light was very distinct, yet dull, not even as bright as a bright full moon. And yet everything was bathed in a blue hue. This light was also apparently not affected by the misty clouds. It penetrated them, and the orb could be seen clearly, which made it look closer, like it was this side of the clouds.

They were both taking deep, meditative breaths.

David spoke first.

"We've got to get outside. Call the others. But let's just sit with this first. Be with it. Reach out to it with our energy. We don't know how long it's going to be there. This might be just for us, but I seriously doubt it."

"I don't think it's a ship," she replied. " And it feels benign to me. It feels like we can trust it. It feels like a spirit guide of some kind, a very big one, needless to say."

She paused, and it popped into her head, a memory that wasn't very far away.

"Remember the Blue Star Kachina from the Hopi Prophesy that Jack shared with us."

In ancient Hopi Prophesy, the appearance of the Blue Star Kachina in the heavens was the sign that the end times were near. End times referred to the end of the Fourth World, and the opportunity to transform to the Fifth World.

David inhaled and exhaled deeply again.

"I'm going to reach out to it with a prayer," he started. "Blue light, blue star, my name is David, and this is Kelly. We are humble servants of this creation, servants of the web of life. Our mission in this world is to live in harmony with nature and with the forces of nature. You have appeared in our heavens on this night, and we reach out to you. We reach out with our energy to connect with your energy. You feel like a very powerful force to us, a very powerful spirit. You also feel like an ancient relative. We reach out to introduce ourselves to you, and if you are a friendly spirit, how we might be of service to you. Aho."

They stayed as they were in the blue hue in meditative silence for several minutes.

The blue sun stayed as it was.

"OK," David started, like he snapped out of a trance. "Let's go outside. See if anything changes. Call the others. Dress warmly. Be prepared to stay out there. Take your bundle. I think a fire ceremony in the meadow is probably what's called for."

Kelly nodded in total agreement. Their minds so commonly worked as one.

It was a chilly night, but there was no snow on the ground. It hadn't snowed much in the mountains of the south-central part of the state of Coronado for several winters now.

They walked outside together in the blue light, which cast faint shadows. They saw the blue sun through the branches of the Oak and Juniper trees. It was as it was before.

As soon as David saw it, he bellowed, "Everybody up! We've got something big going on here! Everybody up!"

Kelly flicked on her headlamp, and went off to ring the dinner bell, which was at the community house. They also used it in emergencies.

David looked across the meadow at Jack's house. The lights were on. Grandpa Jack was an early riser too. Actually, he didn't sleep much these days at all. Next to Jack's house, Chris and Wanda's teepee was also aglow.

The instant David heard the clang of the dinner bell, he saw the lights on Jack's Jeep go on, and it started around the meadow toward the community house.

"Everybody up! Time is of the essence here! Everybody up!"

Red Hawk's teepee then lit up, across the road, at the edge of the meadow, about 100 feet away.

David flicked on his light, and started the short walk on the path through the trees to the community house. In the faint blue light, he really didn't need his headlamp. He flicked it off. In the other direction from the meadow, in a grove of trees next to the rock and mud firewall that surrounded their village, he could see that the lights in Don's house were on. That meant everybody was accounted for.

David arrived at the community house, and he and Kelly waited in silence in the driveway outside, where they had a clear view of the blue sun above their cabin through the trees and the haze.

They could hear Don, his wife Sandy and their two daughters chattering as they approached from behind the house. They clomped up the wooden steps, and around the house on the deck. Don still had his headlamp on.

"This is what we've been waiting for, I have a feeling," Don said.

"I have a feeling," David nodded.

They joined them in the driveway. Everybody hugged. In this community, everybody hugged a lot. Sometimes these hugs were formal, like a handshake or saying good morning. And other times, like this, when they were on the verge of leaping into the unknown, together, the hugs were tighter, lasted longer, and were more heartfelt. They needed this connection. They were nothing without it. And in this community, they took these leaps often.

Red Hawk, his mother and his teenage son approached them down the driveway. They were walking side by side, enveloped in the blue light. Red Hawk had wrapped himself in a beautiful red Lakota blanket, with multi-colored patterns, his arms crossed across his chest. None of them spoke. Words were not necessary. They were walking in reverence.

Jack's jeep rounded the bend of the meadow, and came down the driveway toward them. Chris and Wanda were with him, as always. Jack was in his early 70's, and quite crippled, with a bad hip, a bad back, bad hands, bad eyes, bad everything. He had decided about 30 years ago that he would rather die that go to another mainstream doctor. He was going to live and die the old fashioned way, naturally. Chris was in his mid-twenties, and served as Jack's arms and legs. He had been with him for almost five years now. Wanda was fairly new to the scene. She and Chris were madly in love.

The Jeep arrived at the community house, and turned out the lights. Jack got out on the driver's side, and hobbled and wobbled up to others, leaning on his crutch. Chris and Wanda got out on the other side.

"Is everybody here?" Jack said curtly. There were no hugs here. Jack had his mind on something, and he was all business. He often acted like he was in charge, even though he wasn't. David was. Jack owned the land and most of what was on it, but David had been elected Chief of this tribe.

"Yes, all here," David replied.

David deferred to his elder. He knew Jack had something important to say.

Jack's eyes took in the whole group, and they sparkled in the faint blue light.

"Sorry," he said, grinning. "Good morning."

"Good morning, Jack," they intoned collectively.

Jack took a deep breath, and started rapid fire.

"OK, I've been on the Internet for a couple of hours. I've been up for awhile with this. I first noticed it at about one o'clock. As you can imagine the Internet is in a frenzy, kind of hard to make sense out of anything. I found the major news outlets to be the most intelligible. There are a few things it seems like we know for certain. This thing, this phenomenon, this blue star, is everywhere, everywhere on the planet Earth. This is not just for us, folks. This is really really huge."

Kind of a collective moan rippled through the group, like they were all mumbling, wow.

"OK, another thing is it doesn't seem to rise and set, like the Sun and the Moon. It's there all the time, night or day. As far as I can tell, it appeared last night at around midnight our time. And it appeared everywhere on the planet at that same moment, different times in different places, some day, some night. And I kept hearing over and over again that it was in the northwest part of the sky, just as we can see it is here. I guess that makes sense because most of my sources were in the same range of latitude as us. I guess in the southern hemisphere it would be in the southeast because everything is upside down and that is the equivalent of the northwest. I'm not sure about that."

He stopped, and looked down. He was obviously thinking. Nobody spoke.

"Oh yes, one other thing, this is very cool. There wasn't much on this, kind of ran out of time. But some of the early scientific reports, you know, from the government space agencies, people who analyze objects in outer space, they were saying that this object wasn't behaving like solid matter, or even like a ball of energy for that matter. I don't know the technical language for all this, but their telescopes or their instruments or whatever were having a difficult picking it up. It was like it was there, but it wasn't. They couldn't find it, and they couldn't say where it was. Like they couldn't say it was in between Mars and Jupiter, or it was the same distance from us as our Sun or Moon, or it's at a certain point inside our galaxy. They don't know. They can see it, but they don't know where it is. And it follows from all this they don't know what it is either - a blue sphere, about the size of our Sun, of unknown substance, of indeterminate distance, in the northwest part of the sky."

He scanned the group, person to person.

"You guys remember the story from Hopi Prophesy about the Blue and Red Kachinas? This very well could be what we're dealing with here."

They had all read it, and they all remembered. This was like assigned reading at this community.

"If this is the Blue Star Kachina, can you tell us again what that means, please?" David asked.

"It means that the end-times, or the times of transformation, are near. The Blue Star is like a herald or a warning. It is to be followed by the Red Star, or the Purifier, and then the end-times will be upon us. That's when Mother Earth will begin to fight back with all her fury."

"And we don't know how long we've got, I'll bet," David added.

"Nope. Could be a day, could be a year, could be five years."

And what does all this call upon us to do?" David asked.

He knew the answers to his questions. He asked anyway. He like the way Jack put things. And he was beyond question an expert on these subjects.

Jack beamed, and cackled with laughter, his shoulders bobbing.

"Exactly what we're doing, exactly what our mission is here - to remember the original instructions, and live in harmony with the natural forces and frequencies of this creation and with the world of the spirit. Those who follow the original instructions will survive, and they will be the ones to create the world of the Fifth Sun. Different spiritual systems have different names for all this, but it's all the same thing. This pertains to the whole planet."

He looked deeply into David's eyes.

"And as you know, my brother David, we're as prepared as we'll ever be. We've been preparing for five years. I've been preparing for ten. All we need to do is keep doing what we're doing, every day."

"Thank you, Jack," David nodded.

They had huddled together into a circle. David was in the middle.

"Well," he started, looking around at them. "In this moment, at this time, it seems clear to me what we are called upon to do. We must have a fire ceremony in the meadow. It is necessary that we connect with these energies, with the energies of this blue sun. This feels like a very powerful spirit, like a very friendly spirit. As we all know, the best way to form our relationship with it is through the fire, through our prayers and our songs and our offerings, and raising the frequency of our vibration."

He scanned them all again with his sparkling blue-green eyes.

"Yes, we need to do some sharing. It looks like this is an incredible thing we're on the verge of experiencing, together. But time is of the essence here. Let's wait until we get into the circle. We can share then. Let's get the fire going. So, everybody get your bundles. Dress warmly. We still have a good couple of hours before sunrise. Remember to breathe and pay attention."

He looked at Red Hawk. Red Hawk was like the unofficial co-leader of this tribe. In many ways he was the true leader. David had actually been his apprentice a little over five years ago, when he and Kelly were hiding out in the wilderness of the Lakota reservation. Red Hawk was a shaman in the Lakota tradition. He was trained by his great great grandfather, the legendary Red Cloud, who was a wichasha wakon, which means high priest or medicine man.

"Anything to add, Red Hawk?"

"One thing, quickly, I agree that ceremony is the only thing we should be doing, and we should get moving. But why do they assume it's far away? They don't know what it is, or where it is. Why does it have to be in between Mars and Jupiter, or out in the galaxy someplace? We can all see it clearly and distinctly, in spite of the clouds. Maybe it's just beyond those tree tops out there. Or maybe it's nowhere, at least nowhere in this physical world. OK, let's get moving. Aho."

They all started to disperse.

David looked at Chris.

"Chris, we've got enough wood out there, right?"

Chris was the Firekeeper, a very sacred duty in their community and in indigenous spiritual traditions. Wanda, who had only been there now about six months, was his apprentice. Fire was one of the primary elements of creation, along with the earth, the air and the water. The fire was a grandfather, a guide and a teacher, and a medium to connect with the world of the spirit. Their relationship with the ceremonial fire was one of the most important things in their life. They made all of their ceremonial fires naturally, including the sweatlodges. They didn't use matches, lighters or paper. They used flints and strikers. They caught the sparks on charred cloth that they placed in nests they made out of dried grass, weeds and other natural substances. Regardless of what happened in the outside world, they knew they would always have fire.

"Enough for about 12 hours," Chris replied. "If we need more, we can haul some from the community house. We need to cut again."

"OK, will you two please get it started, and take care of it for us?"

He really didn't need to say this. It was understood. Everybody in the community had duties to perform, and this was one of his. He said it anyway out of politeness and respect. They made a practice out of treating each other this way.

"Of course."

"Thank you."

"I'm going to have to shift where I sit," David whispered to Kelly. We're going to have to shift where we sit."

24

Red Hawk had just been smudged, and he entered the circle. He approached them moving clockwise. David waited for him, as he walked behind them, and took his customary spot on David's left.

David continued to speak in a whisper, so that only Kelly and Red Hawk could hear.

"Red Hawk, if we sit where we always sit, the blue sun will be behind us. That doesn't feel right to me. The blue sun is the reason we're here. I really feel like we should be sitting in between the two lights, the two suns."

Customarily, as chief of this tribe, David's spot was on the west side of the circle, facing directly east, facing the sunrise and moonrise. Kelly always sat to his right. Red Hawk always sat to his left. These were the ceremonial leaders. Jack often sat to Kelly's right, and Red Hawk's mother, Kathy Spotted Deer, often sat to his left, as they did a lot of singing together. But that was not fixed. They did it this way, with the chief facing east, because that's the way it had always been done. That's the way most of the indigenous traditions did it. Red Hawk learned it from the Lakota. David and Kelly learned it from several traditions, including the Maya. With many of these ancient traditions, they decided to go their own way, and not follow them, but not this one.

"I was thinking about that on the way out," Red Hawk nodded. "I agree completely, but this is very powerful medicine. We align ourselves to the sunrise for a reason, and then to realign ourselves to a second sun. That's totally huge. It's like we're adjusting the dial on our energy field."

"But we've got to do it," Kelly said in a hush, as she huddled closer to them. "We're dealing with things we've never dealt with before, forces. We're being forced to make decisions about things we're never even thought about before. There are times when you just have to change. It's unthinkable to do this ceremony without facing the blue sun."

As if sensing something was up, the others hadn't taken their positions yet or started unpacking their bundles. They were standing at the entrance and at the outer edges of the circle.

Grandfather Fire was already burning brightly. David started walking clockwise around the fire, around the circle. As he passed the entrance, he looked up at the blue sun, and he kept his eyes on it as he continued walking. He stopped at a point on the southwest part of the circle, his eyes still on the blue sun. Then he looked back to a point on the ridge where they yellow sun soon would be rising. He lifted up his arm in its direction, as if he was orienting himself. Then he looked back at the blue sun, then back at Kelly and Red Hawk, and he spoke so all could hear.

"It looks like almost a perfect opposition to where the Sun's going to be rising, 180 degrees."

"That's it then," Kelly said with a huge smile. "That's the spot."

She and Red Hawk walked around the circle, always clockwise, and took their spots next to David.

David addressed the group, and explained why they were shifting positions. He also did something else they had never done before. He suggested that everybody position themselves on the same half of the circle as them, so that they could see both suns when the Yellow Sun rose, without moving or turning around. There were only 12 of them, so that was not a problem.

It was starting to get light. There was a mountain ridge above them to the east, and the sun rose very late here. It was still well over an hour away.

The blue sun stayed as it was. It didn't change positions in the sky, and it continued to look down at them like a huge bubble of light blue. The meadow itself, which they named Rainbow Meadow, was high atop a mountain ridge. To the west, the view of the valley below and the mountains beyond was spectacular. Normally, on a dark night like this you couldn't see much. On this night, the mountain tops in the distance and the horizon were bathed in the faint blue hue, as were the surrounding hillsides, the ridge to the east, and all the buildings, barns and domes of their village.

They took their positions around the fire, put down their blankets and tapestries, began unpacking their bundles, and putting all their power objects in their places on their mesas. They always did this in silence. Ceremonies were not the time for socializing. Tonight the silence was absolute.

Each bundle was an expression of that person's spirituality. It was how their spirituality came to life. Music, singing, chanting, and occasional dancing were an essential feature of their ceremonies, and all ceremonies. Almost everybody placed musical instruments on their mesas, a wide variety of drums, flutes, whistles, singing bowls, rattles and shakers. Chris played the didgeridoo. Some of them had small candles burning. Most of them had beautiful bowls with sage, cedar and other medicines in them. Some had conch shells, in which medicines burned, with the smoke drifting up on this calm night. Several of them were pipe carriers and smokers, with their pipes and tobacco and smoking mixture pouches placed in prominent positions. Everybody had power objects, such as stones, crystals, pieces of wood, feathers, bones and horns.

Everything was placed where it was placed for an energetic reason. Each mesa was a careful alignment of powerful forces. Each was that person's vortex or medium to connect with the world of the spirit. Taken together, together with Grandfather Fire, together with their prayers, their offerings and their songs, together with their vibration, they were creating a far greater vortex to connect to the word of the spirit. All together they were like a huge mandala. In this case, it was a medium to connect with the energies of the blue sun. And Grandfather Fire was the center through which all these energies flowed.

Their spirituality was very eclectic. They didn't follow any particular tradition, and their ceremonies didn't follow any set ritual. They were far more loosely structured. David was their ceremonial leader, as well as chief, but he relied upon Kelly and Red Hawk to help with this, and he deferred to them often. They all learned from a variety of traditions. David and Kelly were strongly influenced by the Maya and Red Hawk by the Lakota.

But they shared something in common, along with the other adults in the community, Jack, Spotted Deer and Don, which was one of their primary virtues and strengths, and one of the reasons they were attracted to each other. They all thought for themselves. David learned most of his spirituality from listening to his own heart and his own spirit. And he learned it from his closeness to nature and his harmonious relationship with her. Plus, his human mother, who was murdered when he was four, had been a gifted psychic and spiritual medium. He always believed she shared her gifts with him in a mysterious way. Kelly was precisely the same, minus the exceptional mother. They had been together now for 12 years, and they shared most of their spiritual experiences. Red Hawk got to a point in his spiritual evolution where the rituals of the Lakota ceremonies, which had been the same for hundreds of years, began to feel like a prison to him. And he broke free, precisely as David and Kelly, and started to create his own ceremonies based on how he felt on that day, in that moment.

On this occasion, David's guidance was clear. He didn't ask for help. When everybody was ready, he opened the ceremony by standing up, pointing his wooden flute at the blue sun, and blowing it three times, each time lasting about five seconds, and each time consisting of a low note, followed by a higher note, and returning to the same low note again. The sweet tones reverberated off the hillside behind them. It was the same as he almost always did at sunrise. Then he did something he didn't do very often, but which seemed perfect on this apparently monumental occasion. He asked that they sit in silence for a little while, maybe about a half hour, with each person reaching out to the blue sun, and forming a relationship in their own way, maybe a silent prayer, perhaps an offering, or maybe simply with their meditative vibration of feelings of peacefulness, joy and love. Or perhaps they could simply listen. We usually don't hear unless we first listen.

The blue sun was unchanging. It stayed in the same place in the sky. The new day was dawning, and as it got lighter, the blue hue grew fainter, but it was still there, a new feature of their world. And its shimmery, amoeba-like surface was always distinctly visible. And it continued to be unchanging in relationship to its surroundings. The clouds continued to be mostly hazy, with a lot of thick puffy chemtrails, but there were patches of clear sky, with hints of pale blue. The blue sun never changed. Sometimes it looked far away, and sometimes so close that you could reach out and touch it.

For David, the silence was perfect. Winter nights up there were generally extremely quiet. Their little community really was in the middle of nowhere. That's why they were attracted to it. The nearest road was over a mile away, at the bottom of the mountain. Their nearest human neighbor was over three miles away. They never heard cars or trucks or horns or sirens or trains or any of the other noises so common on the outside. Other than an infrequent helicopter or jet, the only sounds they ever heard were the sounds of nature. On this night, this consisted only of the occasional whirring of night hawks overhead, making a high vibration humming sound that is often mistaken for bears in the distance. And then as it got lighter, they were serenaded by four woodpeckers, one at the edge of each of the four directions of the meadow, whose pecking reverberated around them. And the wind on this night was breathlessly calm, and this in a place that is one of the windiest on the planet Earth. The smoke from Grandfather Fire drifted up in perfect lines, never fluttering.

The firekeepers kept the fire mellow, as they were told. David was mesmerized by the silence, by Grandfather Fire, and by the blue sun. These three elements were all that there was in his world at this moment. That was all he needed. He looked deeply into the flames, and yielded to them. He joined them. And he looked at them with more than his eyes. He looked with his heart and with his spirit, and with the totality of his luminous being. And the fire would talk to him, but rarely in words. The fire spoke the language of the spirit, the language of nature. For most it took years of being with the ceremonial fire to understand what he was saying.

David reached out to the blue sun in the same way. Very few words were necessary. He did use a few, but this was to be a relationship of a different kind. He reached out with his energy to connect, and he also reached out with his energy to receive. If this being was to send any signals or messages, he wanted to be in the proper vibrational state to pick them up. He wanted to be able to understand it, even if it wasn't in the language of words.

How you feel in a relationship like this is also extremely important. The way you feel usually tells you whether the relationship is any good or not. David was tingling with feelings of joy and excitement. This was what he lived for. This was what they lived for. This was what they were on this planet to do. He could feel his joy tingling in the back of this throat and in the tips of his ears, like the energy just wanted to shoot out of his Crown Chakra. His body felt light, like it didn't exist. The only thing that existed was his breath, which flowed in and out like the winds of creation, and which flowed in waves to connect with the breath of the blue sun. And with each breath he opened himself like a flower to receive whatever energy the blue sun sent.

David felt no fear. He had already died too many times for that.

He easily could have just let himself drift off, and disappear into these energies. But he snapped out it. He had alarms built into his psyche that would bring him back to his responsibilities to his tribe. A half hour was up. It was now quite light. Sunrise was about another half hour away.

Kelly was sitting cross-legged on her brightly colored Mayan cushion. Red Hawk had just finished smoking his pipe, and he was on his knees, placing it back on the tapestry of his mesa next to his white leather fringed pouch and a small candle.

David looked back and forth from her to him.

"Guys," he whispered. "This feels perfect to me, this silence, and reaching out in this way. It feels like it has real power. I'd like to keep doing it. Then when the sun rises, I'll blow my horn again, and then I think we should all focus our energies on the two suns and the relationship between them, and between us and them. And we should do this with openness, receptivity. We're here to learn, to be guided."

They agreed, and announced this to the group. They continued as before, silently, each in their own way.

The haze continued, but it wasn't thick enough to dull the Sun's light. The crown of the sun hit the ridge, and the first rays of the day exploded upon them. David pointed his flute at the yellow sun, and blew it as before, three times, and each time a low note into a high note and back into the same low note.

They could all watch the yellow sun rise out the corner of their right eye, with the blue sun in the periphery of their left. As always, it took a couple minutes for the yellow sun to be completely visible. The yellow sun was brilliant and overwhelming, but the blue sun was persistent, unchanging, its outline clearly visible in the bright white sky, its faint blue light distinct.

David was breathing meditatively. The instant the yellow sun was totally visible, the blue sun popped. There was no sound, just a flash like a huge blue flashbulb camera in the sky, sending a wave of blue light into the yellow. Like a flashbulb camera going off in your face, the light was blinding. But this light didn't go away. David's entire field of vision was infused with this yellow light, tinted with blue. All of the objects on his mesa, the earth around them, the trees in the distance, the buildings of their community were all in this field of light. It was like all these objects were losing their materiality, and dissolving into the light.

David looked up, and couldn't see either sun. Everything was bluish yellow light. He then started feeling this light entering his body, and taking him over. It felt like a huge tractor beam taking possession of him. His physical body was there, but it was faint, off in the distance. He was more of an energy body. Everything was energy, pulsating energy. It was like the energy was breathing him. He was at the heart of creation. Everything was perfect. And everything felt perfect. In this moment, there was only one thing David felt, and that was bliss, pure joy at being part of this magnificent creation, of this creative process.

He lost all sense of time.

All he knew was he was possessed by this bluish light, with feelings of bliss, for awhile.

Then he started becoming aware that he was returning, starting to take form again. His breath was now his again, rather than that of the Creator. His materiality was coming back. The outlines of his hands and his body were returning, though they were still bathed in bluish yellow light. The forms of Kelly and Red Hawk next to him were also becoming visible, though they too were still immersed in the light. He felt certain they had been there with him on his journey into the light. He and Kelly had done this so often it was practically assumed. He felt certain Red Hawk was there too. He wasn't as certain about the others.

The light slowly dissipated. David continued to breathe, as his world took shape, and things returned to normal. As his senses returned, the first thing he was aware of was the sound of heavy breathing and sniffling in more than one place. Crying, that's what it was, deep intense sobbing. His eyes came into focus, and he saw that the entire group was in tears. Don and his wife and two daughters were huddled together. Don was holding his 18 year old daughter, Adelle. She was sobbing so deeply her body was convulsing. She had lost all control of herself. But they were clearly tears of joy, effusive, inexpressible, infinite bliss. She couldn't' stop, and didn't want to. Sometimes when spirit touches us, it can hit pretty hard, and knock us for quite a loop.

And this was very contagious. Don's wife Sandy and their 20 year old daughter, Annette, had their arms around each other, and they were crying too. So was Don. And then David noticed the same thing was happening with Wanda. Spirit had clobbered her too. Chris was holding her, as she wailed, her entire body heaving, her breathing like she was in labor. David wondered who started first. He scanned the others in the half-circle, and everybody was in tears, smiling helplessly, as spirit touched them all. No words had been spoken yet, but it was beginning to look like they all had the same experience.

This energy began to sweep over David. He knew he couldn't control it, and didn't want to. He just let it flow. His eyes filled with water, and the corners of his mouth quivered. He and Kelly turned toward each other. Her huge brown eyes were glassy, and she was beaming with an angelic smile. When David saw her, he burst into laughter, his shoulders shuddering. He leaned toward her, and touched his forehead against hers. They gently kissed. Here they were again on the brink of the unknown. What an incredible journey it had been together. The big difference this time is they weren't alone.

David returned to his spot, facing the fire. Then it hit him. Things had been moving so fast that he had forgotten the most important thing. He looked up to his left, to the northwest.

The Blue Sun was still there.

CHAPTER TWO – *The Guardians*

It happened that same day, just an hour or so after they came in from their ceremony.

David and Kelly and a bunch of them were having breakfast in the kitchen of the community house when they heard Jack's voice over the walkie-talkie hanging on the wall. None of them had phones. The signal up there was too weak to be relied upon. Plus, that was a world they had all decided to leave. They didn't have TV either. Their world was very self-contained, and telephones were a distraction none of them needed. Jack had a phone service through the Internet on his computer, and when they needed to telephone the outside world they used that, kind of like the old days.

"Anybody there? More strange news to report."

Don was the closest to it. He pushed the button, and talked into the speaker.

"Yeah, we're here, Jack. What's going on?"

"Is David there?" Jack asked.

"Yo, I'm here, Jack," David bellowed from across the room.

"OK, good. Well, more strange shit going on. I've been hanging out on the Internet, seeing what I can learn, and the weirdest thing happened. They took over the Internet, at least somebody did. My entire screen went blue, and then messages started flashing across the screen, with a voice saying what the messages read. It repeated about five times. The whole thing lasted about a minute. And then everything returned to normal, with the exception of this announcement plastered all over the place. Here's what it says:

> Urgent Notice: there will be an important announcement tonight that affects all the people of the planet Earth. It is imperative that you attend. It will be transmitted at 9:00 PM Eastern Time in the United States of Columbia. It will be transmitted over all forms of available media, over all the channels and frequencies. Please do not be

alarmed. This is not a state of emergency. Everything will be explained tonight. Everything is taken care of. The future has never been brighter.

"And then it's signed, 'the Guardians.' Can you fucking believe that? Who the fuck are the Guardians? They say that like they think we're supposed to know what that means. Anyway, that's it. There's no more information on this anywhere, just this announcement everywhere. You can't go online without seeing it. Same thing with TV and radio, everything is in emergency news mode, and it's posted everywhere. Even the major news outlets are shedding no light on this. Absolutely zero is being leaked. Of course, everybody is assuming it has something to do with the Blue Sun or with something about ET's taking over, or some such thing. But it's all speculation at this point. And as you can imagine, the Internet is going completely berserk. It's pretty close to a state of panic."

Most of them were still recovering from the events of the morning ceremony. Now this. They looked at each other, eyes were vacant, tired. Nobody said anything. The room was numb.

"Anybody there?" Jack could be heard again.

David got out of his chair, and walked across the room. He got to the walkie-talkie, took it off the wall, pressed the button, and spoke into it.

"Yeah, Jack, David here."

He paced back across the room, the receiver to his ear. He took a deep breath, and exhaled audibly with an open mouth.

"I don't know what to make of any of this, Jack. To tell you the truth, my head's spinning. I'm speechless."

"I agree," Jack could be heard again. "This is other-worldly. I'm shitting in my pants too if it makes anybody feel any better."

This brought a few smiles.

"David," Jack went on. "I definitely want you and Kelly and Red Hawk to watch this with me tonight. Everybody's invited, of course, and I think everybody should be here, but you guys for sure. It's at 6:00 our time. I'll make some snacks, and I've got that wonderful fruit juice. I will probably be slamming a couple beers, and anybody's welcome to join me."

Everybody attended. Jack had a large screen TV hooked up to his computer that everybody could see clearly. At precisely 6:00 the screen went blue.

Then an image appeared on the screen. It was the pyramid with the illumined Seeing Eye suspended at its top, which is printed on the United States Federal Reserve Note or Columbian dollar bill. Except this was brightly colored, with a golden aura around a blue eye, in a pale blue sky, with a brown pyramid. The inscription was also included, the same as the dollar bill. This encircled the pyramid, with the words, "Annuit Coeptis" on top, which means Announcing the Birth, and "Novus Ordo Seclorum" on the bottom, which means New World Order.

Simultaneous with the image, printed words appeared on the screen. The first to appear were, "We Are the Guardians."

As soon as the words appeared, a voice said them out load. It was a male voice, very deep in tone, yet soothing and gentle. It was the voice of a benevolent father.

After that, the printed words continued with two to four lines per frame, in large print. And the voice kept saying them in his authoritative yet calming style. The images also changed frequently to match what was said. The theme remained the same. It was mostly esoteric imagery, the kind that is often associated with the Illuminati and the secret brotherhood societies that rule the world behind the scenes. The gods and goddesses and kings and queens of antiquity, from every culture on the planet, were featured, with a heavy dose of the kind of reptilian symbolism that is so prevalent in the ancient cathedrals of Europe and in the crests of aristocratic families. The esoteric symbols of the big banks, the oil corporations and the other huge multi-national corporations were also on display. Also prominently featured were the triumphs and major achievements of modern civilization. Architectural achievements were emphasized, such as skyscrapers, monuments and government buildings in the US and Europe, as well as technological wonders that mimic the gods, such as the DNA double helix and the miracles of computers, both big and small. It was like a promo for how great the world was working.

As David watched, content aside, he couldn't help but marvel at what a beautiful production this was. It was pleasant to look at and to listen to. It was spellbinding.

Here is what it said in full:

We are the Guardians. We welcome you to this broadcast, which will be the most important in the history of the world. We are here tonight to make some very exciting announcements about changes that must be made at this time. So let's begin with the biggest news of all, and this is the announcement of the coming of a new world, a new order, and new more enlightened ways of doing things, of conducting the business of living in this world prosperously, happily and safely. And please keep in mind we are addressing all the people of the world, at the same time, each in their own language. This is how our New World Order will be. All the people of the world will now be one family, under one umbrella, dedicated to the common goal of the greatest good for the greatest number, and reaping and sharing the rewards of this beautiful world of ours. There will be no more separation by borders or by national governments or by systems of money. Everything will be centralized into one common system. We will introduce these changes one step at a time. Tonight is the first step.

We realize this may sound shocking for many you. We deeply regret this. But circumstances in our world dictate that we must take this step at this time. If not, we will be destroyed from within by the ineffectiveness and inefficiency of the old systems. And as we continue here tonight we believe that most of you will be able to clearly see that some very careful plans have been made to ensure the future success and security of all the people of the world. This may seem like a lot at first, but it really isn't. Once you plug yourself into this new carefully designed system, your day to day life isn't going to change that much, only for the better.

And please don't think this is some fly by night plan, made in response to any particular circumstance in our world. This is actually the fulfillment of a plan that has been in place since the beginning of our history, over 6000 years. It is part of the natural cycle of our civilization, and the time has come for us to make the jump in our evolution from an old dying world to a new and completely different one. If we don't, we will drown in the old ways. We have known all these things for a very long time. We have been waiting to take this monumental step for a long time. All the preparations have been made, and all the pieces are in place for us to act now.

You deserve an answer to the question, who are we? For now, we will call ourselves the Guardians. And we will simply say that we have been the authors of all of the events in your world since the beginning of this history. We were the lords and deities of your mythologies. We were the emperors and kings of all the great nations. And recently, when these systems of government were replaced with representative governments, we were the prime ministers and presidents and members of parliament and congressmen. If we weren't actually them, they answered to us. These systems of government were best suited for their times to ensure that societies held together and systems ran as well as possible. These systems have served their purpose. We have reached a great point of culmination in this 6000 year cycle, and these systems are now obsolete, and they must be replaced.

From now on we are also going to begin to operate more directly, like we are here tonight, more out on the open, and yes, more honestly. That is one of the reasons these forms of technology and media were developed to begin with. They were developed to be used on a mass scale for us to be able to communicate with you directly, without the interference of so many intermediaries. Tonight is just the beginning. We'll be communicating in this way frequently in the weeks ahead.

We will be introducing numerous changes in the weeks and months ahead, and we're going to move slowly, one step at a time, so that all of this is easy to do, and not an inconvenience in your lives. Tonight we're going to be beginning with a couple of very basic and long overdue changes with our current systems of paper money. These systems too have become obsolete. These too have served their purpose, and now must be replaced. In the world of money and finances, we too are at the birth of a new cycle. Paper money is no longer consistent with the new paradigm world of business we envision for the people of Earth.

With this in mind, tomorrow, January 17, at 12 o'clock PM Eastern Standard Time, we will issue an edict to the Federal Reserve Bank of the United States of Columbia and to all the national banks of all the other major nations of the world to stop the printing of paper money and the coining of money. We have always had the authority to do this. We have run these banks since the beginning, and created the paper money now in use. This edict will take effect immediately. Then, in 30 days from that time, on February 16, paper money and coin will no longer be deemed acceptable as means of transaction in the new monetary system. And this includes the means used to transfer this old money, including checks and credit and debit cards. Upon reflection, this too is not as big a change as it might first appear. We have been moving in this direction for a while now. Many of you, the sensible ones, hardly use cash anymore anyway.

The new system of exchange will be 100% electronic. It will be administered through a microchip that all people who choose to participate in the new system of exchange will be required to have medically implanted. This is no more complicated than getting your flu shot at the pharmacy. It will be inserted behind the top of the ear. It will not be visible, and even if you look at it up close, it is not much bigger than a big grain of sand. These microchips have long been in use to track criminals and potential criminals, and many of you already use them to track your pets, and some of you your children. In this case, they will be used to store all of your pertinent financial information, in particular your bank balance for making transactions. In person to person transactions, like at the supermarket, the chip can be scanned from several feet away with new state of the art scanning technology, which will readily available to all businesses. Scanning software will also be readily available for the purpose making online transactions. This will be simple, easy to use and inexpensive, and it will be an important part of the new system of exchange. If this seems like space age technology, it is. We've been preparing to unveil this for a long time.

With the introduction of electronic exchange and the elimination of paper money there will come another change that is long overdue. This is the elimination of the different systems of paper money and currency that are used in the different parts of the world. 30 days from now, with the beginning of the new system, there will be no more distinctions between monetary systems, such as dollars, pounds, pesos and yen. All the nations of the world will use the same medium of exchange, and there will be no single reserve currency for international transactions, which the US dollar has been. The new electronic money will be denominated in a new fundamental unit, which we will call the unilect. This will be replacing the dollar, the pound and all the paper denominations currently in use. The value of one unilect will be fixed to the values of all the currencies of the world at the time of the implementation of this new system in one month. The various exchange rates can be determined electronically by the microchip, and everything will then be denominated in unilects.

So if you are one of the wise ones who choose to participate in the new system of exchange, you have 30 days to accomplish three simple things. This will be a 30 day period of transition, in which both systems of money are in place. The first is to receive your microchip implant. They will be available effective immediately at approved hospitals, doctor's offices and pharmacies. They are 100% covered by all medical insurance. The actual procedure takes about a minute. It is no more complicated than piercing an ear lobe and virtually painless. Then it takes a couple more minutes to program the technology, and you're done. The second is to obtain any devices or software you might need to operate in the new system, and receive the education on how to use them. These products and services will be available at approved banks throughout the world, where our representatives will be stationed. We will also be using large worldwide retail technological outlets for this purpose, like Walmart and Costco. These products and services will be available at minimal prices that make them obtainable by all. We are able to obtain the most advanced technology at prices far lower than what is currently on the market. This really is more of a public service. We want each and every one of you to operate successfully in the new system. And the third thing to do is deposit all of your cash and coin in one of our approved banks. One month from tomorrow it will be worthless. And remember, all transactions will be electronic, through the microchip, no exceptions. There will be no more checks or credit cards or debit cards. So make sure you make arrangements with your bank or with people you do regular business with to change these methods of payment to electronic.

That's enough for tonight. Like we said earlier, we are going to be introducing many changes in the days, weeks and months ahead, and we're going to be using these computers and other electronic devices to communicate this with you more directly. We fully realize that for many of you what you've heard tonight raises as many questions as it answers. Again, we want to reassure you that all your questions will be answered in due time. All of this has been carefully thought through, and it is part of a plan that has been in place for a very long time. Our goal for tonight was to give you just enough so that we could accomplish this first step without a hitch.

What you have experienced tonight is the new government. From now on your national governments, your presidents and prime ministers, your representatives and parliamentarians will no longer be in use. They have served their purpose and are no longer needed. This too is not as big a change as it first might seem because they have always answered to us anyway. And please don't fret for these people. They have very handsome retirement packages, and they are well taken care of. All of them have been offered positions in the new system, and many of them will act in that capacity immediately, and help to implement it. As for your local governments, we're going to leave them alone for now. If you choose to keep them running, and if you are successfully able to do so, then that will be up to you. We try to plan as much as possible, but sometimes this is just not possible. We have to let some things run their course, and this is one of those things.

The military and many other government agencies will go unchanged. This mostly applies to the militaries of the powerful civilized nations, and in particular for the United States of Columbia, which is by far the most powerful military in the world. We have been in control of these militaries since the beginning, and this will remain as it is. The one change in this area is from now on this will all be one military, one world army, whose job is to make the world a safe place for the implementation of the New World Order. Most government agencies will remain as they are. They perform necessary public services, and conduct businesses that are essential to the successful operation of the whole system. It's the politicians who have become redundant. The only change with these agencies is they will now serve the new global order, instead of their old national jurisdictions. National security, law enforcement and intelligence agencies will remain unchanged, and will continue to work in coordination with the highest levels of the military, as they have for a long time. And the police will be unchanged at all levels, even down to the local. They have served us well down through history. National and local taxing laws and agencies will also go unchanged.

And please don't try to search for more information about all this. You will be wasting your time. All of the information is in our hands, and we will dispense it when the time is right. All you need to do is the three things we discussed earlier: get your chip, go to your bank and set yourself up in the new system, and deposit all of your cash and coin. Other than that, we expect that you will live your life the way you always do. And when it's time to take the next step, we will contact you with the next round of information. And don't worry about finding it. It will find you. All you have to do is check into your computer or your TV a couple of times a day, which most of you do anyway.

We thank you very much for your attendance here tonight. If you want to listen to this broadcast again, it will be replayed on numerous channels on your cable and satellite servers, and written copies will be easily accessible on the Internet. We look forward to working with you to implement this New World Order, and create the world of the future, where there will be security and prosperity for all. Good night.

The last image was the statue of Prometheus, holding the eternal flame, which is outside the United Nations Building, again one of the Illuminati's favorite symbols for themselves.

Then the screen returned to Jack's computer screen. He clicked it off.

The room was silent. A gentle breeze was stirring in the trees outside.

Everybody was numb. What a day this had been. First, the coming of the Blue Sun, and now this.

David's head was spinning with conflicting emotions. He couldn't deny that he was in a state of shock. It made him feel light-headed, slightly dizzy, and slightly sick to his stomach. With all he'd been through in his life, he thought he got past this years

43

ago. But here it was, dredged up from somewhere deep in his psyche. He was also feeling feelings of exhilaration, which also made him feel light and light headed, but in a transcendent way. It was the way he always felt when he took leaps into the unknown, which he and Kelly had done many times. Now it was time for another. Just imagine, he thought, if he felt this way how some of the others must feel, some of the young ones.

He looked up at the others, and took a deep meditative breath. He looked at the young ones. He looked at Chris and Wanda, who were huddled together on a couch, with their eyes closed. They looked like they might even be sleeping. He looked at Don's daughters, Annette and Adelle, who were sitting on either side of him, with their eyes fixed on David. He looked at Red Hawk's 16 year old son, Erick, who was staring into space resolutely, which was his style. They all looked OK.

David would speak if he had to, but he wasn't ready. Jack relieved him of this.

"May I speak, please, David?" Jack asked formally.

Jack's formality wasn't necessary, but it bespoke the seriousness of this. Now it became an official meeting. Chris and Wanda opened their eyes, and sat up straight in their seats.

David often deferred to him on these kinds of matters anyway. After all, Jack was one of the world's foremost experts. Jack had written and published five books and 4 DVD's, most of which dealt with the international conspiracy, the probable role that extraterrestrial beings play in human affairs, the true meaning of the indigenous prophesies, and spiritual solutions to the apparently hopeless mess humanity found itself in. He was also an eloquent and mesmerizing public speaker, with a knack for speaking with conceptual clarity, which means he could take things that sounded complicated, and make them easy to understand. He came very close to becoming a celebrity in the New Age scene, but in the final count his message was never popular enough to reach a large enough audience. After all, he was telling people to take complete responsibility for their own lives. David loved to listen to him speak. Jack had been taking notes. His tablet and pen rested in his lap.

"Please, Jack, thank you."

Jack inhaled.

"Thank you. First of all, as we all know, as far as the practical aspect of what we've just heard is concerned, there's not much to discuss here. We've been anticipating this, or at least something very similar to this for a long time. We've discussed these things. We've planned for them. Tonight was just a few of the many possibilities we've gone over. This simply marks the next stage of our mission. The only thing that changes is now we have this specific time frame, 30 days. And we're ready to operate without the chip. We don't need their money to do what we're doing. We'll basically just keep doing what we're doing. We also understand that this means we are going to step out of their world, and into a new one of our making, where we depend upon ourselves, and other like-minded souls like us. We also know at some point this will probably make us criminals. But we have decided there's no point in worrying about those things."

He gazed off for a second. Then his eyes popped open, and he shook his head.

"That's the easy part. But there are two other parts to this that really jump out for me. One is the fact that they didn't even mention the appearance of the Blue Sun that rocked the entire world just a few hours ago. 'Under current circumstances,' or something like that, was as close as they came to mentioning it. Now it's pretty god damn obvious this, tonight, has something to do with the Blue Sun."

"But the thing that's really blowing my mind is the way they came out of hiding, the way they came out from behind that curtain that they've been behind for, like they said, 6000 years. And they didn't come out and say it directly, but they were making inferences that made it sound like they weren't from this world. Certainly that's what everybody's going to think, as certainly they should. I didn't see that coming. Man, is that bold, is that brazen! That is like in your face people of planet Earth. And they are rushing their agenda. I don't know maybe they're panicking. At least they were honest about that. They are taking a quantum leap in their agenda, and they are expecting the people of the Earth to take it with them. I don't think most of them can handle it. I don't think most of them will. This could go very badly, and ultimately it could lead to their downfall, which would be the most wonderful blessing of them all."

The entire room was nodding affirmatively. This was the most shocking aspect.

He took a sip of his Lemurian Lager.

"I'm going to miss this when it runs out," he said grinning. Silence again.

"Are you finished?" Kelly asked. "May I speak?"

"Yeah, sorry," Jack replied. "There's more, but let somebody else speak. Aho."

All eyes turned to Kelly.

"Yeah, thank you," she began pensively. "They know what the Blue Sun means, the same as we do. They're totally into the occult. They know about prophesy, and the prophesies about these transformative times span so many cultures and spiritual systems. They know that time is now short, and they know that soon the entire Earth is going to be stressed, even them on their high and mighty perch. This is what forces them to speed up their agenda. They want to get as much of it in place as possible before the big changes come. Because then they won't have control, or at least they don't know how much control they'll have. At least that's how they think. And they're arrogant enough to think that the shift of the ages has to do with them, and the changes they are bringing to the Earth. Somehow it's always all about them. That's why they don't mention the Blue Sun. They don't want to be upstaged. They don't want anybody to think there's something going on here that's not part of their plan."

The meeting ended early. They were all drained and frazzled, and besides, like Jack had said, there wasn't that much to discuss anyway.

Their specific plan was already in place. They reviewed it, and assigned specific tasks. They had numerous trading relationships with neighbors and groups and other communities, like theirs. They needed to contact these, and make personal visits where necessary, to make sure all these agreements and contracts were in place.

The most important thing they had to barter was their precious and sacred spring water. The state of Coronado was in the midst of long-term drought, and many traditional water sources were drying up. Water was scarce and precious. Their land had seven spots where the underground spring water came to the surface, one of which was a real gusher that formed its own creek. This was part of the greater Mount Camille water system. Mount Camille was snow-capped for most of the year, and even during dry times she would receive forty feet of snow at her higher altitudes. Her volcanic soil was porous, and instead of running off, the water would soak directly down into the earth. And then Mother Earth pushed it out into the surrounding mountains in the form of innumerable springs. Mount Camille was like a huge fountain or pump. Their community, which they called Rainbow Village, was located on one of the sources of this water. It was like living on top of an immense river of spring water. They had been selling, and more recently trading, water for years. They dispensed it mostly in five gallon bottles, and many people came and got it directly in large tanks.

One of their vegetable gardens was also used for raising heirloom seed, which they sold and traded. Heirloom means they continue to reproduce generation after generation. Most commercial seed had been genetically engineered by the international agricultural cartel to last only one generation, thereby preventing people from growing their own seed to grow their own food. Red Hawk was the guiding force in this area. He and a group of his fellow Lakota warriors on the Lakota Reservation had been growing seed since they were little boys. Of course this had to be done in secret. His great great grandfather, the legendary Red Cloud, had taught them how to grow, harvest and store seed. He had also taught them about many of the other foods and medicines that Grandmother Earth shares with us, substances that were found in roots, bark, mosses, and parts of plants you never think of. Red Hawk taught David and Kelly many of these things when they lived on the reservation. He was a good guy to have along if you were stranded in the wilderness.

Their land was also thick with oak trees, and they had been gathering and storing acorns for years. Red Hawk also knew the rather precise process for curing acorns, and preparing them for meal and flour, which he taught them. This could become a very important source of food in times of scarcity and need, and its value would increase. Same with the seed, its value and trade value would increase in hard times.

They also had a product they developed and manufactured which had value in the present, and could have a lot more in the future if anything happened to the mainstream energy grid. Don Morrisee was a foremost scientist in alternative energy. He had a long list of credits and achievements, but his most recent invention was a simple motor, which used a conventional electric charge and a series of magnets, which moved and rotated in a variety of directions, to extract energy out of thin air, which was then stored in traditional batteries. Non-traditional scientists, such as Reich and Tesla, had postulated for years that energy is everywhere, even in the space that surrounds us. Quantum science had confirmed this. But nobody had yet figured out how to harness it. And those that got close were invariably sabotaged by the oil monopoly. Don was one of those. Don's motor was complete and working, but he would no longer operate his affairs out in the open. So far the motor only worked on a small scale, but it was big enough to build a backup generator for their solar system, which was greatly needed in the dark winter months. And there was a market out there for small generators that did not run on traditional fuels.

And now they knew for certain they had 30 days to spend all the rest of their money. This wouldn't be too difficult because none of them had much left. They always believed the day would come when their money would no longer have any value. They believed that in the long run tangible goods had more value, and they'd been accumulating and storing them with this in mind. They had made a list here too, and now was the time to make the final purchases.

They had known for a long time that this day would come, this day when the people of the planet Earth would be forced to make a choice between two worlds, two worlds that were mutually exclusive. One was the world of slavery, in which you followed an authority that was external to you. The other was the world of freedom, in which you answer to no authority other than the spirit within yourself. With the coming of a mandatory microchip, it would no longer be possible to have one foot in each world, as it had been for so long.

They knew that many of their friends and neighbors and many of the people in their area in general would refuse the chip. Fortunately, these remote areas far from civilization were places where you tended to find freedom loving and self-sufficient people. In their case at Rainbow Village, the area they dealt with was known locally and unofficially as the State of Jefferson. This consisted of the mountains of south-central Coronado and the north-central part of the state to the south, Olympia, extending from around Mt. Camille to the north to around the town of Tuttle, Olympia, which was 60 miles to the south. The State of Jefferson had quite a history, including a couple of attempts to actually secede from the union. In many ways the State of Jefferson was a state of mind. These were people who no longer saw themselves as citizens of the United States of Columbia.

They also knew that it was only a question of time before those who refused the chip became criminals, or at least expendable, much like the Native Americans in the United States and all the other indigenous people in the other parts of the world. These people simply couldn't be allowed to live in a way that was so diametrically opposed to the established order, especially if they were healthy, happy and spiritually illumined. There's no telling what kind of a destructive influence this might be. This is why it was so important to be remote, beyond the tentacles of civilization. The cities were becoming places of unimaginable chaos that required all of the law enforcement and other resources of the established system to contain.

They knew they knew about them at Rainbow village. They were surrounded by federal and state owned forest land. Helicopters flew over all the time, especially during fire season. But they had decided long ago they couldn't worry about such things. They were committed to doing what was right, regardless of the consequences. Besides, they had a mantra, which is where they found their protection. This mantra was found in virtually all the indigenous prophesies regarding these monumental times of shift and transformation, and previous times of transformation in our ancient past. The mantra was: those who follow the original instructions, and who live a simple life in harmony with Mother Earth and with the forces of nature would survive the Earth changes, and live to create the world of the Fifth Sun. The Hopi believed that the world had already been destroyed three times, and each time the purest of the Hopi survived to build the next world. The same was true now, as improbable as it seemed. They didn't know how this would get done. All they knew was they had to believe it would. It was a matter of trust. They trusted that if they lived in harmony with the divine spirit, then the divine spirit would take care of them, and provide all their needs. Was this like believing in a miracle? Perhaps it was. But this was their shield of armor, and it had gotten them this far.

CHAPTER THREE – *The Frequency Fence*

Three weeks passed.

David, Kelly and Red Hawk were taking a walk through the meadow and up the hillside on a brilliantly starry night. The moon hadn't risen yet. This was the way the sky always was not so long ago. The chemtrails were accomplishing their task. They were gradually turning the sky from blue to white. And most people didn't even notice.

On this night, there were none. The Milky Way was truly milky. It looked like a frothy organic being swirling above them. The planets and stars looked gigantic and were twinkling dramatically. There were numerous shooting stars.

And the Blue Sun was in its place. It hadn't budged in three weeks. It continued to stare down like an eye in the sky. Its blue color was slightly deeper in the clear air, its speckled membrane-like surface more vivid. The blue hue remained faint. They needed their headlamps.

This walk was their excuse for spending time alone together. As this clan's three primary leaders, they felt they needed to do this often, at least once a week. If nothing came of it that was OK. But it usually did.

They hadn't gotten far. They were right about in the middle of the circle of the meadow. They first heard it as a sound coming from over the ridge to the south. It sounded like the soft hum of finely tuned high-tech machine. But the longer you listened it started sounding a chant, like a hundred Buddhist monks delicately chanting.

Mmmmm..

It began its ascent over the ridge as a single point of brilliant light, brighter than the brightest star, so bright it cast shadows, so bright you had to squint. As it slowly rose, the point became a thin vertical bar of light, glowing and sparkling with the same intensity. No solid form could be distinguished in the glow, just pure light, like a shining staff. The entire meadow was lit up. The bar continued to rise, and it became a cross, as a horizontal beam of light, of the same brilliance, rose as part of the structure. This happened four more times, at equal distances, as this lattice-like form took shape, which consisted of the one long vertical bar of light, and five shorter horizontal ones, equidistantly spaced, with the middle one the longest, the ones on either side of that slightly shorter, and the ones on the ends the shortest. When it cleared the horizon, the lattice had the shape of a brilliant sparkly egg.

Mmmmm.

It continued to hum or chant as it moved slowly toward them in the sky.

The sound faded and stopped. It was silent.

It started again.

Mmmmm.

This made it sound even more like a chant, not a engine.

David, Kelly and Red Hawk were silent, immobile, watching, breathing, taking this in.

David thought to himself, "It's singing, powered with song."

It reached a point directly above them, and stopped. The chanting stopped also. Silence again, a silence so absolute it was other-worldly.

Enveloped in the light, David checked to make sure Kelly and Red Hawk were still there. They were, in the radiance. They were both looking up, squinting. Kelly picked up his vibe, and looked back. He looked back up. This ship seemed to have a vibration that carried its own reality. David felt like he was in it, along with them.

The ball of light around the lattice structure started to shrink. Its light started to fade. It continued to contract, along with the structure, until it was a single point of light, no bigger or brighter than Venus or Mars were a moment ago. And this point of light was alone above them in the pitch black sky. All the other lights from a moment ago were not there. At least they couldn't be seen.

Music started again. But this music was far more elaborate than a simple chant, even if it was by a hundred Buddhist monks. It was like nothing any of them had ever heard before, with instruments they couldn't identify. It was high frequency sounds like crystal bowls mixed with primordial rhythms like didgeridoos. It was the singing of a chorus of angels with mathematically precise harmony. And all of this was blended together in perfect tones, perfect rhythms, perfect variations, which took possession of the spirit and flew away with it to other worlds.

When the music started, the point of light started to dance, moving in perfect synchronization to the sounds. At first it moved in waves along a horizontal axis, up and down, back and forth, varying its speed, its amplitude, its frequency. It increased in speed until the point became a solid line tracing the wave-like shapes. Then these lines and shapes left the horizontal axis and started to move around in space, tracing dazzlingly intricate and beautiful shapes and figures, in three dimensions. sacred geometry.

And all of this was in perfect harmony with the ethereal music.

Then the music stopped and it all collapsed in an instant back into a single brilliant point of light, which was directly above them.

Silence again, the same other-worldly silence.

The point of light began to move slowly to the west. When it reached the west end of Rainbow Meadow, it stopped, and started moving clockwise in a circle to the north, then to the east, then to the south, to complete the circle. The area the circle covered was roughly that of Rainbow Meadow and then Rainbow Village to the north of that, which was marked off by a wall of large rocks and earth they had excavated as a fire wall. As it moved in its circle, the point of light began to rapidly accelerate until it became a solid line whirling around above them. It was a perfect circle, and it began to make a swooshing sound, which increased in pitch as the point went faster and faster. It was the sound of something swirling away into a vortex. It whirred higher and higher in frequency above them, and then poof, it was gone.

The stars were back, as before. The Blue Sun was in its spot. The ship was gone, the music, the point of light, all gone. The regular sounds of their world were back. They were back in 3D.

They were standing in the darkness, in the faint blue hue.

They sat down on the hard earth. It was a chilly night, but they were prepared to be outside. Red Hawk had brought a blanket and, as always, a candle, a shell and sage smudge. They were lit. The candle and the smoke fluttered in the breeze.

They talked about what they had seen, and how they felt about it. They knew they had to get back to the others, but for now they had to be together. They all saw precisely the same thing. And they all felt precisely the same way. The experience felt totally positive and benevolent and transcendent. And they agreed that even though they didn't know what it meant, this seemed like a connection and a communication that was meant specifically for them, at Rainbow Village. The ship stopped directly overhead, and the circle so perfectly traced the heart of their community.

They also wondered whether this sighting had anything to do with the one they had had a few days ago. Since the Guardians first went public, three weeks ago, UFO sightings had become much more common all over the world. In particular, in Brussels, Belgium, and that part of Europe, there were an abnormal number of sightings, plus the sighting of a huge shining globe, which many alleged was a mother-ship of some kind. Many people believed this was where the Guardians were physically located, along with their super-computer, which also might be on that mother-ship.

At Rainbow, they had several sightings of small light ships too, but in each case they just passed over, and seemed to be headed on missions elsewhere. That is until three nights ago when they were visited by a large blue ship, which clearly seemed to be probing their area. Unlike the lattice ship, the blue ship did not feel positive and benevolent. It felt invasive and threatening. David, who happens to be highly sensitive to these negative energies, actually felt sick to his stomach as he watched. It was about half the size of the Blue Sun in diameter, and it was saucer-shaped, thicker in the middle like a flattened oval. Like the Blue Sun, it too was not bright and shiny. It was a darker and solid shade of blue. It made no noise. It came from the south over the ridge, just like the lattice ship. It stopped over Jack's house, hovered for a moment, then flashed with a bright yellow light. It was like the flash bulb of a camera. For the next few minutes it flew over the meadow and over all the houses and structures of the community. It stopped and hovered over virtually every structure. It stopped over the gardens, over the orchard. It stopped over the solar panels, over the water tanks. It stopped over the ceremonial circle in the meadow. And a few times it stopped over apparently nothing at all. It didn't flash every time it stopped, but most of the time, maybe ten in all. When it departed, it followed the road to the bottom, flashing a few more times along the way.

The three weeks since the appearance of the Blue Sun and the Guardian's announcement had seen more dramatic change in the world than at any time in the entire history of the planet. The shift of the ages was obviously in full gear. The Guardians plan, as announced that night, crashed and burned almost instantly. Either they had miscalculated the intelligence and the emotional stability of the vast bulk of humanity, or, more likely, they didn't care. They wanted to be able to at least say they had given humanity a chance.

After the announcement, panic set in almost instantly all over the world.

The following day there was a mad rush of selling in all the United States and foreign stock markets. In the first day they lost one third of their value. In the second day they lost another third. Things leveled off there, where the only stocks that continued to have any value were those of the huge international corporations, which it was now pretty obvious were owned and controlled by the Guardians. This part of the world at the top of the pyramid of power continued to function relatively normally, and this included businesses like the defense industries, the big banks, the two remaining phone companies, the public utilities, the technology industries, the agricultural monopoly, and of course, big medicine and the pharmaceutical cartel. This situation was mirrored in all the financial markets all over the world. After a couple of days, portfolios with assets in any stocks, bonds or any of the other trading markets were down roughly 70%.

This rash of buying also struck the consumer markets, and this too instantly, all over the world. This too was clearly panic-driven. Humanity seemed much more willing to spend their dollars or other paper currencies rather than put it in the bank as part of some mysterious and brain boggling plan. But this was more than that even. People were digging into their savings and spending what was left of their assets on tangible goods that would last and keep their value. They were doing this to facilitate their survival in the face of pending disaster. In such times, things like non-perishable food, gasoline and batteries are more valuable than money. Lines at the gas pumps and supermarkets and retail stores were long.

Pretty soon the shelves were empty and the reserves were running short.

The cessation of the printing of all paper money was ordered as promised. Economists had been saying for decades that this massive printing of paper money was the primary thing preventing the world economy from falling into hyperinflation the likes of which had never been seen before. And that's exactly what happened. Consumer prices went up as fast as was mathematically possible. After one week, they had gone up 50%, and the next week they went up another 75%. The Internet was so clogged with traffic that much of it didn't work, and it was hard to buy anything. It didn't take long before everything was so expensive that the existing money was essentially worthless. The Guardians did take emergency measures to fix prices and to speed up the implementation of the electronic money. But the new system wasn't ready to handle the stress being placed on it. There was too much to do in too short a period of time.

There was total chaos in making the simplest of financial transactions. Understandably, black markets arose almost immediately, where people bartered goods and services for other goods and services. The Guardians made it clear this was frowned upon because it showed a lack of cooperation with the new system of money. But there wasn't much they could do. With everything in such chaos, they really didn't have a better alternative. Besides, they never said it was illegal not to participate in the new system. Under their divine guidance, they assumed the new system would work, and that it was financial suicide not to participate. In the current crisis, all they could do is urge people to hurry and get the chip as quickly as possible. After a couple of weeks the new system was starting to work in certain pockets of the world economy, and invariably this involved the military industrial complex and the multi-national corporations and banks.

But it didn't make a lot of difference because most the damage had already been done. There was almost a total collapse of the entire way of life of the civilized world. Things were the worst in the big cities, and the bigger the city the bigger the problems. Looting and mayhem were common in the urban areas of virtually every city in the world. In most cases, the Guardians ordered martial law, and the new world police force was quick to respond, all over the world. This new police force not only consisted of regular police, at every level, from local up to national, but it also consisted of every branch of the military, Army, Navy, Air Force and Marine, and whatever their equivalents were in other countries, as well as police from new-fangled government agencies, like FEMA, which were created to protect national security. In many cities even the firefighters and other government employees, like road construction workers, were teamed up with the new world police force. And this was one part of the new world that was functioning effectively. Obviously, these military forces were in a state of preparedness for such a disaster. All the Guardians had to do was give the word and they swung into action.

Pretty soon the vast majority of humanity couldn't pay their bills and there was the possibility of mass outages of the most essential utilities, electricity, water and gas. The Guardians issued an order that these services were not to be suspended, with the assurance that these problems could be remedied once the new system of money was in place. Obviously, the real ownership of these utilities was high enough in the hierarchy of the ruling elite that agreements like these with the Guardians could be made. And all of these systems were centrally designed in such a way that this was possible. Just flick a switch, and all the electricity in the world goes off, or on.

The Guardians also issued an order that all Internet and television services were to be maintained with the same understanding. These were far too valuable to their system of control and mind-control. This was particularly relevant to the folks at Rainbow Village. Since they had decided that nobody would receive the chip, they knew the day would come when they would not be able to pay their Internet bill. The Internet was their last line of communication with the outside world. Other than word of mouth with the people below that was their only source of news. It was also their only telephone service. When this day came, it would definitely be another huge shift for them, but it was a shift they were ready for. They knew they could get their bill paid if they really wanted to. They had friends down below who had received the chip, and who offered to buy things for people who didn't, usually for a price. And there were other areas where they would do this. But with the Internet, it was a matter of principle. They had made the decision that if things ever got so bad they couldn't pay their Internet bill, then that would be the day that they would fall back upon their self-containment once and for all, and that of their small community down below. No phones, no email, no Internet. That day was drawing near.

As long as they had the Internet, they followed the events in the outside world. Well, Jack did. Everybody else was pretty busy working. The basic patterns for how this New World Order would be stratified became apparent very quickly. The inner cities of every large city in the world, where low-income, poor and ethnic minorities lived, were totally written off. They were left to crash and burn. The streets were either deserted, or they were filled with the marauders who ruled them. There was gun warfare as business owners and private individuals protected their property from armed gangs of looters. Virtually all small privately owned businesses were forced to close down. Windows were smashed. Cars were abandoned with no gas. Corpses were in the streets. And the neighborhoods were the same. They were war zones. There was starvation, sickness and death. Those who were making it were often boarded into their homes. If you had anything of value, you weren't safe.

And the New World Order police were nowhere to be seen, not even the regular police who worked in these areas prior to the crash. They were off protecting people and property that were deemed more important and valuable, as in valuable to the one world order cause. The people in the inner cities were basically left to die. They were apparently deemed expendable, of no use. Somebody would have to clean the whole mess up at some point, but that would have to wait.

In the urban areas, the new police were always sent to the business districts, with the huge corporate banks, the offices of other major corporations and financial services, such as investment houses. Many of these were still in business, working for the Guardians as they always did. These businesses would do what they always do, except now they would do it with the electronic money. Many government complexes, national and state, were also protected by the new military, at least those that performed functions that were compatible with the agenda of the Guardians.

These were important to the Guardians for another reason. Government bureaucrats, at all levels, would be far more willing to receive the chip and to comply with the new system. This is what the Guardians needed, obedient servants. Plus, the Guardians needed their bureaucrats and pencil-pushers to do their busy work and to help create the illusion that this system worked. Many industrial sections in these urban areas and individual factories and corporate businesses were also protected. The general rule was: if it had anything to do with the moneyed-elite at the top of the pyramid of power it, it was protected. All over the world in these areas there were skirmishes with rioters, and some of these had pretty huge numbers, but they were not well organized, and they were no match for this New World Order army. These were not treated like your average protests in peacetime. This army meant business, and they had a job to do. They did not hesitate to use their weapons. Many people, and some soldiers, were killed.

As you moved out of the inner cities and into the outlying areas, the small business districts, the strip malls and the suburbs, you began to feel the presence of the new police more. It was simply not as concentrated because there was more area to cover. But the sky was always filled with helicopters now, and the Air Force and the Navy were standing by if needed. In these areas the same basic rule applied. Military protection was concentrated around most of the major corporations which had moved to the suburbs and which had any connection with the military/industrial/technological complex. Protection was also provided for many of the strip malls, particularly those with the large corporate outlets, like Walmart, Sears and Walgreens, and those with large supermarkets, and particularly those bordering the inner city, where there was more violence. The Guardians wanted the consumption aspect of the world economy to keep working. It was an important focus. They wanted people to get the chip, get it quickly, and start spending the new electronic money at the new fixed prices. The only problem was so much money had been lost in the crash that most people didn't have anything left to spend.

The new police presence was everywhere, but the farther from the inner cities you got the less it was. By the time you got to the affluent suburbs the crisis was much less visible. On the surface, life seemed to go on as usual. Most of these people had some money left. If they had a million before, now they had a hundred thousand, maybe less, and it bought a small fraction of what it did before. But they could get some gas. Lines were long, but they weren't as dysfunctionally long and dangerous as in the city. Many stations were often sold out, or out of business. Many of these people still had jobs, at least those who worked for a corporation or the government. Many of them went to their jobs everyday not knowing how they would get paid, or whether they would get paid at all. Many of them had refrigerators, cupboards and freezers full of food at home, and they could hold out several weeks, maybe longer. These were the people who had the most to gain from the chip and the new money, and these were the areas where recovery was the most likely.

And so far we've only been talking about those who were physically healthy enough and emotional stable enough to get through this crisis, which far exceeded anything anybody had experienced. Such was not the case for vast numbers of humanity, who were stretched beyond their breaking point. This seemed particularly to be the case with mental and emotional disturbances. The epidemic in the civilized world had been going on for some time, with cancer, heart disease and diabetes leading the way. With the chaos of the crash, many of these people couldn't receive the life-saving medication or the treatment they needed. Many of them got sicker. Many of them died.

But this was to be expected. Most of these people were mostly dead anyway. But the hospitals and medical clinics were overrun by a completely different kind of patient, people who had lost everything overnight and were losing their marbles, people who were cracking under the stress of their world being inexplicably torn apart, and people who had nowhere to go because they were so steeped in helplessness and irresponsibility that they couldn't manage what the Guardians were asking of them. In short, people were going crazy and doing really stupid things.

Plus, as you might imagine, the hospitals were in as much a state of chaos as everything else, probably more. Not only was the volume of patients far beyond what they could handle, but also many of the finest and most prestigious doctors simply disappeared. And this happened all over the world. It was widely speculated that they were recruited to work at hospitals that served the ruling elite, including the Guardians, many of them secret hospitals or hidden at underground facilities. The hospitals and clinics also suffered what every business and government world-wide suffered. Lots of people at every level just weren't coming in for work. After all, the world is coming to an end. Why should I bother to go to a job I hate and might not even get paid?

The same basic patterns held in every segment of civilized society. Things were falling apart faster than the Guardians could build it back up with their electronic money and fixed prices. You could see this clearly in education, particularly colleges and universities, anything that was not free. College tuition was the kind of money everybody had lost. Nobody, excluding the filthiest of the rich, could afford this anymore. It was now a question of putting food on the table, gas in the car, and setting things up so you could survive. So students stopped going to classes, and either had no place to go, with no money, or they went home. As with the doctors, many of the foremost professors disappeared, and lots of people at every level just didn't come in for work. And yes, many of the larger universities became hotbeds of protest and violence against the new system. And yes, they met the same fate as those in the ghettos. This was a new world, and this was war. These students, world-wide, who were sometimes lightly armed, stood no chance against the New World Order Army, which used all the latest in high tech weaponry against them.

Now with the crash the Guardians came on the TV and the Internet every day. The message and the tone was always the same. Everything was going to be OK. Things were already turning around. They urged people to get the chip, and go to their bank, and get themselves plugged into the new system. As soon as enough people did this, things would turn around, and everything would return to normal, better than normal. They continued to hammer on the theme that this was a better world. They didn't talk about the chaos, the violence, the murder, the sickness, the death, or the collapse of a way of life that had been in place for thousands of years. And they never said anything about the Blue Sun that had occupied a place in the heavens.

And the real problem was always the same. It always came back to the same thing. Too many people around the world had lost too much, and now there was no way to get it back. And the

Guardians never said anything about this either. Vast hoards of humanity were simply being left to die, and their only hope was to trust some mysterious entity that sounded like it was from another world, and who was telling them to receive a microchip implant that had the technological capability to do a lot more than check your bank account.

And the Guardians never talked about bailout plans to help the billions of disenfranchised, or anything like that. Theirs was not a humanitarian agenda. Government programs like unemployment compensation had been completely blown away by the inflation and the crash of the money. They were insolvent and had to close their doors. There was no talk of replacing them. So the billions of disenfranchised had few choices. It was either wait to die, or turn to some form of crime. This was even true in the suburbs where people were banding together and stealing and committing other crimes just to get by. Never in the history of our world was it more painfully obvious that the true agenda of the ruling elite was genocide. There were simply too many people in the world. These numbers had to be reduced dramatically in order for the New World Order agenda to succeed. How they would clean up the mess was a good question.

Or you could do what they had done at Rainbow Village. They had prepared for this day. They were off the grid, living almost completely independently of the outside civilized world for five years now. They were prepared to live without the fiat money of the established system. They produced most of what they needed, and they had alternative mediums of exchange for what they didn't.

One of the most important ways they prepared was to find a place for their community that was remote, as far away from the big cities as possible, and in an area that was thinly populated. This way, in the event of a crash and a police state, the likelihood of police action against them was greatly diminished because they were too small and too far away. Jack had done some research, and FEMA actually posted maps, which showed the zones of the greatest intervention and the various levels of intervention in the event of a national disaster. Rainbow Village was so remote it was in a non-intervention zone, which meant it was a waste of resources for FEMA to go there. And now that the crash and the police state were a reality, this is how it proved to be. Other than the frequent helicopters and several UFO sightings, they had been left alone. Life went on pretty much as usual.

Such was also the case for most of the surrounding area, the State of Jefferson we talked about earlier, which included the small towns of Rushville, about 25 miles to the northwest, and Mount Camille. Most of this area was far more unaffected by the crash and the crisis than the outside world. These were farmers and ranchers, people who knew how to take care of themselves. Many had lived this way for generations, and those who had moved here all did so for the same reason. They wanted to learn how to live off the land, and they wanted to do it. They wanted to be close to nature. And they liked being far away from the big cities. It's one of the things that drew them here. Most of them didn't have very strong affections for big government either, and didn't appreciate being told how to live their life. And most of them were hunters, another attractive feature of this area. Most of them had firearms, more than just a couple, and were well versed in the use of them. Alternative forms of energy, such as solar and wind power, were also common.

Like the folks at Rainbow Village, many of these farmers, ranchers and country folk were also survivalists, meaning they believed the crash of our civilization was inevitable, and they prepared for that day. Many of them had already formed networks to exchange and share products and resources, and they were prepared to form one large network in the event of an emergency. Rainbow Village was a part of these networks. This is where they traded water, seeds, acorns, acorn by-products and Don's motor, which created quite a stir in this network.

Almost nobody, including the folks at Rainbow, understood the extent of these underground networks until the crash, when they sprang into action. Rushville was actually the scene of an armed revolt by the local citizenry, most of them from the surrounding countryside, which worked like clockwork and was successful. As was happening in many small towns, the police and the firefighters in Mount Camille and Rushville all disappeared, probably assigned to higher risk areas. In Rushville, three of the local cops actually defected and stayed home. And they did confirm that they had been ordered to the north, possibly as far as Johnsport, the closest large city, where there was significant turmoil. This was the extent of local law enforcement, and these three cops joined with the local vigilantes to form a new and indigenous police force, one that followed the old-fashioned organic law of right and wrong, and one whose primary purpose was to protect the people of Rushville from outside interference not of their choosing.

They first struck in the middle of the night, two days after the Guardians made their initial announcement. After two days of hyper-inflation, the collapse of the money and utter chaos, it was pretty easy to see what direction things were headed. The scene was also ripe for looting, especially with no police. Rushville was a small town of about 10,000. Most of the businesses were small and local, catering to ranchers and farmers. It was a very popular resting spot for truckers, located as it was off of a major interstate highway. There was not a lot to loot.

There was a Walmart, and this is where the local militia first struck in the middle of the night. They arrived by the truck load, over a hundred of them, mostly men but a fair share of women, fully armed with rifles, pistols and fully stocked ammunition belts. But they were not there to protect the store from looters. They were there to appropriate. This was war. They were there to take by force vital resources that belonged to the enemy, and which could be very useful to their cause. Walmart sold motor oil and lots of other kinds of fuels, fluids and resources used to run machinery and other accessories for machinery. This was their target, and they took all of it, including everything in the warehouses. They didn't take it to sell, for profit. They took it to further their cause, which was to help the freedom loving people of the State of Jefferson to live independently and sustainably in the face of an unspeakable tyranny that wanted to not only rob them of their property, but their soul.

There were also four gas stations in Rushville, and on the following day these too fell to the network of the local rebels. However, no force was necessary here. All of these stations were run by local people, and all of them had previously been approached by the leaders of the vigilantes. They had discussed the possibility of exactly what was happening down to the smallest details. The vigilantes clearly elucidated what nature would compel them to do in such a scenario. They would use force to take as much gas and oil as necessary, but what they were asking for was cooperation. They made their case to convince the station operators that it would in everybody's best interest for the gas and oil to be used for the cause of helping all the local people to be free. They also offered their protection in the event of any mass crisis that threatened their reserves of gas and oil. One of the operators joined the network and agreed to cooperate before the crash. The others kept an open mind. When the crash hit, after two days of lines and chaos and crushing inflation, the other three closed their doors, and called the leaders of the network for protection, and to start making plans for the gas and the oil. They were on the scene in less than an hour.

The same basic thing happened with the propane reserves. One of the gas stations sold propane in bulk, and there were two other small businesses, privately owned by local families, which sold propane to residential customers. As it turned out, these local families were close personal friends of the leaders of the vigilante network. They were also big fans of the concept of local sovereignty with the State of Jefferson, and they were sympathetic to the cause of the vigilantes. So they were an easy sell.

And then there were their contacts, the drivers, as well as the drivers of the gasoline trucks for the gas stations. As stated earlier, Rushville was a popular spot with truckers. Many of the veteran truckers were well known and well connected in the community. Many of them lived in the area. And they too had been approached by the vigilantes. In many cases they delivered to them directly. And with them too, the case had been made to join the side of freedom and local autonomy versus the lies and the deceit of the New World Order. When the crisis hit, on the same day the gas stations closed their doors and called upon the vigilantes, two of the gasoline trucks and one of the propane trucks showed up with full loads that were being pledged to the cause. And with all the chaos and confusion out there, there was still the possibility they could return for more, until the gig was up.

On the night David, Kelly and Red Hawk saw the ship, it had been almost three weeks since the crash, and Rushville was still in a state of armed revolt, under the control of the vigilante network. No outside force had been used against it. And there was no other legal entity in the area claiming to have authority. For the time being at least this area seemed to have been cut off from everything that was happening in the outside world. Most of the local government was shut down. None of the courts were in operation. The network of the vigilantes was expanding all the time and they managed to keep all the essential community services in operation, like trash collection. They made arrangements to pay workers in goods and services, and often they drove the trucks and did the work themselves.

The hospital remained open, but was more of a state of chaos than anything. The two pharmacies were also open. One of them was at Walmart, but the vigilantes did nothing to prevent the normal operation of the store. They had simply appropriated all the oil and other vital fuels, whatever machinery that was of value, and anything that was essential to their cause. But no representatives of the new system were showing up, as promised by the Guardians, to implant the microchips that were so vital to its success. There were three banks in town, all of which were small branches of larger banks, and all three closed down. The banks were supposed to be the primary place where people learned how the microchips worked, again from representatives sent by the new system. Now the closest banks were in Tuttle, in the state of Olympia to the south, well over an hour away. So that door was closed too. There were no representatives sent to anywhere in Rushville. It was like it had dropped off the map.

And that was just how they wanted it at Rainbow Village. That's why they moved there. It was part of their plan. The revolt in Rushville and the early success of it was a total surprise to the folks at Rainbow. This had not been part of their plan. They had several connections with the vigilante network for trading purposes, without even knowing the extent of the network or their plan. Now that they knew they were delighted. Suddenly, their world was bigger, and they had allies they didn't even know existed.

Nobody really knew how many other enclaves like Rushville there were in the country or in the world because there was virtually no coverage of this on the new Internet. You could find some information by working and digging deeply, but once you did, half of it was disinformation planted by the powers that be. Every such story was scrambled by disinformation. The folks at Rainbow were aware of several other smaller communities in the western US, like theirs, but nothing on the scale of a city the size of Rushville. It was logical to think that such a thing could happen in remote cities in other freedom loving places, or in similar places in other parts of the world, but nobody knew. The Internet had lost almost all its credibility.

And in these early weeks, the vigilantes had the local system up and running pretty nicely. They had even implemented a plan to use the old dollars, deflated to their pre-crash values, as a medium of exchange. They also implemented social programs to make sure everybody got fed and got basic essentials. And medical care was provided in the form of first-aid, given by nurses and other healers, and also herbal medicines and alternative healing that they were now free to do. This was the kind of medicine that most people were looking for anyway.

Most people believed it was only a question of time before armed force was used by the New World Order army against Rushville. A lot of that depended upon how much chaos there was in the more populated areas to the north and south. As long as they were needed there, the military would stay there, and not move into any remote non-intervention zones. After three weeks, things in the large cities to the north and south, Johnsport and Heatherton, were still very messed up, and the folks in Rushville were feeling pretty safe that they had more time. And who knows? Maybe they'd just write the area off completely. Other than murder, there really was no purpose to a military attack. All the vital resources, the gas, oil and propane, had already been taken, and it was not out in the open where it could easily be found. Besides, the freedom-loving people of Rushville and the vigilantes understood that they stood no chance, with their small army and their rifles, against the New World Order militia, with their choppers, missiles, lasers and all the latest high-tech weaponry. In the event of attack, their plan was to head into the hills, where they would be difficult to find. This was already their base of operations. They were the farmers and country-folk. This was a true guerrilla movement. Other than murdering everybody, you couldn't fight them because you couldn't see them.

At Rainbow Village they never thought about armed resistance. They knew this was a battle they could not win, and they didn't even want to think about fighting it. They had guns, and they believed in defending themselves, like against an intruder or a thief. They also hunted. But using armed force against humans, even in an attack, was just not their style. Yes, they believed they were in a war, a war where the prize was humanity's soul. They also believed with every fiber of themselves that they were going to win, win without firing a single shot. There was only one way to do this, and this was to fight this battle on their own turf, a turf that was unfamiliar to their enemies. For the folks at Rainbow Village, and anybody else on the planet Earth who expected to win this battle, the battleground was that of the spirit.

They also believed that for them to win things on planet Earth would need to shift energetically in such a way that the balance of power was tilted in their direction. Virtually all of the indigenous prophesies from every culture on Earth speak of these things, and they all agree. And now with the appearance of the Blue Sun, the collapse of the old paradigm system, and the appearance of UFO's that feel prophetic, things in the world are obviously shifting. The prophesies are coming true. The balance of energetic power may have tilted in their favor.

David, Kelly and Red Hawk had the same dream that night.

David and Kelly had done this often. This was the first time Red Hawk had joined them. David and Kelly confirmed this the second they woke up. The eyes opened simultaneously, and all they had to do was look at each other.

There are two kinds of dreaming. Ordinary dreaming, the Freudian kind, is when our intra-psychic contents are projected outward, and shown in visual and symbolic form. It's like watching a movie of what's going on in our psyche. Ordinary dreaming can be a very helpful tool in our personal growth. And then there is dreaming that is inter-dimensional or dream journeying. This is the dreaming that is part of the spiritual training of the shaman. It is when our consciousness or our spirit leaves our physical body, and has an actual experience in another dimension or world, and then returns to this world, usually. One of the major differences between journeying and ordinary dreaming is during journeying we are aware of what's happening. We know we are dreaming, and we have volitional control over much that happens. Dream journeying usually happens during sleep, but not necessarily. That is when our defense are down, and we are the most open. Many advanced shamans can do it in a waking state, volitionally, and they can also be evoked through ceremonies, through meditation practices and through plant teachers, like peyote and ayahuasca. When you return from such a journey during sleep, the feeling is always the same. You know instantly it was not an ordinary dream. You may not know why. You just know. You know you were touched by spirit. And you know that the message, whatever it was, is extremely important on your spiritual path. We feel blessed to have such experiences.

David and Kelly knew instantly. They really didn't feel like they had to say anything, but they did anyway, just to make absolutely sure. They each confirmed a couple of the major details of the dream. They didn't need to say any more.

The next step was to check with Red Hawk. They were certain he was there too, and they couldn't wait. It was about five o'clock, and it was still totally dark. They flicked on the light, and went downstairs to get dressed. They didn't talk.

They heard him come up the steps to the deck, and then knock on the door.

Kelly was closest to the door. She was still in her underwear. It didn't make any difference. She flicked on the outdoor light, and opened the door.

Red Hawk stood motionless on the deck, the light shining on his face. His eyes went to hers, and then to David's. Then he nodded.

Again, nothing else needed to be said.

"Come in," David nodded back.

Here was the dream:

They were in a teepee, sitting equidistantly around a small wood fire. The teepee was made of fine white clothe that was faintly aglow. The cloth had a transparency to it, and when you looked at it, you could see an ocean of big bright stars twinkling through it all around. The floor of the teepee was the same cloth, and when you looked down you could see the same sea of stars. It was all around them. They were suspended in a brilliant sea of stars.

Each of them felt like they could see everything at once, the fire in front of them, the teepee faintly glowing, the stars all around.

There was no sound, not even the crackling of the fire.

Suddenly there was faint humming sound, like distant chanting, like the motor of the light ship they had seen earlier. The flames of the fire then shrunk, and collapsed into a symmetrical circle of coals that perfectly fit the circle of stones surrounding it. As the humming continued, a cylinder of light began to slowly rise from the circle of coals. It too was faint and transparent and had a misty quality. It continued to slowly rise until it reached the top of the teepee, where all the poles crisscrossed each other. It passed through that, and stopped a few feet above the teepee. There the light grew in intensity, brighter and brighter, until it was a ball of sparkling light atop the cylinder.

The humming stopped.

A voice came to them from the ball of light.

It was the voice of a man, a gentle man. It was a voice that was soft, yet firm, with a melodious, soothing tone.

Greetings David, Kelly and Red Hawk. My name has no equivalent in your language. I call myself Kaleen because I like the sound of it. I am from another galaxy. It doesn't matter which one at this time. It is unknown to humankind anyway. We'll have plenty of time to talk of these things soon, if all goes according to the divine plan. I am here by the request of an intergalactic council, which consists of beings from all the known galaxies and dimensions that share the common objective of following the natural laws of the universe, and not going contrary to them.

We communicate with you at this time in this way because by intergalactic law this is what is allowed. Just like in so many of your science fiction stories, we follow a prime directive that forbids us from interfering in the natural evolution of the people from other worlds. Our enemies, those who do not follow natural law, follow no such directives. Several groups of them have been meddling with affairs on planet Earth for hundreds of thousands of years, rewriting her history, and enslaving humanity without them even knowing it. As you know, this continues at this time.

Things have now come to a head in this great battle between the forces of good and evil that has been going on since the beginning of time. The Earth is really a very special place in the universe. Her current challenge is being watched by a multitude of us. Its outcome will affect the energetic balance of the universe. As you know, The Earth has reached a critical time in her development. She is in the midst of a sea of shifting energies of every possible kind, physical, spiritual, cosmic, mundane. The ancient indigenous prophesies spoke of these things thousands of years ago, longer. The opportunities and potential for change are vast, and the outcome has yet to be determined. The forces of darkness, those who do not follow natural law, those who now call themselves the Guardians, understand all this. And now they believe that in order for their agenda to survive they must speed things up to match the shifting energies they find themselves in.

One of the ways they are doing this is by increasing the involvement of malevolent extraterrestrial beings, like themselves, as well as extraterrestrial technology. We are watching all this very closely. There is little we don't know. We have our ways. They know about Rainbow Village. They believe that people like you and a mission like yours are the greatest single threat to them. If what you're doing ever spread, it could be very contagious, particularly with the world falling apart the way it is.

We learned that a plan had been formed to destroy you, through the use of extraterrestrial ships and weapons. To put it simply, they were going to blow you away. That seemed like the most practical way to them since you were so far removed and so immune in most other ways. This whole area of intervention versus non-intervention is very delicate, but this was clearly a case where intergalactic law stipulates that we can intervene in a protective way. Attacking you in this manner is not a part of your natural development. This is different from most of the atrocities they commit because in these cases they have tricked humanity into giving them their consent. Once that happens, almost anything can be justified. We cannot go to war against them on your behalf, at least not at this point, but we can take steps to prevent them from taking unfair advantage of you in this way. And we are fully capable of doing so. They know who we are, and they won't mess with us. They will never admit it, but they have a deep inner fear that we have the advantage over them because of our connection with nature and with spirit. However, this is what they renounced. So they are going to have to live with that.

That was us in the sky above you tonight. But that wasn't just some fancy kind of light show. The first part was a greeting and the gift of sharing with you a vision of who we are. It was celestial art that touches the spirit, as it touched yours. It expressed our essence. The way you were feeling when you saw that, that's us. The second part, where the point of light formed a circle around Rainbow Village, was the actual construction of a frequency fence. You can't see it now because it is invisible energy, but it is still there. This is your protection. This marked your area with a beam of energy with a frequency that is designated in an intergalactic declaration that is very old. The forces of darkness know this very well. It has been used many times before. It declares that any extraterrestrial force used against the area such marked will be met with retaliation by our intergalactic forces. Like we said, they won't mess with this. They don't want any cause for us to get involved.

That is the extent of what we can do for now. Rest assured we are watching carefully, and we will help in every way that the laws of nature allow. Like we said, understanding these laws and the violations of them is delicate and more complicated than it might seem. People often say, right is right, wrong is wrong, why don't you just get involved fully, and do the right thing? It doesn't work that way. If we were to do that, it would influence the outcome in an unnatural way. We can't have that. It creates an energetic imbalance that affects the entire universe.

Unfortunately, the forces of darkness pay no attention to such rules. This may seem like this gives them an unfair advantage, but much of that is just on the surface. Beneath the surface there are many forces at work that give us the advantage. Many of these forces are beginning to manifest, and others will be manifesting soon. The biggest advantage we have is we are acting morally. In a divinely ordered universe, good always triumphs over bad, eventually, if not in this world, then in some other. The forces of darkness are a formidable adversary because they are tricky and deceptive, and they know how to get around the rules. Look at the havoc they are wreaking on Planet Earth that they are able to do because humanity gives their permission. The power of free will is indeed awesome, and this is a power humanity is giving away.

If everything goes according to the divine plan, the time is coming soon when we will be able to communicate with you in the normal fashion, and we will be able to help more. The current situation must run its course and resolve itself. The new forces we speak of must surface, as was foretold in the prophesies. The energy of transformation on Planet Earth must reach critical mass, which means that for the first time in a very long time the energetic balance will be tilted in our direction. Once this energetic point is reached, the forces of darkness will not stick around and fight because they know it is impossible for them to win. They will leave and find another world to infest. And you can rest assured they've already got one lined up. This has been going on a very long time. Unfortunately, much of the help we will provide at this time will be sifting through the ashes of what's been left behind and cleaning it up. But we must begin where we must begin.

You will know when this time comes. You will know because you are plugged into these shifting energies. This will be the time of the coming of the Fifth Sun. You will know because you will see us in your sky. You will see us at the sunrise of the Fifth Sun. And we will beam ourselves down to your village. We will meet you in person. We can't hug like you do because our bodies are no longer physical, but we can join our energy with yours, like we did with the ship tonight. And we can talk about working together to create the new Earth.

There are others like you scattered about the Earth, not as many as we would like, but it will have to do.

We commend you on doing your work as superbly as you have. This is exactly what is needed. Rainbow Village will be a prototype for those that follow."

CHAPTER FOUR – *The Inspection*

Three months passed.

The Blue Sun held its place in the sky.

The world continued to move deeper into the field of transformative energies.

It was late morning on a pleasant day in May. The winter and spring had been wet, in the form of rain, and nature was moist, and ready to burst into its summer growth.

In the old days, this would have been a bright blue day, with a sprinkling of cotton ball clouds. On this day, with the ever-present chemtrails, the sky was its customary hazy white, with faint smudges of blue trying to poke through. The chemtrails were so thick you couldn't see them behind the haze.

Everybody was working. This was the busiest time of the year for the gardens, the time of moving from inside to outside. The root crops were already planted outside, and the soil was being plowed and prepared for the first planting of the summer seeds, green beans and zucchini. Much of the work was still being done inside, in the greenhouses, preparing plants for transplanting, particularly tomatoes. Tomatoes, both fresh and canned, and their seeds were one of their primary products for exchange. Kelly even made a tasty tomato sauce that she canned, and traded commercially, underground of course.

The community also had three new members, who had been there now a little over three weeks. Ian and Claudia were a young married couple, in their early thirties, and Peter was Ian's father. Up until now, they had lived down below on a farm, just a few miles down the road. They were their closest neighbors, and they were already a part of the Rainbow family. In addition to being farmers, they were builders, including Claudia.

Jack met Peter as soon as he arrived on the scene, 10 years ago. Peter had already been living there for over 20 years, with his wife, who had recently died. Actually, they met when Jack got a flat tire at the end of Peter's driveway. Jack is not the handiest guy in the world, and he was trying to figure out how his new jack worked, when Peter came out, took over, and changed the tire in a few minutes, talking the entire time, explaining how everything worked. It was love at first sight, mutual. Jack quickly learned that Peter was a master handyman. He understood how everything worked, and he could fix anything. Jack hired him to build his house, as well as design and build the water system, which pumped the spring water from the Earth on one side of the meadow, piped it up the hillside to two huge storage tanks, and then gravity fed it to the houses and spigots below.

Ian and Claudia built the other houses, and many of the other greenhouses, barns, sheds and other buildings of the village. They also had an excavator, a backhoe, and a lot of other heavy equipment, as well as more chickens, two horses and three goats, which they brought to the circle of Rainbow Village. They were handy people to have around. There was nothing they couldn't do. Jack had been badgering them to build up there, and join the community, since before there was a community. Jack loved Ian and Claudia as if they were his own children. The idea was always appealing to them, but they were already very self-sufficient, and they were very skeptical about the people who were going to show up for this grand experiment. Then when such obviously extraordinary people started showing up, like David and Kelly and Red Hawk, this definitely got their attention. And then when Don Morisee, along with his family, shows up, the inventor of this incredible little motor that extracted energy from open space, well, that blew Peter's mind so totally that he started thinking they might be doing something very special up at Rainbow Village. Then, about a month ago, their well water ran dry. That was the last straw. They also had a source of spring water, but that also was running too low. So they decided to make the move up, where the water was abundant, and where there was strength in the numbers of this community of extraordinarily gifted and wise people.

During this time, the Leadership Council of Rainbow Village, which was David, Kelly, Red Hawk, Jack and Kathy Spotted Deer, also had to say no to several people who asked to join the community. Actually, over the years they had to do this on a pretty consistent basis. In the early years, they said yes to a lot of people who didn't work out, and invariably this left deep scars, particularly since they were all people who they trusted, and who they thought they knew. This was such an all in or all not in situation. It was very similar to a marriage, where people pledge their lives to each other. The trust had to be absolute. Without this, the answer had to be no. And the profile of those who didn't work out was always basically the same. They were people who didn't bring much, other than the pledge of their labor. Just look at how much Peter, Ian and Claudia brought to the circle, in addition to building two more houses up there for themselves. They were actually investing in this project, putting themselves into it in such a way there was no turning back, even if they wanted to.

Look at Chris and Wanda, and what they brought to the circle, two young hippies, children of the universe, not a penny of money to their name in a long time. Yet they gave themselves up to this project, to this mission. They literally sacrificed themselves for it. They wanted nothing more to do with the outside world. They agreed to be Jack's servants, for as long as he lived, in return for a place on sacred land to put their teepee and food on their table every day, and the pledge they would be taken care of when Jack departs this world, in exchange for their continued service to the land. They let their drivers licenses expire. They mailed back their Social Security cards, saying this contract was non-binding because they signed it when minors and without proper informed consent of the nature of this contract, and how deceptive, manipulative and evil it was, the Mark of the Beast. They had no medical insurance, no insurance of any kind. They had no mortgages, no loans, no debt, no ties to the old paradigm system of any kind. In the eyes of the outside world they didn't exist anymore. Rainbow Village was their world. Mother Earth was their world, in conjunction with those in their area who made the decision of freedom over slavery.

Those who didn't work out always believed at first that their commitment was absolute, and then at the first sign of stress, it wasn't. And since they didn't bring anything, other than the promise of their labor, it was easy for them to turn back, and return to their life in the old paradigm. The life up there turned out to be just too hard for them and the remoteness too much to bear. It's one thing to visit a sacred sanctuary and have ceremonies there.

It's quite another to live at a sacred sanctuary, and give your life to it. It will break the spirit of most.

The hardest thing the Leadership Council ever had to do was say no to prospective community members. It was an awesome responsibility, which usually affected the lives of those involved deeply. Invariably these people were friends. In the early days, Jack sponsored ceremonial events on the spring and autumn equinoxes, which lasted as long as five days. He did these in conjunction with three elders he had met on his own spiritual quest, two men, a Maya and an Aborigine, and a woman, a Pueblo from New Mexico. They were all shamans, trained in their own traditions. These events were usually attended by 30-40 people, and everybody was invited to spend time there both before and after to help with the huge amount of work this required.

Then, five years ago, when David, Kelly and Red Hawk arrived, they assumed the ceremonial responsibilities. The ceremonies were held for a total of seven years, and as a result, quite a little family grew. There were always people staying there, either outside in tents or teepees, or in their campers, in their trucks, or crashing in the loft of the community house, or simply sleeping on Mother Earth. People were always coming and going, but there was always a core group. Jack and the elders were always pushing the vital importance of exactly this kind of sustainable community, one that made no compromises with the old paradigm established system. People were permitted to stay there, in exchange for their work on the land, lots and lots of hard work. They continually reminded people of the need to decide which world they were going to live in, old paradigm or new. It was not possible to have one foot in each world.

When David, Kelly, Don and his family arrived, building two more houses, followed by Red Hawk and his family and all their worldly possessions, the emphasis began to shift away from the ceremonial events, and more in the direction doing the work of building the community. Chris was soon to follow, making his life-time commitment to serving Jack and the land. This was the first time Jack had ever had permanent help, and they dove into the work with a boundless enthusiasm. For all of them, this was a dream come true.

This was also the time when the others started drifting away. Perhaps it was because the place just wasn't as much fun anymore, for them. Hanging out, and just following your own spiritual path didn't work anymore, when the core group was working ten hours a day. Maybe it was because they were being pushed to make a decision, to make a commitment. Maybe they got tired of hearing about the inevitable collapse of the old paradigm mainstream system, to which many of them still had very strong roots, which pulled at them. Most of them complained about financial pressures. Rainbow Village was a full time job, and it didn't pay any wages, and in those early days, they didn't grow enough food, and they didn't have enough of the other necessary resources to live communally and sustainably. People were still responsible for their own food and other personal necessities. Most of them didn't have the money to build a house there or the ingenuity to figure out how to build one without money. And they didn't have the desire to live in a tent or a teepee forever. These were the kind of forces that they allowed to suck them back into the old paradigm. But whatever the forces, it almost always came back to one thing. They weren't ready. They weren't ready to leave the world that they knew, and take that final leap into the unknown.

After the crash, the Leadership Council had to say no to many of those who had drifted away. With their old paradigm world caved in around them, they asked if they could come back, bringing only their poverty and their pledge to work. It was a painful decision, but an easy one. With the addition of Don and his family, their family numbered 12, and that was just the amount of food and resources they had. And they were also nearing the limit of the capacity of the solar system and backup generator. If somebody new was going to come, they would have to bring something. And with the coming of Peter, Ian and Claudia, that's what they got. The circle was enriched.

On this day, as with most, they were all outside working. The newcomers were devoting all of their time and energy building their houses. These were simple structures, consisting of a few rooms, kitchen and bath, and designed to take care of life's basic necessities, shelter, food and plumbing. They were also designed to be finished quickly, before winter at the latest. They were on opposite sides of the community. Peter's was on the same side of the meadow as Jack's, a little to the west and a little higher up, a great honor, since Jack had always said he didn't want anyone else to build on that side of the meadow. And Ian and Claudia's was on the other side of the community, on the other side of the mud and rock firewall, near Don's. They were off by themselves in a grove of oaks and junipers. Peter still had the ranch down below, and the three of them were staying at both places for a while. There was a lot to move.

Everybody else was working on garden projects, either out in the fields or in the greenhouses. It was so odd that the world outside was falling apart as it was, and here at Rainbow Village they were just hitting their stride, precisely as they had visualized it. They were working to serve the creation and to build the world of the Fifth Sun, while the world outside collapsed under the weight of its unsustainability. They had become the self-contained unit that they had planned.

For a long time, the Internet, which was also their telephone, had been their last link with the old paradigm world. Three weeks ago, the time finally came when they lost their Internet signal. They stopped paying their bill as soon as the Guardians announced the electronic money. Then when the economy crashed, there was a grace period for the Internet to give people time to get chipped and to pay their bills again. It was too vital to the Guardian's propaganda. As long as they kept getting the signal, they kept using it to keep track of what was happening out there, at least the version that was reported on the Internet. And as far as they knew, the grace period had never officially ended. All they knew was their signal stopped. The Internet was in just as much a state of chaos as everything else. Some people were getting it, and some people weren't. Nobody knew what to expect.

One the surface, the loss of the Internet made absolutely no difference to the folks at Rainbow Village. Everybody did what they always did, and they were not influenced at all. Yet beneath the surface, this had a subtle and very powerful affect on all of them. Everybody still had an email address, and most of them would check that every few days. Everybody also used it to purchase products with the old money on credit cards. They still had a regular mailbox at the bottom of the road, which they kept to receive these deliveries. And they all used the Internet to search for vital information they couldn't find anywhere else. Unlike most people, they didn't use the Internet for entertainment. They had several TV's and a nice library of DVD's for this purpose.

None of these things really mattered anyway. They knew it was only a question of time before the Internet was gone, and as with everything else, they were prepared. They no longer needed the Internet to survive. But when it actually happened, the world felt profoundly different to them in a way none of them had anticipated. There was a finality about this that felt very powerful. There had always been the tiniest crack in this door, and now the door was firmly slammed shut. There was no opening it again. There was no going back. That mainstream old paradigm world was now totally gone. They had no idea what was happening outside their community and their local network. From now on the only way they would know these things would be by word of mouth with their neighbors and trading partners, a very flimsy source indeed. As fate would have it, few of them had family or close friends on the outside that mattered. Most of them were estranged from their families because of their unusual lifestyle. Peter did have three other children who lived in other parts of the country, and Red Hawk and his family had many relations back on the reservation, but they said goodbye when they left.

It felt very much like dying, which is something those on the spiritual path do over and over. With each transformation, we die, when we let go of those parts of ourselves that no longer serve our spiritual purpose. They all knew all this. There was nothing new in any of it. They had each experienced this when they made their original commitment to make the leap into the unknown of living at Rainbow. Now with the slamming of this final door, these feelings reared their head again. The old world was finally put to rest, no more crack in the door. Their world would never be the same again.

And then, just ten days ago, another huge change rocked their world. That was the occupation of Rushville by the New World Order forces. Actually, this included Mount Camille and other points to the north. As far as they could tell, to the north these forces were the most heavily concentrated in the populated areas surrounding Johnsport, and that was about 300 miles away. Then south of there, they thinned out, in what used to be mostly farm country, but much of which now was desolate, with the drought. But these places didn't get the attention Rushville did, a place of open rebellion. To the south, these forces had reached as far as Tuttle in Olympia, which was about 60 miles away, and separated from Rushville by an imposing range of mountains.

Like everything else, this was something they had to learn about through their grapevine. They knew something was up because on the day of the occupation a fleet of helicopters flew over. They were accustomed to the helicopters of the government forest service and the fire fighters, but nothing like this. Not only were there lots of them, they were bigger, more modern and high tech, and they were armed for battle. They flew over very low, conspicuously low, and you could actually see the machine guns anchored in the cockpits and the small missiles on the bottoms.

It took a few days to learn the other details. These forces also came by land, with truck loads of soldiers on the main highway, accompanied by tanks. When they arrived at Rushville, they found a town, a community, which was doing quite nicely without any connection to the outside world. There was no resistance to this invasion. Most of the people and families continued to live in their homes, as before. Even though the government and the banks had shut down, and nobody was chipped and technically there was no money, they were conducting commerce in basic goods and services using the old paper money at fixed values, which they had agreed upon, and through trade. Food was provided by local farmers, and distributed through autonomous local markets. And all of this was being orchestrated by the band of local rebels, who had appropriated most of the oil, gasoline and propane, in addition to other vital resources. At the time of the occupation, these rebels were nowhere to be seen. They had fled into the hills, which was the plan all along.

Again, this had no direct impact on Rainbow Village. They went about their business as always, no changes. The military helicopters continued to occasionally fly over, sometimes at low altitudes, but they seemed uninterested, on other business. And yet again, in those same subtle and intangible ways this too was felt by all of them. The question of whether the Guardians would just let Rushville be, like all the other ghettoes, because it was too far away and too insignificant had been answered. They were here now, closer. They were in the valleys below. This shield of immunity had been penetrated.

Wanda was the first to hear it. She was walking from the chicken house area, with a basket of eggs, back to the community house. It was the blaring of a man over a hand-held loudspeaker. This alternated with the eerie wailing of a police siren. She walked down the road toward the gate to get a better look. She only stopped long enough to glance. At the gate there was a white police wagon, with its red lights twirling. Behind it there were several other unmarked vans. Beside the police wagon there were several men in plain clothes, one of whom was speaking into the loud speaker, and behind them there were others in military uniforms. It sounded mumbled and indistinct, and she didn't stop long enough to decipher it.

She turned back up the road, and headed toward David and Kelly's house. David was home, and didn't hear them. He was on the computer, with music playing.

"OK," he responded calmly and officially. "Go get Kelly and Red Hawk. And if Jack doesn't come down, go get him too. And spread the word to the others to stay out of sight. We don't want them to see any more than they have to. And if they do force their way in, nobody answers any questions."

Wanda took off. Others had noticed, and they were starting to mill around the community house. Wanda told them to stay out of sight. Before she could run up to Jack's, his yellow Jeep was coming down the road in their direction.

David gathered himself and took a deep breath. This was it. He hadn't had a confrontation like this in over ten years, and the last time had practically killed him. He, and then Kelly, were once criminals of the highest order, who the system wanted eliminated in whatever way. They were fugitives. This was why they hid out on the Lakota Reservation for over two years, where they met Red Hawk, and why they had to live the way they currently were, totally outside the mainstream system.

Their crime was not something you see on the six o'clock news. Actually, they hadn't even broken any laws. They were wanted by the highest levels of government because they were seen as serious threats to the established order due to certain extrasensory powers they had. In telling this it is necessary to back up in our story, and lay some groundwork. The traditional version of history we are fed by our schools and by the propaganda system is a monumental lie, the purpose of which is to be one of the weapons that is used to enslave us. One of the most monumental omissions of this history is that extraterrestrials arrived on Planet Earth far before the beginning of our so-called history, hundreds of thousands, perhaps millions of years. They came for the purpose of colonization, and they formed great civilizations that were highly advanced technologically. There was also a lot of inbreeding between the ET's and the indigenous human women of those times, producing a race of genetic hybrids, part ET, part human. It was these hybrid bloodlines that went on to rule and dominate the world and all of its people. In more recent times they took the form of the gods and goddess and the kings and queens of antiquity.

The ET's were not only extremely advanced technologically, but also mentally and psychically. At the highest levels of their hierarchy, they knew how to shapeshift, which is also something that many shamans and priests and priestesses in indigenous human traditions know how to do. This means they knew how to change physical form, in this case from ET to human, and back again, by an act of their will. The ET's, at least this strain, were also reptilian in appearance, for lack of a better word. David's crime, which Kelly picked up from him, was he could see the hybrids for what they were. He could see through the human form to the reptilian that was within. This always followed the same pattern. The skin turned a pale shade of green, like a swamp, and the head was surrounded with a faint aura of the same color. The eyes were those of a serpent, with thin vertical black slits in the whites of the eye, extending from the top to the bottom. And when David was in their presence he also sensed them with feelings of nausea and revulsion. These hybrids were mostly in positions of power, the royal families throughout the world, high level bankers and business executives, lawyers, doctors, high level politicians, police and law enforcement at all levels, with high concentrations in federal agencies like the FBI and CIA, and celebrities from TV, movies and entertainment. They were the ruling and moneyed elite of the world.

Of course, David and Kelly did not have all these sightings in person. They had them on TV, on the computer, in photographs, and through any other medium in which these images could be displayed. David inherited this ability from his mother, who had been a gifted psychic and medium. She started having sightings when he was a small boy, and one month later she was ritualistically murdered, with her heart cut out, and hung from a bridge at midnight on the night of the full moon. She warned David of this in a letter she wrote before she died, which David's aunt showed him when he was old enough to understand, age 14. David's first sighting was one of his prestigious college professors at a large university in the Midwest US, where he was studying to be a medical doctor. The professor was giving a lecture at the time, when David saw him transform into the reptilian features. As soon as David saw him, he glared back with his snake eyes directly into David's. He knew this young man was seeing him, and there was no greater crime. If enough humans learned to see beneath the mask, then the gig would be up. If enough humans learned the truth, they would set themselves and the rest of the human race free.

From that day on, David was a fugitive. The world was no longer a safe place for him. And David and Kelly devoted their lives to someday exposing this truth, and playing their part in setting humanity free. Since then, they had not had many direct sightings because they had always lived in remote locations, apart from humanity. The state of Jefferson seemed to be fairly clean of the hybrids. They were also very careful about who they interacted with. The only sightings they had in that area were most of the state troopers who hung around Mount Camille and Rushville. Other than that the last sighting David had was police officers in Johnsport over ten years ago. They tried to shoot him, and David only escaped through a miracle of his spiritual powers.

And now here he was again, about to confront the very people he had been avoiding for so long. The law enforcement people who were at their gate were probably pretty high ranking, at least a few of them. This was a group that was crawling with the hybrids, the reptilians. But he was the chief of this tribe, and this was a responsibility he must face. The time had come. Maybe things would be different now.

He walked outside. The loudspeaker continued to blare, intermittently with the siren. Kelly and Red Hawk were already huddling in the driveway, waiting for him. Jack arrived in his yellow Jeep and joined them.

"It's show time," Kelly said with a grin, as David joined.

"We've been over this a bunch," David said, with a shrug. "Let's go do what we've got to do and say what we've got to say, or not."

They walked down the driveway in silence, with Jack, hobbling on his crutch, following behind. The gate was not far away, and it was located after a turn in the road, so you could only see a little bit of the community. You could see the chicken house area, Jack's house on the other side of the meadow, and the garden plots in between, with their extensive fencing. The gate was closed, not locked.

As they got closer, they began to distinguish what they were dealing with. The red light continued to twirl. The man with the loudspeaker stopped speaking, and put it on the hood of the police van. He then gestured to somebody inside, and the light stopped.

As things started to come into view, David was bombarded with sensations. The two men on either side of the man who had held the loudspeaker were dressed the same, dark gray suits, white shirts, and no tie, the same outfit worn by the hybrid police David had seen many years before. They also looked similar, average height, with athletic builds, boney cheeks and pale skin. The one on the left was totally bald and the one on the right had short stubbly brown hair. As soon as David could distinguish their features they both instantly transformed into hybrids, with the reptilian eyes. And just as before, when he saw them, they saw that he was seeing them, glaring back intensely, almost incredulously. This never happened, not with normal humans.

David looked away. He had seen enough. He wanted to make as little eye contact with them as possible.

He nudged Kelly with his elbow.

"See em?" he asked.

"I see em."

As they continued to approach, David focused his attention on the man in the middle. As he did, the hybrid on the right crossed behind him, and had a very brief, but animated, discussion with the bald one. They turned to face the man in the middle, and the bald hybrid moved closer to him, almost touching, and said a few things directly into his ear in a muffled but very emphatic voice.

The man in the middle raised his arm, with his palm facing forward.

"Thank you for that. I'll take care of it," he said calmly, with a slight grin.

It was clear who was in charge.

David studied his features for a few seconds. Almost instantly, it popped back into place. He had seen this man before. Interestingly, he remembered the way the man was dressed. He was dressed the same on the two occasions he had seen him over ten years ago. He was wearing a brown tweed sports jacket, with a white shirt, collar tucked in, clean faded jeans, with a crease, and well worn brown cowboy boots tucked beneath his jeans. He was the picture of coolness. As David scanned up, the face popped back into place too. His looks were as undistinguished as his clothes were distinguished. He was bald on top, with short, neatly cut hair on the sides. His face was robust, with ruddy skin, pock-marked cheeks, an ever-present smirk that ended in dimples, and a mischievous glint in his eyes.

David didn't remember his name. He was a high-ranking cop in the Johnsport Police Department, over ten years ago, the same time David had his run-in with the hybrid cops, and the same time he met Don Morisee. David and Kelly had been guided to Johnsport from the Lakota reservation as part of their spiritual journey, and through a miraculous divinely-guided series of occurrences they met Don Morisee. Don then introduced them to a group he was working with, which consisted of scientists, spiritual teachers and other foremost experts on the energetic alignment of December 21 2012 and the phenomenon of the shift from one age, which was dying, to another, which was being born.

David remembered that this cop was a renegade, a double agent of sorts, a cop who marched to the beat of his own drum, and who did what he believed to be right, as opposed to strictly following corrupt police policy. David first met him at one of Don's groups meetings. He recognized David and Kelly from police photographs, and he warned them of their peril. It was at that same meeting where David met Jack. And then David and Kelly saw the renegade cop a few days later at a spontaneous mass rally where David spoke on the importance of breaking free from the system and learning to live sustainably, in harmony with nature and the divine spirit.

"Frank Jacoby," Kelly whispered, tilting in his direction, like she was reading his mind.

That was it, Frank Jacoby, Lieutenant Frank Jacoby.

As they got closer, they could see the marking on the side of the police van, which read United States Government Police. Behind that they could see four other large vans. There may have been more, but you couldn't tell because of a turn in the road. All the doors had been opened, and uniformed soldiers were standing in the road, alongside the vans, in readiness.

They arrived at the gate, and looked at each other.

"I am Lieutenant Frank Jacoby," the man in the middle bellowed officially.

David put up his hand.

"Please, wait for the old man."

"Certainly," he replied with deference.

They waited as Jack hobbled up. He arrived, leaned on his crutch, looked up at the Lieutenant, and spoke with a gasp.

"OK, what is the nature of this visit?"

"I am Lieutenant Frank Jacoby, United States Marshall's Office," he repeated in a tone that was a strange blend of pomposity and playfulness.

The lieutenant took a few steps forward, separating himself from the others.

"Please don't be alarmed. This is a routine inspection ordered for this region by the New World Order. As I'm sure you are aware, due to certain glitches brought about by the recent economic problems, this area did not receive the resources necessary to help people get started in the new system. We are personally visiting every home to see if we can find those who need help. With much of the Internet also not working, many people have been stranded, and cut off from this information, particularly out in the boonies like this."

He continued to bellow, even though they were just a few feet away. His tone was official and deadly serious, and yet there was an odd lightness to it, like he was simply playing a game circumstances forced him to play.

They looked at each other in silence.

The two hybrid cops continued to glare at David and Kelly. In their past encounters, just seeing them like this was enough to have them killed or at least arrested with the key thrown away.

David sifted through what was before him. Jacoby hadn't asked a direct question, so there was nothing to reply to. He certainly wasn't going to offer any information of any kind. He also didn't want to stir things up by acting or saying anything belligerent or suspicious, like ordering them off private property without the proper warrant. After all, they were already there, with all the guns, and the law wasn't what it used to be.

"OK, we understand why you're here," he stated plainly. "We are not in need of any help. And we do have all the necessary information."

Silence again, as everybody stood their ground, and continued looking at each other.

David's statement covered all the points Jacoby had mentioned. So, there was nothing further to discuss. Apparently, that was not the case.

"For the record," Jacoby continued in the same tone. He was not being unpleasant. "May I ask who the owner of this land is? There was no mailbox on the main road, and we're a little lost out here, as I'm sure you can understand, don't even trust our GPS that much."

Silence again. David intended to politely refuse to answer the question, on the basis of the fact it was none of their business. But he waited. Then Jack spoke up.

"David, my I speak, please?"

"Yes, certainly."

Jack was well versed in these matters, in the organic law of the land, at least the way it used to be. His eyes rose to meet Jacoby's.

"Lieutenant Jacoby," he began plainly and politely, like David. "With all due respect, we don't want any trouble. But we are under no legal obligation to answer any more of your questions unless you can show due cause. United States Marshall, and you're a high ranking official. If I'm not mistaken, you investigate criminal matters, and there is no crime here. But because it's on the public record, you can look it up over at the government buildings, if they're still open, I will answer this final question. I am the owner of this land. My name is Jack Wallace. I've owned it free and clear for years now. Now, with that said, we would like to ask you to please depart these premises."

Jacoby grinned. He enjoyed this, but what was he up to?

"Certainly, Certainly, we'll leave. But as I'm sure you are aware, there was an armed rebellion against the government of the new order in Rushville and the surrounding area. These rebels stole valuable resources from privately owned companies, and I assure you that makes this a criminal matter. At this point, they've fled the scene, and there is every reason to believe they are hiding out up in these mountains. Actually, we know they are, and they are clearly guilty of treasonous crimes against the state. You wouldn't happen to know the whereabouts of any of these criminals, or you wouldn't be harboring any of them, would you, or any of these resources?"

Of course, they were not going to answer his question. But at least now he was being honest. They were on a fishing expedition. It was also clear that they were not going to forcibly enter, at least not on this day. They were hoping to stumble upon information, or find people stupid enough to give them information or to let them in. And all the guns and manpower were on hand just in case they stumbled upon some rebels, and found themselves in a battle.

They looked at each other again in silence. There really was nothing further to say.

Kelly couldn't resist. When she thought about it later, she didn't know why she said what she did. Perhaps it was just the human in her, reaching out to another human. At this point, there didn't seem to be any harm.

"You know we know you, my husband and me. We've met. It was a long time ago, over ten years. It was in Johnsport. You were with the Johnsport police then."

Jacoby's unshakable demeanor shifted for the first time. It was like a flinch in the normal rhythm of his behavior. It was obvious Kelly's comment had struck a nerve, nicked his armor, and he didn't want his colleagues to see this. He looked back at her, deeply into her eyes, and he held this look for a moment. It was a look that said, "Don't go there. Leave it alone." When he had held it long enough, he replied with his previous playful pomposity.

"I assure you, young lady, that has no bearing on why we're here today. Now, if you would be so kind, would you at least let us through, so we can turn our vehicles around? That's a thin road, and not much room to turn around."

"No, Lieutenant Jacoby," David was quick to reply. "You may not enter beyond this point. Actually, you've been trespassing for quite some time now."

Smirk in place, Jacoby looked back and forth between them.

"Something to hide?" he went on. "Seems harmless enough, one citizen helping another citizen, even though we are cops. What could be so important you don't want us to see?"

They stood their ground, waiting. There was nothing else to say.

"They're not going to let you do it, you know," he continued, not skipping a beat. "You're all smart people. You understand that. It may have seemed like a good idea at one time, but the world's a lot smaller now. And they're not going to let you do it. You might as well get used to that, and adapt."

They all had the same thought. What was he up to? Why was he saying these things? Was he bluffing, or did he actually know something. None of this felt like a threat. In an odd way he might even be trying to help out.

"We don't need to come in. We know what you've got going on back there. There are aerial photographs. Everybody knows. It's well known you've got houses back there and other buildings. It's also well known you didn't get building permits for any of them. You're sitting ducks, man. What about those solar panels? We know about them, you know. Did you get the proper permit and pay the proper fees for that, not to mention the penalties when you do get busted. Being out here in the middle of nowhere, out of the reach of the law, obviously isn't going to protect you much longer, not in this new world. After all, here we are knocking at your gate."

David's heart was pounding. Even though this was the last thing they wanted to hear, it didn't come as a shock. They had always known that big brother was watching. But they couldn't stop listening to this man. There was a strange allure to his words and to him. As long as he was going to spill information, it would be silly not to listen. And there was still the nagging question of who he really was and what he was really up to.

And he wasn't done yet. As he continued he paced back and forth a few steps, like an orator.

"This might seem like a stretch, but we're a lot alike, you and me. I used to be like you. I understand what you're doing. I was a staunch Libertarian, very principled. It was all about freedom, the freedom of the individual to do whatever the hell they please, as long as they don't harm others, or interfere with the right of others to that same freedom. God, I've said that so many times it's etched into my neurons. And it was the sole purpose of government to protect that freedom, nothing more. We've obviously strayed pretty far off this course in the modern world. You people own this land. You're not hurting anybody. You should be able to do whatever you please, right? You've got your own enclave, your own jurisdiction in the eyes of god, or whatever higher power you want to call it. You believe you are not bound by the laws of this government because it has broken its sacred contract with you. You believe you are bound by a different set of laws, higher laws. We used to call it the organic law of the land, such as in the common law and in the original US Constitution. And you are bound by your spiritual laws, putting service to your god, or whatever you call it, first, and by the laws of your own conscience."

He stopped, and looked at them all again, a look that was not unpleasant.

They were all startled by his words, not only their eloquence but their accuracy. It was a pretty nice summary of what they believed and why they were doing what they were doing. This was the guy David and Kelly had met in Johnsport.

Jacoby's grin broadened, his dimples deepening.

"You see, I do understand. But none of that amounts to a hill of beans in this world today. You might be totally in the right. And I'm sure you can make a good case that all this is completely legal. But it doesn't matter. There's only one thing that does matter. They're not going to let you do it. And I tell you that as a fact that's as clear as day. You guys are like the Indians on the American frontier, and look what happened to them. They are going to do whatever is necessary to eliminate all this. Today is just the first step. It's like a warning shot. You guys are lucky you got me, an old softy. I've got a couple of deputies back there, a couple of agents, who want to bring you two in right now."

He pointed to David and Kelly with his eyes.

"They see something in you. I don't know, something that requires further investigation. They feel very certain about it. And I don't understand what they're basing this on. I don't understand the evidence. They kind of just want me to trust them. There are a lot of strange things going on in the world today, a lot of things I don't understand. And I just keep doing things the old fashioned way. But you can rest assured of one thing. When we get back to Rushville, with our mobile units, and with our fancy new technology, they are going to investigate you. And they're going to file their report. And then I have a feeling all hell's going to break loose."

He looked at all four of them one more time, placing his eyes on each individually and holding them there for a moment. He then turned around, waved both his arms at his men, and bellowed.

"OK, let's back down and turn around! We're going back down! We're finished here!"

After a few steps, he turned around, and spoke to them again.

"If you remember one thing that was said here today, remember this. They're not going to let you do this. They're not going to let you do this. The sooner you realize this, and adapt, the better off you're going to be."

He turned around again, walked back to his vehicle, and got in the back seat. It took them several minutes for them to back down, and depart.

There was nothing new in anything Jacoby had said. They had known all these things as possibilities for years now. Even the eye contact between David and Kelly and the hybrid agents was something they knew they were going to confront at some point. On one level, you might say things looked rather bleak. They had looked bleak before. After all, David and Kelly had been fugitives, and had lived underground for a long time now. The same was basically true for Don and his family. And Red Hawk and his family came from the reservation, where the natives were slaves, and their way of life was illegal.

And now this, it was all pretty much the same thing. Here they were, a community of 15 farmers, on the spiritual path, and they were up against the greatest military force the world had ever known, which also just happened to be in cahoots with extraterrestrial forces with powers far beyond anything the world had ever known. This was beyond David and Goliath. They had no chance.

But they were accustomed to this. Nothing had changed. And they didn't see it in this way anyway. They didn't see it in this way because their world was a world that involved a lot more than this. Their world was far more than linear variables in a material world. Theirs was a world of the spirit, and this is where they placed their trust. If they were to fight this battle with guns, bombs and the high technology of the old paradigm system, they would be wiped out instantly. No, they chose a different set of weapons. And this choice was based on the fact that there were many other forces at work here, higher forces, forces with more power than guns and bombs, forces with the power to transform the universe. And they couldn't even say for certain what these forces were. All they knew for certain is they received guidance from spirit to live in the way they were, and this was the way to remake the world. This is where they placed their trust.

Yes, theirs was a very different world. It was a new paradigm world, a world in which these higher forces gained ascendency. Theirs was a world in which the mysterious Blue Sun appeared in the heavens, heralding that the time of transformation was soon to come. Theirs was a world where they awaited the coming of the Red Sun. They didn't know when, but this would be the sign that the time of transformation had arrived. Theirs was a world in which they had been contacted by Kaleen, an ET representing a galactic confederation that had pledged to protect them from ET forces working with the Guardians. Theirs was a world that was built upon the foundation of their prayers and ceremonies, which connected them with the world of the spirit, and with supernatural powers that went far beyond this world.

This was their world, the world they trusted. This was where they derived their power. And if they were to persevere in this great challenge, these were the weapons they would use.

Jack Allis

CHAPTER FIVE - *Battle in the Ethers*

Three weeks passed, three weeks that were delightfully uneventful. It had been a while since they experienced a period like this.

There was no follow-up on the investigation by Lieutenant Jacoby and his forces, not yet. The flyovers by the military helicopters had stopped, as had the customary flyovers by the government forest service helicopters. The sky was a quiet place again. And there also hadn't been any UFO activity, either of the friendly or unfriendly kind. It was like the old days.

They had been without the Internet for a month and a half now. They had no idea what was happening in the outside world. Just as they had pictured and planned it, their outside world now consisted of their immediate neighbors, within about a 15 mile radius, most of whom they knew through their trading networks. These were good people and they liked them. And there were a few social functions and gatherings, but in general Rainbow Village had become the self-contained unit they had always envisioned. And occasionally they would invite people or small groups in from the outside. There was another small sustainable community about 20 miles from them, and they stayed in touch with them. And now they were growing, with the arrival of Peter, Ian and Claudia, and the pending arrival of Wanda and Chris's baby. She was a couple months pregnant.

Everything they knew they knew through word of mouth within this very thin network. And this wasn't much. Most of these people had also declined the chip, and many didn't have the Internet or TV either. Much of their knowledge of the outside didn't go much past Rushville. They did know that Rushville had been militarily occupied, but that many of the people still resisted the chip and compliance with the new system. The guerrilla forces had disappeared into the hills, and apparently had not yet been challenged militarily. They knew several of these people and groups and traded with them.

The Blue Sun had been with them four and a half months now. It remained perched in its spot in the sky, unchanging, always there, day or night, clear or cloudy, the dim blue light emanating from the amoeba-like sphere. What a four and a half months it had been, the four and half months of this story, so far. As was prophesized, it had been the herald of the great shift, the transformation from one world to another, or transmutation actually because the new world was being created from the ashes of the old world, which had died. It was the sign that the time of change was upon us. And according to one Hopi Prophesy, it was a sign that the coming the Red Sun was near. When the Red Sun appeared, it meant that the time of change had arrived in full force. And this would be the time when Mother Earth would play her part in this transmutation in all her fury.

In the mainstream system and in the mind-control media, there was still no official explanation for the Blue Sun, not even any fabrication passed off as science by any of the science and outer-space agencies. The Guardians never mentioned it in any of their pronouncements. It simply defied all the laws of the universe as they knew them. And considerable efforts were made by these agencies. Work from the ground, like with the most-advanced telescopes, always proved futile. They could never determine or even estimate its size, its location or its substance. Emergency space probes were sent, some which left this atmosphere, but none of them ever got any closer to it, and the measurements from outer space were equally confusing. The same was true of any measurements that were taken by satellites in the existing system. There were discussions of a manned space probe to the Blue Sun, but it was hard to sell a program about which virtually nothing was known. For all they knew, it wasn't even in this solar system, or in this galaxy, or in this space-time continuum. None of the news stories ever had anything conclusive to report, and they always ended by saying that the most extensive research at the highest levels would continue until an answer was found.

Pretty soon even the news stories started to dwindle, and people stopped thinking about it, at least the people who were stuck in the mainstream system. Just like chemtrails, they didn't notice it or bother to notice it anymore. After all, with all the chaos of the Guardians and the New World Order system people were out of their minds worrying about other things. The folks at Rainbow Village and the others who thought like them believed that the Guardians and those at the highest levels of the mainstream system did understand what the Blue Sun was and what it meant. After all, most of them were extraterrestrial hybrids who have ruled this world for hundreds of thousands of years, and they had knowledge of things esoteric. They had knowledge of the prophesies and of the ancient teachings of the indigenous peoples of the planet Earth. That's why they fear them so much. The Guardians understand that the Blue Sun is a spiritual portent of these transformative times, and that it can never be explained by science as we know it.

Yes, what a four and a half months it had been. At Rainbow Village, they believed they were living with a vibration that resonated in harmony with the natural forces and frequencies of these transformative times. That was actually their entire mission in this world. It was all very simple really. It consisted of two parts. One was to live in harmony with the Earth and with the forces of nature. If they served Mother Earth in this way, then she would take care of them and provide all their needs. The other was to follow the spiritual path, connecting with spiritual energies and forces through their prayers, through their ceremonies, and through their service to the web of life. This was the primary source of their power. Without it, they were nothing. And ultimately, if they were to persevere in this great challenge, this could only be done through their connection to the power of spirit.

They had to believe these things. If they didn't, their world would crumble. The concept of having to believe is found in most indigenous, shamanic metaphysical systems. The shaman has to believe in the mysterious powers of the supernatural and their ability to energetically merge with these powers and use them. If they don't believe this, their shamanic world will topple around them, and they might not even survive.

At Rainbow Village, and every other sustainable spiritual community in the world, there was one more thing they had to believe. They had to believe more change was coming, bigger change, much bigger change. In their current world, there was no longer any status quo. If things stayed the way they were, then their great mission would fail, and they might not even survive. If things stayed the way they were, then it was only a question of time before the New World Order would come after them. They knew that Frank Jacoby was totally correct. This new-fangled world government police state would not allow them to do what they were doing. It was too heretical and too dangerous, particularly if it worked and if it caught on.

They had to believe that more profound change was coming, as was prophesized. This would have to be change so profound it would change the nature of their world. They didn't know what any of this meant, specifically, only that they had to continue to believe, believe in their connection with Mother Earth, believe in their connection with spirit. All the prophesies and the ancient teachings said the same thing. Everything else would take care of itself, sometimes as if by magic. The power of the supernatural is indeed fantastic, once we acquiesce to it.

They had to trust these things. They had to believe in them, even if sometimes they weren't certain what they were believing in. Maybe it had something to do with the coming of the Red Sun, or something similar to this. They were already certain that the coming of the Blue Sun played a vital part in this. Maybe these final changes would be triggered by transformative Earth changes, volcanoes, earthquakes, tsunamis, meteors, massive storms with destructive winds, lightening and torrential rain or snow. Or maybe they would be triggered by a final collapse of the old paradigm system. Since the Guardians had come out of the closet, there was a semblance of a system that was up and running, but it continued to run on very wobbly legs. It could topple any day. The high-tech world of the New World Order was far more vulnerable than most people thought, connected as it was to an intricate system of satellites rotating the Earth and to a few central computers in various parts of the world, and ultimately to one central computer, the Beast, in Brussels Belgium. If one strand of this massive web went out, the whole thing could go down. And if the old paradigm system was to crash, then Rainbow Village and the other sustainable communities in the world would not only move to a position of equality, but superiority. This is what they planned and trained for, to survive when all else failed, and to be the launching pads for the new world.

And there were many other possible scenarios that could tip the balance of power in their favor. Perhaps the extraterrestrials, friendly or hostile, would get involved. It was pretty obvious to them that the Guardians were probably negative ET's, or at least hybrids, and the only reason intergalactic law permitted them to do what they were doing was because humanity had given them their consent. Yes, there was deceit, manipulation and trickery involved. But the fact will always remain that in a universe where certain beings are blessed with free will, they also have the responsibility to use it to make the proper decisions. There are no excuses. In addition, other benevolent ET's were participating as much as intergalactic law would allow. And as Kaleen had told them, they also knew that they were protected by intergalactic law because they had never given their consent to this slavery. They had chosen to take complete responsibility for their own lives, which is their god-given right. This was an incredible source of power for them, the strength of which they had no idea. They had watched as the energetic frequency fence was put in place on that night. They didn't understand its powers. They didn't have to. And they had total trust it was still there.

Maybe it would be one of these scenarios, or a combination of them. Maybe it would be some other, or perhaps one beyond their imagination. They understood that the powers of the supernatural were capable of almost anything. They had to believe in this, and they did. They trusted it. They trusted that there were forces at work here with the power to rearrange their entire world, both inside Rainbow Village and outside. Their job was to live with a vibration that resonated in harmony with these forces and powers, which meant to acquiesce to them, to merge energetically with them. This is what would allow them to use these supernatural powers to their advantage, to accomplish their mission, to flourish into the future

Yes, all these things were going on in their world. All these events and forces were swirling around them, not far from their borders. And now, with the visit by US Marshall Lieutenant Jacoby, their bubble had been pierced. The enemy was at their gates. And with the participation of the ET's, this drama was playing out in their skies. The folks at Rainbow Village could not ignore these things. They felt it every day. The world was squeezing in around them. Something was going to happen. They knew not what. Something had to happen.

And yet, this last three week period had been delightfully uneventful.

It was now early June. Even the weather was nice. Winter weather in these mountains challenged the spirit, and this past winter had been no different. There had only been splatterings of snow, and the snow-pack in the high mountains was still too low to remove doubts about the drought. Most of the snow was melted now, except for Mount Camille and the other higher peaks. The winter had mostly been dark, cloudy, rainy and windy. Late spring and early summer were always the best. The sun was shining. The temperature was pleasantly warm, not so brutally hot like in July and August. The nights were crisp and cool.

This three week period had been a reminder of how wonderful life at Rainbow Village could be if the world would just leave them alone. This had been their intention all along, to be able to live independently of an outside world that had gone mad and was destroying itself. And now it was happening. They were doing it. And it was working. And it felt so good to all of them that it was working so well. They were a self-contained unit, a separate world if you will, with the capability to sustain themselves almost entirely, with a little help from their trading partners, who were allies in their cause. And they were happy in their self-contained world. They didn't need anything else. They would continue to dabble with their immediate outside world, but they didn't have to.

How does something like this work? They were such a small community, 12 people, now 15 with the newcomers, and soon to be 16 with the birth of Wanda's baby. And David and Kelly wanted to have a baby too, as soon as things settled down, which never seemed to be. Ian and Claudia wanted to have children too. But they were such a small community, in the middle of nowhere, in a state of nature, with no distractions, no TV, no Internet, no nothing, just the Earth, the trees, the other animals, the gardens, the Blue Sun, the silence and each other. Wouldn't people get bored in such a setting, just working in the gardens and chopping wood all the time? Wouldn't they get bored and unhappy because of the lack of stimulation that you have in the cities and outside civilization? There's not a whole lot to do in the woods, and on the farm life is just a routine of unending chores. It's like camping, forever. Everybody wants to go home from camping. Wouldn't they get bored with each other? There are only 15 of them. That's a pretty small world. It's just not enough people to make life interesting. Wouldn't they start to get on each other's nerves? Maybe it works out for the adults, but the children need a larger peer group than that. It's not fair to them, or so the argument goes.

How do they make this work? What do they do every day that allows them not to lose their minds with boredom? What is the key to their joy? The primary thing they did every day was work. This was a working community. Nobody was there for a free ride. If you were, you were gone. And they worked at what they loved. Their work was their mission in life. It was their true purpose. It was the reason the divine spirit of a living universe put them in this world. This started with growing their own food and preserving it, including the seeds for the future, and it branched out from there to all the other aspects self-sustainability. They were there to learn how to do what humankind had forgotten, which was the cause of its demise, and that was how to live in harmony with nature again. This was a calling, this work, an honor, and they took pride in it. It gave them joy.

But there's more to life than work, as we all know. Work is never the total answer. All work and no play leads to an imbalance. They had discovered the gift of not wasting time, ever, and doing their work efficiently, which meant getting it done, with ample time left over for the other things in life. What were these other things at Rainbow? What else did they do with their time? The practice of their spirituality, both as individuals and as a group, was very high on the list. This was something they all shared. It was an essential part of the foundation of this community. They didn't practice any fixed spiritual system. They each followed their own individual path, but they did share a few things in common. One was their reverence for nature, attuning themselves vibrationally to her forces, frequencies and cycles, and finding spirit there. As the Hopi were so fond of saying, everything we need to know about this world or the world of the spirit we can learn from the growing of corn.

And practicing their spirituality was something that required attention, daily attention, not the one hour a week variety. It required time. It required practice and development. Like anything else, the more you did it the better you got at it. With young people, particularly white people, this takes a lot of work at first. With the elders, it becomes a way of life. They don't have to try as hard.

Participating in and practicing our spirituality means anything we do to connect with the spirit. Prayer is an essential feature of this. Prayer is when we talk to spirit. It's when we give thanks for all the blessings of this creation and pray for guidance to serve according to our purpose. We really should pray every day, at least once. We should pray before we eat our food, when we begin our work, and when we do things that have special spiritual meaning, like planting seeds. Ceremony is another way to connect with spirit. There are many different kinds of ceremonies. In addition to some form of prayer, they usually include music, singing and chanting, and playing our sacred instruments, drums, flutes, shakers, singing bowls, didgeridoo, and the like. They also usually include some form of fire, whether this is a fire circle outside, or a candlelit altar inside, or just a single candle. Sometimes they include the ingestion of medicine plants, such as marijuana, peyote or wachuma. And there are many other types of ceremonies, such as sweatlodges and pilgrimages to sacred sites.

At Rainbow, they had at least two fire ceremonies every month, one on the full moon and one on the new moon. Some were very short and simple, just lasting an hour or two. The most sacred days of the year were the winter and summer solstices and the spring and fall equinoxes, which, interestingly, correspond to the four major holidays in the old paradigm system, Christmas, the 4th of July, Easter and Labor Day On these days the ceremonies were more elaborate, sometimes lasting all night, sometimes a few days. Sometimes they took hikes and pilgrimages to sacred sites. There were sacred sites on their land, and they were plentiful in their general area, the greater Mount Camille vortex and the State of Jefferson. There was the magnificent Susquana River, which flowed just a few miles away. And this was volcano land, with lava caves, and other dormant volcanoes to the north and south, including Meteor Lake.

Yes, their spirituality took time and work. But as David, their spiritual leader, always said, what better thing do we have to do with our time? Everybody had a bundle. Everybody had their own altar. And both of these are constant works in progress. Our altar is where we arrange our power objects, which means imbued with spiritual power. Typical things you'd find on an altar were musical instruments, pipes and tobacco pouches, candles, conch shells for the burning of herbs, crystals, other stones, jewelry, animal bones, horns and skins, and any other artifacts that we have gathered on our spiritual journey. Our bundle is a large handbag or pouch, which we pack with our sacred objects and take to ceremony or on pilgrimages. It's like a mobile altar. Both our altar and our bundle are powerful expressions of who we are spiritually. They embody and carry our spiritual energy.

So with community work and spiritual work their time was getting pretty full. And there was leisure time too, time to just do nothing. Everybody needs to take a total day off once in a while, rest the mind, which is usually what gets overworked. But with this group these days were few and far between. This wasn't much of a do nothing group. They had a community meeting once a month, which was mandatory and for community business only. And they had a community dinner once a month, either in the community house or up at Jack's. This was the social highlight of the month. It was not an obligation. It was a party. Beer, wine and marijuana were often involved, which were brewed and grown by their neighbors and trading partners. The energy was usually uproarious. This was a genuine source of joy for all, often moving outside after dinner to sit around a social fire, watching the stars and the Moon, and often staying up quite late, for them. Another source of fun and entertainment was watching movies. Jack had a fine library of DVD's and even some old VCR cassettes, which he watched every day, with a standing invitation for others to join.

And that's pretty much it. That's how they filled their time. And for everybody it was more than enough. They had rich and full lives. Rarely did any of them feel the need to look to the outside for anything other than trade. And since the New World Army now occupied all the small towns around them, the world outside their enclave was increasingly dangerous anyway. The majority of them had partners in the community with whom they were deeply in love. And this was recently added to when Erick, Red Hawk's sixteen year old son, and Adelle, Don and Sandy's 18 year old daughter, fell in love. None of them ever needed to leave the place. The only exception was Annette, Don and Sandy's 20 year old, who had recently started dating a neighbor, who she met at a yard sale. They were together constantly, and he spent much of his time at Rainbow, with the possibility of even moving there someday.

That's what they did with their time, and nobody was bored. But it's only a partial answer to the question why it was working so well What else was it that allowed them to succeed, where so many others had failed? The entire village was sparkling clean, all the houses and teepees, even the sheds and the barns with the animals. Yes, there were places you could never keep clean, like the chicken coop or any of the animal barns, but even they were organized. Everything was in its place. There was never any trash strewn around. Even their junk was organized, and it wouldn't be where it was for long. Tools were always put back. Weeds were always picked. Dishes were always put away. Kitchen counters were always clean and clutter-free. They considered this too an honor, and this too gave them joy.

Many other communities have set out to do this, and the vast majority has failed. How did they manage to be so clean and organized? There is the misconception that this would take extreme amounts of work that would take too much time, and would actually throw life out of balance, and create unhappiness. Such a thing is often called obsessive-compulsive, meaning there is something deranged about it. But at Rainbow they did this with relative ease, and all within the rhythm and flow of the calm and peaceful lifestyle they had created.

And they did have a few secrets that allowed them to pull this off. One was they weren't afraid to have rules. I know this may sound odd to some, but there are some groups for whom rules are a problem. One such group I refer to as white, New Age, hippies. It seems that a top priority in their world is that everybody is allowed to do their own thing, and rules are contrary to this spirit. They are seen as oppressive and unenlightened. Of course this leads to chaos, and any time anybody attempts to implement rules, there is a natural resistance to them, which the community is unable to manage because there is no respect for rules. It goes around it a circle. They all say wash your dishes and put them away when done, and nobody does. They believe that people just shouldn't be allowed to tell others what to do. A great example of one of the problems this causes in white New Age hippy communities is the children, who invariably are defiant and out of control, because their parents don't know how to say no, and the children don't know the difference between right and wrong. Compare this to an indigenous community, in which the children are obedient, and when an elder says no, and the children simply obey, no questions asked. Nobody throws a fit. Nobody has a tantrum. Nobody requires an explanation.

At Rainbow Village, the rules were clearly stated, and there were lots of them. The rules were made by their tribal council, which consisted of David, Kelly, Red Hawk, Jack and Spotted Dear. The entire community met in an open meeting once a month to discuss the rules and procedures and possible changes to them. The walls of the community house and the other common areas, such as the barns and sheds, were covered with signs that stated the rules. And this included everything, from how to separate the trash, to cleaning your own drain screens, to where to throw your used toilet paper, to removing all personal clutter from all counters and common areas. There was never any confusion. The rules were staring you right in the face. The only excuse was you weren't paying attention. And with this group, nobody played any games. Everybody followed the rules. They respected them, and they could see the results. And interestingly enough, when they had visitors, the place was so immaculate that the visitors would automatically clean up after themselves in ways they never would normally.

Another one of the secrets of their success was an individual thing. It was something that was preached by their leadership council as one of the most important aspects of following the spiritual path, as was taught in most shamanic traditions. It was something that was brought to this circle by David and Kelly, who had learned it and practiced it in their own trainings, and which was a key to their own incredible spiritual connectedness. Red Hawk too had always practiced it, but he had a different name for it. And it was something that this entire group accepted readily, and endeavored to live by.

This was the simple act of paying attention. Red Hawk called it the impeccability of a warrior. Paying attention is one thing that is so lacking in our world, which is responsible for so much of the chaos and distress that exists. Paying attention in this sense, in the sense of the shaman, is to pay attention to everything, every detail in our lives. Nothing goes untouched. Nothing is neglected. Everything is looked at. Everything is analyzed. A conclusion is reached, and then everything is put in its place, or disposed of all together. A warrior's world is one of perfect order. A warrior knows where everything is, and what it's doing there, what its purpose is. If something has no purpose, it is thrown away, responsibly. Because a warrior is not afraid to throw things away, their lives tend to be minimal and trim. Everything they have in their life has use, and is used. Everything is accounted for. There is no clutter. There is nothing that is just randomly there. Rainbow Village was a community that was minimal and trim, no fluff.

When a person begins to pay attention in the way of the warrior, it is the difference between being awake and being asleep. And this applies to the biggest things in life, like our spirituality, as well as to the littlest things, like picking up after ourselves. The vast majority of humanity is sleep walking through life, paying attention to only a tiny fraction of what there is. They are literally turned off, and energetically this is why people get sick. When we start truly paying attention, everything changes. It's like flipping a switch, and everything comes to life. It also makes life harder in many ways, but this is a responsibility we heartily accept.

Not paying attention is the single reason for the sloppiness and disorganization with most people and communities. It all sounds so simple and self-evident, and it is. Nothing could be easier. Once we learn how to do it, it doesn't take an additional speck of our energy. When we pay attention to our material stuff, we know where it is, and whether that's where it's supposed to be. When we pay attention to other people, we can make certain our stuff is not in their way or in anybody's way. When we pay attention to the rules, we know where everything goes and how the system works. We can take refuge in the rules. They can protect us from friction. You don't have to like a rule, but you do have to follow it. Everybody was paying attention and living like a warrior at Rainbow Village. If you weren't, it would energetically throw everything so totally out of balance, so quickly, that you would just have to leave. This hadn't happened now in years.

Paying attention is also an essential component of our personal growth and spiritual development. If we want to change and evolve in these areas, the first thing we have to do is wake up. In the old paradigm culture, which is so imbalanced and dysfunctional, we are programmed from our earliest days in a way that cuts us off from the rhythm and flow of the natural forces in ourselves and in our world. It's this energy that gives life its vitality, its spark.. We live in state of numbness to our thoughts, our feelings and to the world around us. We're so numb we don't even know we're not paying attention.

When we begin to pay attention, the process can be very challenging because we are entering a world with which we are completely unfamiliar. When we wake up to what's happening in our physical bodies, we often feel anxiety and pain, which we then must learn how to work through. In most cases, we have to learn how to breathe for the first time, getting our air and our energy moving and flowing. It's much like coming to life. When we wake up to the reality of our thoughts, what's going on in our minds, we usually discover patterns that trap us in lives of misery and angst. In most cases, we need teachers to help us overcome these things. We need teachers to show us how to relax and how to get our body's energy back in balance. We need teachers to teach us how to think and how to change our thoughts in line with how we see ourselves and what we want in this world.

In addition to paying attention to ourselves, it is also necessary to pay attention to the world outside ourselves, particularly the natural world. It is in the world of nature and the forces, frequencies and cycles of nature where we often find spirit. And paying attention here again means paying attention in the way of the shaman or warrior. It means paying attention to every detail of this glorious creation. It means paying attention to all the natural forces of this world, paying attention to life's seasons and cycles, to the Sun, the Moon, the other planets and the stars beyond. It means paying attention to the four primary elements of this creation, the fire, the earth, the air and the water, paying attention to our brothers and sisters in the web of life, the other animals, the four legged, the birds, the fish, the reptiles, the insects, all the plants, the sacred trees, the medicine plants that grow in nature, the vegetables that grow in our gardens, and paying attention to every other aspect of this creation. When we pay attention closely enough, we invariably discover unseen forces and intelligence at work in the natural world. This is one aspect of the world of the spirit. Once we start to see these things, we see a world that is so mysterious and unfathomable that it could not possibly exist by random chance. We begin to see that everything in this world, including us, is created as part of some grand, cosmic design.

At Rainbow Village, everybody paid attention, like a warrior. This was a creed they lived by. It was one of their distinguishing characteristics, setting them apart. And it was another important reason for why the whole thing was working so well. You could feel it in their presence as individuals, and much more so, multiplied many times over, as a group. When they gathered for community dinners or any other community gathering, the space around them bristled with energy and vitality. Everybody was awake and fully present. Everybody paid attention to everybody else, meaning everybody talked to everybody, and listened. The volume was always very high, like at a party where people are having fun. There were no cliques. They weren't needed. They were beyond that. Nobody was just hanging out or lolling around, ever. There was never any same old, same old. This group was alive, like an organic being, charged with the vital energy of creation.

Everybody fed off this energy. They were all better as individuals as a function of being a part of this group. Some social systems take energy, instead of renewing it, and they drain themselves and everybody in it. This one was a self-charger, and there was no telling how high the charge might go, if it was left to run uninterfered. This is also one answer to the question posed earlier about why they never got bored. In an atmosphere like this, boredom wasn't even an option. The simple act of 15 people paying attention raised the energy so high it was impossible. It created an energy field that was exponentially beyond what they could create as 15 individuals.

Which leads us to yet another aspect of their group chemistry that charged everything up even more, and this was the fact that they all truly liked and admired each other. Nobody had to fake it, and nobody did. They were all best friends. It might even be true to say they all loved each other, depending on how you define that term. There were five families now, stable, non-dysfunctional and loving families. David and Kelly were married and best friends for eternity. There was Red Hawk, his mother and son. There was Don, his wife and two daughters. There was Jack, Chris and Wanda, who were like his children. And now there was the extended family of Peter and Ian and Claudia.

And across these families, there were many other friendships that were profound and eternal. For two years on the reservation Red Hawk had trained David and Kelly in the traditional ways of the Lakota and how to live off the land. They would spend weeks together hunting, trapping, harvesting medicinal plants and working in the garden. Red Hawk's mother, Kathy Spotted Deer, was present that fateful day when David was guided to meet Red Hawk's great grandfather, Red Cloud, a Lakota elder and medicine man, whose final teaching was with David, when he told him that he saw that he was a white man with special gifts and with powers strong enough to play an important part in changing the world. These were relationships that were clearly interwoven by destiny, guided by the force of the spirit.

Such was also the case with David, Kelly and Don Morisee. When David and Kelly were on the reservation, they were guided on a dream journey one night to the jungles of South American, where they met the Togi people, an indigenous tribe that had never had any contact with civilization. During this journey, they also had a vision of a scientist in his lab in Johnsport Coronado, and they were told they must find him as the next step on their own journey. They had no idea why, only that it had something to do with the great shift of the ages. They knew nothing else, not even his name.

And their actual meeting with Don was no less miraculous, guided by the supernatural as it was. David was in Johnsport, and he had been chased into an abandoned building by two policemen, who were reptilian hybrids, guns a blazing. It was a familiar script in those days. He saw them as they were, and they saw that he saw them, a most serious crime. They had him trapped in a second floor room, and his only chance of escape was to dive out the window. He tried to do a flip, but lost control, and landed headfirst on the sidewalk, knocked out cold, with serious lacerations on his body. But Don Morisee was standing right there. He had been guided to that spot, at that time, in a dream the previous night. He had no idea why, but he followed the guidance. When David came flying out the window, crash landing at his feet, it was all crystal clear. He threw him in the car, with Sandy at the wheel, and they took off. By the time the cops got to the window, they were out of sight. They nursed David back to health, and introduced him to their underground group in Johnsport, which was devoted to the shift of the ages and making it happen. It was at one of their meetings where they met Jack and where they met Lieutenant Frank Jacoby. And the rest is history.

All of the relationships at Rainbow Village had this power of being guided by spiritual forces. When David, Kelly and Don attended that meeting in Johnsport, they shared the same vision and the same agenda. Their calling was to use their unique knowledge and skills to help build a sustainable community that would be one of the bases from which to create the new world. And they had a few prerequisites about which there was no compromise. It had to be remote, far away from the tentacles of civilization, and it had to have a source of natural spring water. This community would also make no compromises with the old paradigm system. That was part of its spiritual base. It would be its own sovereign and self-contained entity. Of course, this was not the most popular point of view, even at a meeting like this. Making that final break with the old paradigm world was always the final issue. Most people really struggled with that. Many people also resisted the idea of small communities because it defied the idea of one global community, which was also very popular in the New Age.

Meeting Jack was another match made in heaven. They had everything except a place to manifest their plan. Jack had that place, but he didn't have the practical knowledge and skills to make it happen. And they were exactly what Jack was looking for.

He shared their vision. He wrote about it in his books and DVD's. It was like they stepped out of the pages of one of his novels. He had owned the land for a few years, and built his house and the solar system, with the help of Peter, Ian and Claudia, as well as the community house, which was one big room, with a kitchen, a bathroom and a loft. Those were the years he had the equinox ceremonies, and there were always people staying on the land. However, the sustainability part of it wasn't happening. The people Jack was attracting were a constant disappointment to him. Most of them were more interested in their own spiritual quests, as well as the social aspect of Rainbow, having fun in other words. And the experience was a transient one, as opposed to a life-long commitment. The place always ended up looking more like a hippy crash pad than a sacred sanctuary. This was infuriating and a total disillusionment to Jack. He started to think the right people just didn't exist.

Jack had no real hope that anything would come of the meeting in Johnsport. He found out about it through his grapevine, and it was appealing to him because they were trying to keep it a secret. He agreed that was the only way such a thing could work. But he had to force himself to go. He simply did it because he hadn't done anything different in a while. And though he was a renowned author on the shift and the spirituality of it, he hadn't been invited to speak. Everything changed as soon as he heard David and Kelly speak, which Don had arranged. It was like he was waking up from a dream. Here was this young couple who had been living sustainably in the hills of Lakota reservation for two years, under the tutelage of a young Lakota shaman. And they told their whole amazing story that night. They talked for hours. They talked about Red Cloud's vision. They talked about their dream journey where they were guided to find a scientist in Johnsport, Don Morisee. And their message was identical to that in Jack's books, emphasizing making a total break with the old paradigm system and creating our own communities where we reassume taking care of ourselves.

Now suddenly Jack was the one who felt guided, something he hadn't felt in a long time. He hadn't been that impressed with the conference so far. It seemed like a bunch of people who were talking about something he was already doing. Now these two young people were an answer to his prayers. How is it they weren't connected with any specific project yet? He had to talk to them quickly, or they might get away. Jack could walk in those days, and when the talks were finished, he attempted to make his way through the crowd to David and Kelly, but he got stuck. There were too many people stuffed in this private home, and it seemed like most of them were moving in the other direction. Jack stopped, yielding to the crowd, but he kept his eyes and his energy focused on David. He would not let this moment pass. Jack had the distinguished presence of an elder, with his long silver hair brushed back, down to his shoulders, piercing blue-green eyes that commanded respect, and a definite glow. When Jack wanted to he could really sparkle. He always stuck out in a crowd. David was swamped with people, but the instant Jack stopped, David turned his head, and his eyes went directly into Jack's. David remembers that he felt something. He felt drawn to this stranger, and he always followed these impulses. He broke away, pushed through the crowd, and introduced himself to Jack. Jack remembered that he called him grandfather. The rest was easy. Jack told him what he had in southern Coronado, just seven hours away, and David agreed to come and look. When you're flying on the wings of divine guidance, decisions make themselves with ease. After spending a few hours with Jack, and hearing what he already had in place, and where it was in the Mount Camille vortex, they didn't even really need to see the land.

Of course, David had to ask if Don and his family could come along, as well as Red Hawk, his mother and his son, who were waiting on the reservation. They too were a part of Red Cloud's vision. Jack knew of Don's work, and vice versa, and both were honored. By the end of the next day they were on the land. And at sunset on the day after that David, Kelly, Don and Sandy decided they would make this their home. This was where they would build a sustainable community that would be a base for the creation of the new world. One week Later Red Hawk arrived with his family and all his worldly possessions. Rainbow Village was now finally born. In an instant Jack had gone from the brink of giving up to the manifestation of his dream.

All of the relationships at Rainbow were guided by the spirit in this way, mysterious and unfathomable. It was the same with all the young people. Everybody had a story to tell. Everybody had a vision or was touched by the spirit in some way that led them to this sacred spot. And in every case the guidance was unmistakable. There was no saying no to it. Jack often said his experience felt like he was squeezed by the forces in his life to this place and to these people, like out of some giant cosmic tube.

Relationships that are guided in this way have more energy, more power than relationships that aren't, exponentially more power, and more staying power too. This was another of the reasons for their success as a community. When you have one of these relationships in your life, this can be a force to be reckoned with. When you have more than one, this power is multiplied many times over. And when you have many in a single community, all crisscrossing each other, like at Rainbow, this force can become invincible. That's how it feels, and that's how it arranges itself in our minds. When we follow spiritual guidance in our lives, and begin to experience miracles as a result, we begin to think and feel that anything is possible. And it might well be. When a group of 15 people do this together, there is no telling the limits of what they might manifest.

So we say these three weeks were delightfully uneventful, and we know that this is just an expression because when you live the way they did at Rainbow, nothing is uneventful. When you pay attention like a band of spiritual warriors, something is always happening, even when it isn't. But these three weeks allowed them to just be, without any outside static. It allowed them to do their thing, the thing they were on this planet to do. And it allowed them to feel their power, those feelings of invincibility. It allowed them to experience their success. This enterprise was working perfectly. At a time when the world outside was falling to pieces, Rainbow Village was doing just fine. They were living sustainably, in harmony with Mother Earth, with a little help from their neighbors. And they truly loved each other. They were happy, healthy people, with the fullest of lives. There was nothing missing. Their beautiful creation at Rainbow Village was a constant reminder that anything is possible. There was nothing more they could do to serve this creation.

As soon as David saw it, saw the image in the sky, he thought of it.

He thought of what he had heard Peter talking about recently. Peter still had lots of connections in the outside world. His house, his property, his farm were still down below. He was well known locally. He still had customers for his handy work. He didn't use the Internet much himself, but he talked to people who did.

One of the latest scuttlebutts on the Internet was the report that people in vast numbers around the world were seeing huge images in the sky. Nothing else was known about this. Nothing was reported in the mind-control mainstream media, which was now so obviously controlled by the Guardians. But it was reported at enough places by enough people that there was no doubt something was happening.

The reporting on this was very sloppy and imprecise. The Internet was still a mess. Much escaped the censorship and control of the Guardians, but most of this was wild gossip by a lot of crazy people. So you really had to do your due diligence to get at the truth. But a picture was emerging that these images were similar to the ones that were shown on the TV screen the night the Guardians made their epic announcement. There was apparently a wide variety, and the images were both people and things, but the basic theme was always the same. The human ones were simple depictions of how the Guardians saw themselves and how they wanted humanity to see them. The images were of men and women who appeared to be divine or enlightened beings, with beatific, enraptured, regal expressions. None of them were reported to be specific people from any particular religion or philosophy, like the Virgin Mary or Sir Isaac Newton, but this was the aura they had. Many were reminiscent of the busts and statues from ancient Greece or Enlightenment Europe. The message was pretty clear. These were all-knowing folks, and the people of planet Earth would be smart to follow wherever they led. And the things depicted were always related in some way to the utopia that the Guardians were selling to the people of Earth. There were celestial cities in the clouds and transcendent palaces on mountain tops. The Seeing Eye from the Seeing Eye Pyramid was projected, as was an illumined double-helix DNA molecule. And on a few occasions it was reported that an image was projected of the sky catching on fire. Or maybe the sky was catching on fire.

Apparently these images would appear. They'd remain for a few minutes, and then disappear. It was hard to determine what kind of an effect they were having. Ostensibly it didn't seem to be much. They weren't causing any riots or anything like that. Most of the world was already in a pretty high state of panic anyway. The people of the planet Earth had already been subjected to so much with the coming of the Blue Sun and then the actions of the Guardians. Everybody's reality had already been stretched way beyond the breaking point. Now there was one more thing, and it wasn't that big a deal.

As soon as Jack heard this, he immediately speculated it had something to do with chemtrails. In the conspiracy community, it had long been believed that the purpose of chemtrails was not one single thing, like controlling the weather or protecting us from global warming. That would be the cover story, but there were other purposes that were less obvious and far more nefarious. There was a high likelihood that more than one thing was being sprayed and at different times. It is widely believed by reputable folks that some chemtrails may consist of nano-particles of biological material, like viruses, which alter human DNA, shutting us off from our higher consciousness, and benumbing us, making us more robot-like. There are other reputable folks who believe some chemtrails might consist of nano-particles of artificial intelligence, like tiny computers, which also get into our DNA, and reprogram our humanity out of us, making us more like machines or robots.

And then there were reputable folks like Jack who believed that some chemtrails consisted of something like electronic particles or particles with a technology not of this Earth. And the function of these particles was to create a medium in the sky that could be used for laser projections or any number of other possible things, like, for example, setting fire to the sky. The laser projections could be used for both intimidation of the masses and mind-control. This is what appeared to have already started. And these are only a few possibilities for this medium that was being created in the sky. Perhaps some other big-bang event in the sky was being orchestrated by the Guardians to help them achieve their objective of enslaving the people of Earth.

All of this flashed through David's mind when he saw the image.

He was walking through the meadow.

He just happened to look up. It hadn't done anything to attract his attention. And there it was, perched in the sky above him: the face of a reptilian or a reptilian hybrid, glaring menacingly at him. It was large, large enough that he could distinguish specific features, and it appeared to be about the same distance away as the clouds were.

At first it didn't move. But David could feel the eyes glaring at him, and he stared back. It looked the same as they always did. They did indeed all look the same. The head was more oblong than round, with a pointed chin. The skin was a pale green, covered with scales. It always made David think of a swamp, and the stagnant clumps floating on the water. There was also a faint aura surrounding the head of the same color. Against this backdrop the huge eyes were what stuck out, glaring hypnotically. They were twice the size of human eyes. And the pupil was a black, thin, vertical slit that stretched from the top of the eye to the bottom. The vertical slit was surrounded by the bright white of the rest of the huge eye. The eyes popped off the face like a flash and grabbed a hold of you. The rest of the face paled. The nose and ears were small and undistinguished, little knobs surrounded by scales. And the mouth was long and thin, with no lips, stretching from ear to ear, and expressionless, like a shark. Normally in the past, when David was in their physical presence, he felt them with feelings of anxiety and nausea. He wasn't feeling that now.

It continued its glare, motionless.

David thought of Kelly. She could see them too. He knew she was back at the house, about 100 feet away. It was quiet. If he yelled, she would probably hear.

"Kelly! Kelly Archer! Front and center we've got an issue here."

His eyes darted back toward the community house. Sandy and Annette Morisee were sitting on the porch.

"Sandy!" he yelled. "Ring the bell, please! General alarm, ring the bell, please, Sandy! We've got an issue here."

They only rang this bell in serious emergencies. Everybody knew what it meant. It was one of those triangles made out of thick metal with a heavy metal mallet. They hadn't rung it since the night of the Blue Sun.

Sandy jumped up, and rang the bell as loud as she could. You could hear it for miles.

David looked back up. The reptile eyes were still glaring.

He heard the screen door to his house slam, then looked back, and saw Kelly running down the path in his direction.

Adelle, Erick and Spotted Deer were working in the fields. They stopped, and when they saw David, they looked up too. Ian, Claudia and Peter were working on Peter's house up the hillside. They stopped working, and they were looking up too.

Kelly arrived at David's side. She had been focused on him, and hadn't seen it yet. When she did, the sight sucked the air out of her.

David was numb. In the past he had always managed to escape them, and it was always nothing short of miraculous, requiring significant help from the supernatural realm. But now it seemed there was nowhere to run, nowhere to hide. Plus, he had no idea what he was dealing with. Obviously, the hybrids had located them, which probably meant the Guardians too. But nothing had actually happened yet, other than this image, which did seem to be alive in some way.

He grabbed Kelly's hand, and didn't say anything. He took several deep breaths, and waited. Time stood still, every instant an eternity.

He looked around. The others were coming. The alarm bell meant to congregate, so they were. Peter, Ian and Claudia were on the way in their truck. So was Jack in his Jeep. And everybody else was moving in from all around. Nobody was missing.

Then the image spoke. The long thin mouth grinned fiendishly, from ear to ear. The eyes seemed to bulge even wider, and never blinked. The face became more animated, occasionally moving from side to side or up and down. The mouth moved ever so slightly when speaking, but the words clearly matched the movement of the mouth.

In spite of all this, it didn't feel to David like this was a living being who was actually speaking to them in the moment. It felt like an image that had been prefabricated, and then sent. And the words it spoke didn't feel like they were happening in the moment. It felt like they had been recorded, and then fit to match this image.

The tone of the voice was masculine, smooth, enticing, excessively polite and just condescending enough to be cute. It sounded like the devil himself was speaking.

This is what they heard.

"David, David Rhodes. And you, Kelly, Kelly Archer. At long last, we meet again. Once our hybrid guards spotted you that day with Federal Marshall Jacoby, it was easy to identify you. It looks like our fishing expedition into the wilderness achieved some results after all. We hadn't stopped looking for you, you know, though there were some who thought you might be gone, or perhaps transported to another world."

"You are to be praised. You are formidable adversaries. And look at your creation here, at Rainbow, that's right, isn't it, Rainbow Village. Look at what you've created here. It's really most impressive. You're actually living independently from the one world paradigm we are introducing to raise the standards of Planet Earth and all of its people."

There was the slightest of pauses.

"May I ask a question, please?" David bellowed. "May I ask a question before we proceed?"

This was the only thing David could come up with. He felt helpless, but he had to try to do something. This way they could at least test to find out if there was going to be any interaction here, instead of just being talked to.

But the voice continued, talking over David's question like it wasn't heard.

"This is what we cannot allow. As we know you know, this is the great work of the ages, and it has been in the planning for many centuries, since before the beginning of your history. And it mustn't be stopped. It cannot be stopped. And certainly you cannot stop it. There will be no deviation from the plan, like yours. To succeed it requires total unanimity. Energy must not be wasted on divisiveness. Ideas must not enter the mind of humanity that are deleterious to the implementation of this illumined system. The entire world must be involved, no exceptions. It is energetically imperative."

"And we know the two of you, David and Kelly, well enough to know that you would rather die than join our great cause. And we're certain the same thing can be said now about your accomplices. Again, we applaud your courage and heroism. But the time has come to do what we must. We must now put an end to all this, and you."

With that, the face nodded, with the slightest of grins.

And it vanished.

Everybody had arrived, and gathered around David and Kelly.

All eyes were still on the sky.

"OK," David said. "Pay attention. This isn't over."

A tiny flame appeared in the sky where the face had been. It was a light red. It was like the flame of a single candle, and it was fluttering, like in a breeze.

David instantly remembered what Peter had said about setting the sky on fire.

"Full fire precautions!" he bellowed decisively. "Everybody to their stations!"

They'd been over this a lot. There were wild fires every summer, though only once had one gotten close enough for them to implement their emergency system. Everybody had a job to do, and they all scampered off to do it.

They had an intricate irrigation system, with sprinkler systems on top of all the buildings to protect against fires. They also had two five-hundred gallon tanks of water on trailers, with hoses, which they used to water down the trees and the shrub inside their fire wall and along its perimeter, as well as to actually fight a fire if it came to that.

They watched the sky together.

The tiny red flame continued to flutter. Then it started to multiply, with other little flames leaping out and separating themselves, and then others, and then others, like cells dividing. It grew in a shimmering red circle above them, and as it got bigger they started to hear faint sounds, like the distant sound of rushing water or a waterfall. It made David think of the sound of a flamethrower. At first the fire appeared to grow sideways, horizontally to them. Like the face it was hard to discern where it was, how far away, or whether it was even a real fire, or just an image, a scare tactic. It grew to about the same size as the face, and then the growth of the fire switched directions, and started moving downward, in their direction, in the direction of the community. It started at a single point in the middle, with a single flame, brighter than the rest, which started moving slowly toward them, fluttering, shimmering, with other flames fanning out from it, moving in the shape of a cone toward Rainbow Village. As it got closer the sound like roaring water got louder.

For one of the rare times in his life David was frozen. Everything was happening so quickly. He was usually so good at thinking things through and taking action, in an instant. But nothing was coming to him. He looked around. Most of the sprinklers were on, but the trucks were still being hitched to the large tanks. There was no way of knowing what was going to happen, and whether the water would help. He was starting to worry about his people, and whether they should take cover. Jack had a shelter built into the side of the ridge next to his house, which consisted of two gigantic iron trailers, covered with about ten feet of earth. It was your basic bomb shelter, complete with plumbing, electricity and stored food. Jack had built it for natural or unnatural disasters, like this. They could take cover here.

He looked at Jack's house. Jack was in between his house and the shelter, leaning on his crutch, looking up at the approaching fire. Chris was busying himself with the sprinklers and other precautions.

Everything was happening so quickly.

The fire was getting closer. David was beginning to actually feel its heat. Even if he ordered it, they probably wouldn't be able to make it to the shelter on time.

They needed a miracle.

David and Kelly had had so many divinely guided miracles in their lives. He wondered if they one left.

He closed his eyes and prayed, "Divine Spirit, help us."

Then they heard it.

A humming sound began to emerge from the rushing sound of the fire cone.

Hmmmmm.

It started at a medium pitch, and slowly rose in frequency, as it grew louder.

Hmmmmm.

David opened his eyes and saw a circular band of light start to appear in the sky. It was faint at first and then got stronger, until it was a solid golden yellow line, the color of a star, tracing the border of the community above them. The fire circle was approximately in its center.

Mmmmmm.

The hum shifted to yet a higher octave.

You could barely hear the flamethrower sound anymore.

David and Kelly looked at each other.

"The frequency fence," they both gasped in unison.

Mmmmmm.

Higher and higher the pitch ascended, like a celestial chorus.

The circle of fire, or the image of the circle of fire, or whatever it was, started to fade. It could no longer be heard. It was dissolving, becoming fainter. There was no longer the feeling of heat. Pretty soon patches of blue sky were showing through. It was now no more than a hazy mist. And then, it was gone.

The sky was as it was before.

The hum had hit its crescendo, and as the fire faded, the pitch started to drop.

Mmmmmm.

When the fire was gone, the circular band of light remained.

After a few seconds, the humming stopped.

A few seconds more, the circle of light went out, in a blink, like someone had thrown a switch, and probably did.

The day was as it was before.

The sprinkling on the rooftops was the only sound that could be heard.

David and Kelly stood in silence, waiting, waiting to see if it was actually over.

Everybody else was pretty dispersed, taking care of their water responsibilities.

Then he started hearing the muttering and chattering of the people in their various spots.

Peter, Ian and Claudia were the closest, at the sheds, attaching their truck to one of the trailers with the water tanks. Ian and Claudia were screaming with joy, high fiving each other.

"Did you fucking see that?"

Jack's Jeep had started up, and was headed around the bend in their direction.

David was still holding Kelly's hand. He still felt possessed with the energy and power of what had just happened. It was like a beam of energy had taken hold of him and wouldn't let go. This demanded his total attention. He had felt this way before, and he knew what he had to do.

He let go of her hand, put his arm around her waist, and drew her to him. He turned to speak into her ear, without looking at her.

"This isn't over. Let's be with this energy with our energy."

She was feeling everything he was feeling, and he could feel it. He knew it.

"Yes," she replied softly, not looking at him.

He continued to hold her against him. They were one body.

They both closed their eyes, mirroring each other, reaching out with their energy.

The energy field around them was palpable. Everybody picked up on this. Nothing needed to be said.

Jack got about 50 feet from them, stopped the Jeep, turned off the engine, sat, and waited. He'd been through this before. Ian and Claudia stopped their celebration. Everybody was quiet, watching David and Kelly, waiting. The only sound was the sprinklers, which nobody was going to turn off quite yet. This moment had taken over.

David and Kelly couldn't hear anything anyway, or see anything.

They were outside themselves. They were enveloped in the energy field that surrounded them. They were still aware of their physical bodies, and but their consciousness was not inside them.

Then they felt the energy field take a hold of them, even stronger. It was like a warm sensuous fluid flowing through them. The feeling was one of elation, lightness and lucidity. They had reached a higher dimension, a higher frequency of being.

As all of this was happening, Red Hawk was out by the solar panels. He had fastened his truck to the other water tank trailer and was preparing to start watering the trees. He had also been watching and listening carefully. When the frequency fence disappeared, he felt all the same things David and Kelly did. He too had entered this energy field, this higher dimension.

Then all three of them heard the voice, a voice they had heard before. It was gentle, firm and melodious, all at once.

> Hello my friends, David, Kelly and Red Hawk.
> This is Kaleen again, from the Intergalactic
> Council. Yes, we are communicating with you now
> more directly, in more of a conscious state, more of
> a state you can reach volitionally. And it will
> continue to be more and more this way, as long as
> you continue to raise the frequency of your
> vibration, and as long as we continue to make
> progress in this great challenge to save Planet Earth
> from the forces of darkness. You are now even able
> to initiate this communication, as you did today,
> even though you weren't aware of it.
>
> As far as the events you just experienced, that
> wasn't as close a call as it might have seemed. As
> always, we closely monitor the actions of the other
> side. They hide nothing from us that is of any
> significance, and this attack against you was a clear
> breach of the intergalactic law that they do not
> adhere to. It was so obvious that it almost seems
> like they did it just to test us or tease us, though
> you'd think after all this time, they'd know. And
> ultimately, they will pay the consequences for these

acts. Hopefully, with the situation currently on Planet Earth, that time is near. Not only did they use technology that was not of this Earth, the attack itself was carried out by extraterrestrials, though with hybrids the distinction can often be very fuzzy.

Yes, they could have incinerated you and your entire community. They have that capability and they are using it in other places. The frequency fence protects you because you never gave your consent to be ruled by them. It is a violation of intergalactic law for extraterrestrials to intervene in the affairs of indigenous peoples against their will. And we are watching over to enforce that law. They also have the capability to project the types of images you saw, and they are doing that in more and more places as a weapon of intimidation and subliminal mind control. As yes, these occurrences in the sky are made possible by chemtrails, which provide the proper atmospheric medium for them.

Please take heart. We know that today probably shook you to your limits. As always, we are your allies, and we are doing as much to help as we can, even though you are not always aware of it. Things are not as bleak as they might appear. The new world that the Guardians are trying to create continues to teeter on the brink of collapse. Their grand project just isn't working, and if it continues to be stressed, it probably will break once and for all, even beyond the ability of the Guardians to repair. Things will be such a mess that they will be forced to admit defeat. They may be forced to try to find other worlds to infest.

This, of course, is the grandest blessing imaginable. Yes, this would mean more hardship and worse for vast multitudes of humanity. But there is nothing we can do about this. It is the greatest tragedy of all that humanity has allowed itself to be tricked into choosing this world, which is now punishing them. It is a great blessing because it gives us the fresh turf from which to build the world of the Fifth Sun. And we are permitted to tell you that more changes are coming, big changes, changes that will rock your world even more. These too are part of the alchemy that will help to create the new world. Welcome these challenges and see them for the blessings the universe designed them to be.

We commend you on the excellence of the work you are doing. And please know that you are not alone. There are other communities like yours around the world, not a lot, but enough, communities that are living according to the ancient ways, in harmony with the forces and frequencies of the natural world. The time is near when your community and the others, will lead the way, along with us, your brothers and sisters from the stars, in building the new world. The time is also near when we will be able to work more closely with you, and we will be able to meet in person, so to speak. That will be a most blessed day because that will mean that the world of the Fifth Sun has dawned, and the frequency of Planet Earth is in resonance with ours. Farewell until that day when our energy fields can embrace.

CHAPTER SIX – *The Coming of the Red Sun*

Two months passed. It was mid-August.

It was the new moon in Leo. And in the Mayan Calendar it was 13 Ajpu, the fruition of the 260 day Mayan year, where the energies of this world are at their highest frequency.

David and Don were up at Jack's for dinner and a movie, boy's night out. They were expecting Peter also because they were going to watch his favorite movie, an old frontier western, *Rio Bravo,* with John Wayne and a star-studded cast. But Peter was conspicuously late. He had gone out earlier to pick up a machine part for the tractor, and was expected back in the late afternoon. It was now almost Sunset.

They were also in the midst of a thunder storm. A dark bank of clouds with almost constant lightning and thunder had been approaching from the northeast for a couple hours. It was now almost upon them, and it was beginning to rain lightly. It hadn't rained in a couple months. There had barely even been a cloud, which was normal for the summer months. This was an extremely dry and hot time, with temperatures often as high as 105 degrees. The danger of forest fires was extremely high, particularly in lightning storms like these, in the high altitudes, where the lightning strikes the ground so often. It was not unusual to be very smoky during these months, even from fires hundreds of miles away. But this summer there had been none, so far.

The chaos in the world outside Rainbow Village continued to mount. The New World Order instigated by the Guardians was falling apart, and it wouldn't be able to hold up much longer, at least not in its current state. The system of fixed prices to control hyperinflation wasn't working because so many consumers had been totally wiped out that there weren't enough buyers, for anything. Nobody was making any money, not the huge multi-national corporations, not any of the national governments. The Guardians attempted to solve the problem by implementing a system of price controls, where prices were allowed to rise to new fixed levels. But this had no effect. If they were to manipulate the system so that profits were being made again, they would have to raise prices so much that they would be bringing back the same inflation they were trying to eliminate. Bottom line: the international economy was dead.

But this was only the tip of the iceberg. The Guardians were achieving none of the objectives of their New World Order. The vast majority of the people of the planet Earth did not receive the microchip. As far as all the poor people of the world are concerned, and they are a substantial majority, this is totally understandable. The Guardians weren't thinking about poor people when they put the system in place. Poor people were expendable. They were simply in the way.

But where the Guardians really miscalculated was with the vast middle class in most of the countries of the world. Middle class is defined here as those people with jobs, and enough money to own a home, support a family, send them to the schools of their choice, and have enough money left over to retire, and spend their final years in comfort. The Guardians were counting on this middle class to be the cornerstone of the new system. After all, these people were already subservient and dependent upon the system for whatever prosperity they had. They were also, for the most part, already mind-controlled, believing that reality was what they heard in the mainstream media, having given up one of their primary virtues as human beings, the ability to think for themselves.

So it seemed like a no-brainer. These people would have no choice but to jump aboard the ship of the new order. And perhaps most of them would have if they hadn't been decimated by the first wave of hyperinflation and the collapse of all the existing money. As it was, the choice to receive the microchip and participate in the new system was never a choice at all. And this doesn't even take into consideration the other-worldly aspect of the Guardians plan, which freaked most people out, and opened a lot of eyes.

However, we're still just brushing the surface. When you open your eyes and when you have all the facts, it's pretty easy to see that the Guardians' true objectives were not economic or profit based. It's far more diabolical than that. Once again, it's necessary to back up and look at the whole picture. The Guardians were extraterrestrials or extraterrestrial hybrids, who arrived on this planet far before the beginning of our so-called history, perhaps hundreds of thousands, perhaps even millions of years. It was during these ancient times that they created many highly advanced civilizations, many of the ruins of which we can still see today. Their most commonly cited purpose was colonization and the extraction and exportation of the Earth's abundant natural resources.

However, this too is little more than a cover story. One of the most common traits of the negative ET's was and is their desire to create life and to create worlds that were of their own making. Yes, this is the same as playing God, or the creator, or whatever you choose to call the divine spirit or the natural forces and energies that created this universe and our Mother Earth. They possessed a highly advanced knowledge of genetics, computers and high technology, and these would be their primary tools to manipulate life, to create artificial intelligence, and ultimately to transform the natural world into a synthetic one, which they controlled. This amounts to a rebellion against the creation and against the natural and spiritual forces that created it.

There are those who equate this with the Lucifer Rebellion from ancient Christianity. They say that Lucifer and his band of "fallen angels" were actually lightworkers, who energetically descended from higher dimensions into the material 3rd dimension. Like other lost souls or "wanderers," the heaviness of this dimension caused them to fall victim to a common form of spiritual amnesia, in which they forgot who they were, where they came from, and most importantly how to get out. This is what has motivated them over the millennia to try to circumvent the laws of nature in order to find a way to get out. This circumvention of the laws of nature is the hallmark characteristic of the Guardians and the leadership elite on planet Earth for thousands of years. Farfetched, yes, but let us remember we must always examine all the possibilities, no matter how silly they might seem.

And in fact, this is actually what they've been dong. The human race has been massively tinkered with genetically. We know that half the strands of our DNA have been turned off and are called junk DNA because they serve no purpose. They're just there. Nature doesn't program anything to have no purpose. So it is reasonable to conclude that this was done artificially.

And as our new paradigm science now tells us, the purpose of our DNA goes far beyond the simple passing along of genetic characteristics, as we are told. When functioning at its full capacity, our DNA transmits and receives chemical and energetic signals that connect us with our higher consciousness and with the higher consciousness of the universe. So the result of the genetic tinkering is to shut us off to these aspects of ourselves and of life, which makes us more docile and easier to control. A very good case can be made that the entire Caucasian or white race is a genetic hybrid, part human and part ET, which would explain why they have so little sensitivity to our Mother Earth, destroying her in the way they are. This is unthinkable to an indigenous human. It also explains why they have been so dominant over the indigenous people of this world. And as we discussed in an earlier chapter, a very good case can also be made that some chemtrails consist of nano-particles of viruses and nano-particles of artificial intelligence that also get into our DNA when ingested.

The Popol Vuh has what appears to be an interesting version of this. The Popol Vuh is the most ancient of the sacred Mayan texts and is the basis of Mayan spirituality. It is very similar to what the Bible is in traditional Christianity. Like the Bible, it is also extremely symbolic, cryptic and coded and not at all easy to understand. In the Mayan creation story, it tells how the Lords, as they are called, who are also referred to as the builders and the sculptors, made three attempts to create humans, which resulted in failure. The first was the mud people. The second was the wood people. And the third was the monkey people. One possible interpretation here is that the lords were from other worlds, and they were genetically experimenting with the indigenous humans who were here at that time. It wouldn't be the first time it has been suggested that the Maya are descended from other worlds.

This genetic tinkering is also pervasive with other domestic plants and animals. The whole GMO controversy has now been well publicized even in the mainstream media. It is commonly known that there is a conspiracy by corporate agriculture, at its highest levels, to poison humanity and to alter our DNA. The vast majority of the vegetables and fruits in the corporate supermarkets are genetically altered. That's why they look so uniform and perfect, and that's why they don't rot when you take them home. An apple is no longer really an apple. Its essence and vitality as an apple have been removed. It's like it's been sterilized. It's synthetic. And with bottled and canned items there are chemicals like artificial sweeteners, MSG and hydrogenated oils with toxicity levels that are off the scales. The same is true with meat, poultry and dairy products. Everything is genetically engineered. Even the seeds that are sold by corporate agriculture are genetically modified to last only one generation, thereby preventing us from raising our own seeds. They too are sterile. In the corporate mindset there's no reason for wild or natural animals or plants to exist anymore. Like the Indians hundreds of years ago, they get in the way, and there is the risk they might even fertilize the other genetically modified animals and plants and bring them back to life.

And it's the same everywhere. The entire world is either being poisoned or genetically altered, and sometimes they go hand in hand. They are poisoning the air, poisoning the water, and poisoning the soil. And we know from our indigenous metaphysics that everything in the web of life is energetically connected with everything else anyway. So if you poison one part, you poison the whole thing anyway, eventually. But to the Guardians these things make no difference. And they are doing these things by intention. It's not some mistake or miscalculation or ignorance. They know exactly what they're doing. The ultimate objective of the New World Order is to replace everything in the world with its synthetic equivalent. Then they can say that they created this world. And they would be correct. And this would be a world that they would control completely.

So the ultimate objective was not profits or money, though they certainly have had a good time running the show down here in the 3rd dimension on planet Earth for so long. And they have also entertained themselves thoroughly playing their insidious game to outwit humanity, and turn them into slaves, robots, a work-force. It's very much like a game of cat and mouse with them and a challenge to see if they can pull it off. No, this was not about money. It was about control, controlling the human race, controlling the forces of nature, and becoming the gods of planet Earth.

And now, none of it was working. Until the appearance of the Blue Sun, this ancient plan was pretty well on track. Humanity was thoroughly brainwashed and willing to believe anything. And the rest of the world was also being slowly, incrementally transformed into its synthetic equivalent. With the coming of the Blue Sun, the Guardians apparently felt the urgent need to speed things up and kick the plan into a higher gear with the elimination of paper money, the mandatory microchip and the new one world government headed by them.

The gamble didn't work. And now it was becoming clear there was nothing that could be done to make it work. With the failure of the price controls and the second round of hyperinflation, the world's system of money was completely dysfunctional. Only at the highest levels of the pyramid of power and in a few segments of government was there any semblance of a working system. For whatever reason, the human race had basically rejected the microchip. This was a central feature of the plan. When the ET's first arrived millennia ago, the Earth was such a pristine place to run their experiments. Now it was a total mess, a cauldron of death, despair, chaos and insanity. They had turned it into an unsuitable place to implement their plan. If things deteriorated much further, perhaps they would be forced to abandon that plan.

The Guardians were beginning to show signs of giving up. Of course, at Rainbow Village they heard all these things through their very flimsy grapevine. Peter and Annette, Don's oldest daughter, and Josh, her new boyfriend, who still lived down below with his family, were the primary purveyors of this information. And the grapevine had it that the Guardians' messages to the people on the Internet and TV were greatly diminished, other than the repeat of the same old messages telling people to get the chip and to get involved in the new system. There was nothing new, and it was starting to look like there wasn't even a plan anymore. Everybody remembered how the Guardians had said they would be in continuous contact with the people regarding the steps of the plan.

It was also reported that the Internet and TV were becoming increasingly dysfunctional. It had been hit-and-miss before whether people even received them, and now it was getting worse. It wasn't even clear if the Internet was still free, or whether people needed to pay, or how. One piece of gossip that was picking up steam was the report that the Guardians and other high government officials and entire government departments were moving to underground installations, and to other secure facilities, spanning the globe, which had been created for this purpose. This even included satellite fortresses that were rotating the Earth. Rumor also had it that things were functioning much more efficiently in these isolated installations, and to hell with the rest of the world.

What was left, and what was still plain to see in the outside world was the new world military and police force. They were as conspicuous as the Guardians were inconspicuous. Rushville had been militarily occupied, with the prime directive to facilitate or enforce the implementation of the microchip. Unlike the early days, when there were no chips and no personnel to implant them and to show people how to get involved in the new system, these personnel were now on hand. This meant that the police needed to make sure that the hospital and the pharmacies stayed open, as well as the two specified banks.

However, few people in Rushville received the chip. It just didn't make any sense for people who didn't have any money, and who were doing quite well prior to the arrival of the military, with the local autonomous economy that was supervised by the vigilantes, and pegged to the old paper dollar at its pre-inflation value. As soon as the military arrived, this economy was abandoned. The rebels knew the new army would not allow this, nor could this system survive once it was contaminated by the outside system. Even the gas stations were abandoned, with most of the gas and oil missing. But most of the people of Rushville continued to feed themselves and survive through a secret black market under the tutelage of the rebels.

Other than the implementation of the chip, there was apparently no plan for the military to govern. It did attempt a few things, such as opening and operating the gas stations, with some shipments of gas and oil coming in. But the prices were so high, there were few buyers, other than the military and police, who were able to afford it. But a bigger question remained. Who was in charge? If it was true that the Guardians were AWOL and with all the heads of state and parliaments abolished, there was no government. Nobody was running the show. And there was no way for the people to know. Were decisions being made at the highest levels from secure installations and relayed to the outside? If so, to whom? It could only be to the military because nobody else was available. Were these decisions being delegated to the high level government agencies that were protected by the New World Order, such as the CIA and FBI? Or were these agencies too off in the same bunkers as the Guardians? If nobody was making these decisions, what then? Had the military become an unofficial autonomous governing body? History has told us repeatedly that whenever any military is exclusively in charge, disaster is soon to follow in the form of murderous police states. It was also reasonable to assume that this new world military was not operating as a coordinated unit. In all probability, it was as splintered as everything else, which meant that the military in different geographic locations would be operating as separate autonomous units. This final scenario was potentially the most dangerous to Rainbow Village. If the military in Rushville was self-governing, this presented a far greater threat to them.

Nobody knew the answers to these questions. However, at Rainbow, one thing was for certain. The military presence in the area was escalated as never before. The fly-overs by the military helicopters were now common, at least a couple per day, and sometimes it was almost constant. But they always seemed to be tending to other business and not interested in Rainbow, at least not at this time. They were either en route to Rushville, or they were on surveillance missions for the rebels. At this time, Rainbow, for whatever reason, did not seem high on the list of suspects. This seemed a little odd, since David and Kelly had been identified by the reptilian hybrid cops and were considered criminals of the highest order to them. After all, they already tried to wipe them out once with fire from the sky. Maybe their old friend Frank Jacoby had turned in a favorable report. UFO sightings were also common during this time. Most of these were not too terribly significant, nothing more than lights the size of stars moving through the sky, apparently on missions elsewhere. The sky was a busy place. They hadn't heard from Kaleen, and the frequency fence hadn't been used, to their knowledge, since the day of the fie storm.

They knew that the military helicopters were on missions of surveillance for the rebels and for the stolen gasoline and oil. Raids were ongoing, both on the local population in Rushville, as well as on the farms and the forests in the surrounding areas. Most were unjustified, and there was no resistance, so nothing came of it. In a few cases, some of the stolen gas and oil were found in barns and in storm cellars. Numerous people were arrested on the suspicion of being a rebel, usually with very flimsy evidence that amounted to little more than they were highly armed and with sufficient food and resources to live sustainably. There were several armed skirmishes, one of which could be clearly heard from Rainbow. And one of the helicopters was even shot down, by a high powered rifle, and some sharp shooting. But for the most part, the rebels knew it was pointless to resist forcibly. After all, it was missiles and tanks against rifles and hand guns, hardly a fair fight. At Rainbow, they were certain it was only a question of time before one of the choppers landed in the meadow for another inspection.

David, Don and Jack were sitting outside on the deck, watching the lightning and thunder storm approach. They were each drinking a cold beer. The weather in these mountains was totally erratic and unpredictable. Anything was possible at any time. This storm had been slowly approaching for a couple hours, and when it finally arrived, it stopped. There was a clear line demarking the dark cloud bank, and it was directly overhead, and not moving. To the west, there was still blue sky, with the sun setting. It continued to rain lightly, but with huge drops. To the east it was solid black, a combination of the storm and the night. The lighting was not the dangerous kind that came in bolts that struck close to the ground. It was higher up, in the clouds, fluttering, like a flickering lamp. The thunder was not the explosive kind, but rumbling, and higher up. And it was constant. For two hours now, there were practically no gaps in the thunder.

And usually, there was more than one pocket of thunder rumbling at the same time, like stereo.

Peter finally arrived. He pulled up in his truck, and parked in the driveway beneath them. And as soon as he got out and slammed the door, he started talking, rapid fire and animated, which was his style.

"Almost didn't make it home tonight, gents!" he shouted up at them. "Almost didn't make it home!"

He circled around and started up the stairs to the deck.

"They almost fucking arrested me!" he continued to bellow, halfway up. "They didn't handcuff me, but they stuck my ass in the back of their police car, while they ran some sort of check on me. I sat there for, I don't know, about 10 minutes. Then they let me go."

He got to the top, and stopped. They were sitting around a glass table. He nodded at them, and rolled on.

"I went to Howard's to get that fitting for that gasket. I get there, and there's two cop cars, you know, with the red lights, and a van that was marked United States Marshall's Office. I knew this didn't look good. I probably should have gotten right out of there."

He grinned impishly and went on.

"I guess I was feeling frisky. I don't know. I haven't done anything wrong, except associating with you revolutionaries, and all the others too. I wanted to check it out, play innocent, and see what was going on."

He walked over to Jack, who had a practically full beer on the table in front of him. Peter took it, took several long gulps, and put it back. Peter didn't drink. He was a recovering alcoholic.

"So I walk in, didn't even knock. I never do. And there they were, two plain clothes feds sitting at the dining room table, with three other cops standing there. Howard's wife was at the table too, pretty upset."

The thunder continued rumbling. Peter took the last chair, and sat down with them.

"So there we are, staring at each other, and I say, 'Is Howard home? I'm here to pick up a machine part.' Janice, his wife, says that he was just arrested, taken away. Then she introduces me as a friend of theirs."

He opened his eyes wide and took a deep breath.

"I'm starting to feel not so good about the whole situation. The one fed, his name was Crowe, gets up, comes over, identifies himself, and says he'd like to ask me a few questions. And it wasn't like he was asking my permission, you know. I wasn't about to assert my rights. After he asked me my name, and what I do, he asked me if I had the microchip."

He looked at each of them individually, and nodded again.

"Yeah, that's the first question now. 'Do you have the microchip?' Can you fucking believe that? And then he asks me about the nature of my business with Howard. I tell him about the machine part. Plus, we're friends. And he asks me how I was going to pay for it. Is that weird? I tell him it was a trade, and what for. And then he starts asking me if I know anything about Howard's activity with the local vigilantes who are now enemies of the state, I think he called it."

He looked at each of them again, and shook his head.

"I don't. I'd bet my life Howard's not one of them. I know almost everything that goes on around here. And I know who most of those dudes are. And Howard's not one of them. He's like us. He's got guns, more than us, and he's totally capable of taking care of himself and his family independently, and not about to march to the tune of the new order. They've got the wrong guy, unless those other things are a crime now too."

He sighed, gazing off into space. He looked up, and continued more softly.

"I pleaded with him a little on Howard's behalf, took a chance, said what I just said. Howard's an old fashioned farmer, like all of us, who doesn't like the current political situation, and is not about to join. But he's not guilty of any crimes. I think he was starting to like me, a little, trust me. He got a little personal then, asked me if I had any guns, asked me if I knew the identity of any of the other vigilantes, but I felt like he was softening up a little. He kind of got in my face again on the whole issue of me living here for 30 years, doing business with all these farmers and ranchers, and claiming not to know who was involved. But I think he was getting tired, or maybe he was just losing interest."

He laughed.

"That was when he had one of the uniformed cops escort me out to the car. He was starting to be polite to me for the first time. That gave me some assurance. He assured me it was all procedural, and that they just needed to do a standard check. So I sat in that damn car for what seemed like an eternity, and my life flashed before my eyes. If they're arresting innocent people, why not me? After all, I'm closely associated with somebody they just arrested, and I've got exactly the same profile. And who knows what's going to pop up in that background check. I don't know what's in there. I don't trust any of it. And then he comes back and tells me I'm free to go."

He shook his head again and blew out his mouth.

"Shew. I was scared, man. I'm not ashamed to say, I was scared. I haven't felt like that since I was a teenager, and got caught blowing up mailboxes with cherry bombs."

Peter was finished, fully vented.

They chatted a bit more. Peter's experience reminded them of how they had all been feeling for awhile now, ever since the occupation of Rushville and the visit by Jacoby and his thugs. For David and Kelly the world outside hadn't been a safe place for a long time, over 10 years. Don had been hiding for a long time too, along with his family. And now everybody at Rainbow Village could feel it. The enemy was drawing near, and the enemy wasn't playing by any cogent set of rules. Time was running short.

The storm continued to advance slowly. It was now dark. The lightning continued to flicker, lighting the clouds. The thunder was still almost constant.

They went inside to eat. Jack had made a huge Cobb salad, with all their favorite ingredients, and toasted garlic bread. Everything, including the butter and the chicken, was raised at the farm. They ate in Jack's living room, watching *Rio Bravo* on his big screen. The theme of the virtuous sheriff facing the impossible odds of a gang of outlaw cattlemen seemed appropriate.

They finished eating, and continued watching the movie, fun lovingly, letting go of the heaviness of the day, making comments and cracks, laughing together, having a light and wonderful time.

Amidst the constant rumble of the thunder, they heard voices and commotion outside. It must be the young people, home early from their trek into wilderness. Chris, Wanda, Erick, Adelle, Annette and Josh, her new boyfriend, had gone off into the mountains earlier that day on an overnight ceremony. They all followed the Mayan Calendar, and they believed 13 Ajpu to be one of the holiest of days, followed by 1 Imux, which is like the beginning of the Daylord cycle.

Steps were then heard on the stairs outside.

Chris knocked, peered through the window, entered, and saw them in the other room. The others followed, all taking off their shoes.

"Wimped out, huh!" Jack bellowed playfully. "You gonna let a little rain and lighting interfere with your ceremony?"

Chris was smiling in his customary ebullient way. He was truly an angelic young man.

"We took no gear, man," he said laughing. "I mean, nothing. Only a couple of us had raincoats. There hasn't even been a cloud in a month, man. So yeah, we decided to come back, rather than suffer, getting spoiled."

"Sit down," Jack offered. "Can I get you something, tea, juice, a beer. We're watching *Rio Bravo.*"

"No thanks, that's not why we came up," Chris shook his head excitedly. "We saw it. We all saw it, the red star or the Red Sun, or whatever you want to call it. It had to be it."

This got their attention. Nobody had to say anything. All eyes were on Chris, or whoever wanted to talk. Jack had already clicked off the set.

"It was in the east, the northeast," Chris said, as he pointed back in that directon, his eyes as big as saucers. "Kind of low on the horizon. The clouds were moving in, and you really couldn't see much. And then there was a weird break in the clouds, for about 15 minutes, and there it was, shining through. I don't think it was a ship, could have been. It wasn't moving, at least perceptibly. It was much smaller than the Blue Sun, about twice the size of Venus or Mars at their biggest, maybe a little bigger. And it was bright red. You know how they always call Mars the red planet. Well, it never looked that red to me, just slightly."

He nodded excitedly, his green eyes sparkling.

"This was red, no mistaking it, blood red, red like the reddest rose, and shining brightly, much more brightly than the brightest star. You almost had to squint. And I think all of this was highlighted by how it was all alone in this hole in the sky, with everything else blocked out, by the clouds. And with the lightning and thunder lighting everything up, it was truly surreal. It felt like an omen that was just for us. And I have no idea what that means. We watched it for about 15 minutes. Then the clouds covered it up again."

He was breathing heavily, eyeballing all of them.

"Chris," Erick interjected. "You're forgetting something, the halo. It had a halo."

"Oh yeah," Chris went on, not skipping a beat. "It had a halo, not really a halo. It wasn't a ring around it. It was embedded in a circle of very faint red light, like an aura. You almost couldn't see it. You had to look very carefully. But it was there."

Chris was finished. The room was silent, except for the thunder.

"Anything else?" Jack broke in. "Anybody, take your time. It's important that we know everything."

Chris scanned the other young people.

"No," he shook his head. "We talked about it for quite awhile. We all agreed at what we saw. We saw the same thing. And we all agreed that it wasn't a ship."

"How did it feel?" David asked. "That often helps us to understand what we're dealing with."

"Yeah, that's what I mean,' Chris replied. "This didn't feel like a ship. We prayed to it, David. That's how it felt. We reached out with our energy to connect with its energy. We introduced ourselves as spiritual beings, servants of this creation, and we prayed that it share its message with us. This felt like a celestial happening. And I'm going to say it again. It felt like an omen just for us, the six of us off in the middle of nowhere, the six of us who are the next generation of Rainbow Village. It felt like a very big and powerful spirit that is going to help us shape our destiny together and that of the entire planet."

David felt a tingle go down his spine. It sounded like his words coming back to him from this young man.

"Where was it again, Chris?" David asked, leaning forward in his chair. "Can you show me? I know there's clouds up there now, but can you point to where it was in the sky."

"Don't even get up," Chris replied. "We can do it from here. Northeast, due northeast, and I'm pretty good at reckoning those things. I know these mountains pretty well. And it was about two and a half inches above the horizon, like about how high above the horizon Venus is when she first appears."

He held his thumb and forefinger apart to show how far, and placed it right in front of his eyes.

"Awe," Jack grumbled playfully. "I really miss the Internet at times like these. This would be so much fun, watching the world go nuts the way they do. But we're going to have to figure these things out for ourselves from now on, aren't we, like in the old days, the very old days?"

"And what about this storm," Don jumped in. "That's the first thing I notice. Like Chris said, there hasn't even been a cloud in a month. And now this storm blows in out of nowhere. The red star's supposed to be all about Earth changes, right Jack. I wonder if there's a connection."

The storm had picked up speed. It was now overcast everywhere, and completely dark. It was raining steadily, and the thunder and lightning had diminished to almost nothing.

"The first thing we need to do is have a ceremony," David said pensively. "If this thing is as big as it sounds like it is, we need to connect with this energy, commune with it, like Chris said."

He stared off into space, and took a deep breath.

But I don't have a sense of this yet," he looked up, shaking his head. "I need to just be with all this for awhile. And I have to see it for myself. If this is the Red Star, the Red Star Kachina, there's so much we don't know. It could clear up any minute, and that would answer a lot of questions. I need to talk with Kelly and Red Hawk. My gut instinct is to have a ceremony tomorrow before sunset, the same time these guys saw it. But let's hold off on that. Let's be on ceremony alert."

He shook his head again.

"I know I'm not going to sleep much tonight," he added. When it clears up, I want to see what's up there. And I'll ring the bell. And we'll see what happens next. I think an immediate fire of some kind would probably be in order. We could do it in the little pit next to our house. The wood's already split, on the porch."

"We do know one thing, David," Jack chimed in. "We know it's not omnipresent, as in always visible, always there, like the Blue Sun. It's behind those clouds, and we can't see it. The Blue Sun is up there in its spot, like always."

David nodded.

The patter of raindrops danced on the roof.

"OK," David started officially. "I'm going to go home, talk to Kelly. Let's spread the word. Erick, can you please tell your father and grandmother, ASAP. And Peter, can you please call Ian and Claudia on the walkie-talkie, let them know."

Everybody went their separate ways.

David didn't even want to try to sleep. After talking with Kelly, they turned on their two salt crystal lamps, lit a bunch of candles, and went up into the loft to lie down, and rest, listen to the rain. The skylight was just a few feet above them, so they were always very close to the weather.

They did this often on special spiritual occasions with the lamps and the candles.

There were few things in life that felt better to David than lying in the dim light with his beloved.

The rain sounded like it stopped twice. Both times they got up and went outside. But both times there was still a misty drizzle, with thick clouds and no stars.

Back in bed, the rain pattered a steady rhythm on the glass above them.

David was on his back, with Kelly nestled alongside him. He closed his eyes, and focused on his breath, like in meditation, breathing deeply, attentively. In spite of the excitement of the day, he was very tired. He cherished his sleep and his dreams. The gentle staccato of the rain was mesmerizing.

Ringa, linga, linga, linga, linga, linga, linga, linga, linga, linga, linga, ling.

Ringa, linga, linga, linga, linga, linga, linga, linga, linga, linga, linga, ling.

David's eyes popped open.

The bell was ringing.

He had fallen asleep.

It didn't matter.

There it was, its red glow shining brilliantly into his eyes. He felt like he could reach out and touch it.

The Red Star, the Red Sun, the Red Star Kachina of Hopi Prophecy.

It was perched in the middle of the lower half of the skylight.

He knew it instantly. He didn't need to think.

The sky had cleared up. The rain had stopped.

It was precisely as Chris had described it.

It was far bigger than the biggest star or planet. It was bright red, encircled by a faint aura, and shining spectacularly. Even in the dim light of the loft, it cast a faint shadow. It didn't appear to be moving, though obviously it was, since the youth had seen it on the northeast horizon. Now it was practically in the middle of the sky, moving like one of the planets.

"Holy mama," David yelped.

Kelly woke up with the bell too, and saw the same thing.

The Red Sun was slightly behind them in the window. They got up, swung around, and sat on the bed to get the best view.

They both sat cross-legged, and breathed deeply, reaching out with their energy to connect, and to receive energy in turn, reaching out to feel the presence of the being before them.

David's energy field merged with the red light effortlessly. The beam touched his spirit. He felt joyful and at peace with it. He was transported outside of his physical boundaries. He felt like he wanted to stay in this place forever.

They were both speechless, but they knew they needed to speak. They needed to gather with the others.

"Well," Kelly finally muttered. "It definitely isn't a ship."

David continued to bask in the energy he was feeling. He felt like reaching out with a prayer, but the words were very heavy.

"Will you please reach out with a prayer for both of us?" he finally whispered. "Then we need to go be with the others."

Kelly closed her eyes and let the red energy wash over her. She sat with this for a moment, and then prayed ever so softly.

"Red Star, Red Sun, my name is Kelly Archer, and this is my husband and soul-mate, David Rhodes. We feel you very strongly. We feel you are a very powerful spirit. We also feel you are a friendly spirit, come to help Mother Earth at these critical times. We feel that you are also a relative of the Blue Sun, who has been with us now for six months, and who was such a herald of these transformative and very challenging times we now live in. The Blue Sun was almost instantly a very powerful guiding spirit for us. My husband and I and the others in our community are servants of this creation, servants of Mother Earth. We are here to create a better way of life, a way of life that is in harmony with the divine spirit of a living universe. We feel that you too resonate with these energies. We pray that you hear our words and connect with our vibration and send us the blessing of any guidance you might have. We yearn to get to know you more deeply and work with you to heal our Mother Earth and free her from her captivity."

She inhaled through her nose and exhaled out her mouth.

"Mmmm, Aho," she finished.

"Aho," David echoed softly. "Thank you."

They continued to sit in the red light in silence. They both knew it was what they had to do. They didn't have to talk about these things anymore. This communion was not yet over, whatever that meant. During all this, the bell rang a few more times, and the chatter of the others at the community house could be heard. Jack's Jeep also arrived and Ian and Claudia in their four-wheeler. No matter, they blocked this out.

They waited, in the red energy. They were outside themselves, in the red energy. There was nothing else, just red energy and timelessness, the feeling of belonging there. And of course they knew they were not alone. They both knew the other was there, in the red light.

It popped into both their heads at once. Words were spoken, but there was no sound, in a voice that was impersonal, not male, not female, not necessarily even human. It was as though they heard it, and yet they didn't. The words were implanted, and there they were.

The words were:

"You are prepared. Nothing else need be said."

As soon as this was said, David and Kelly came out of it, returning to their bed, sitting on their butts, looking out the skylight at the Red Sun. They didn't know how long they had been gone, but it didn't seem like long, a few minutes. The star was in its same place. The others could still be heard at the community house.

They looked at each other, and smiled. They had done this many times before.

Confirmation was still required. They couldn't operate completely telepathically, not yet.

"You are prepared," Kelly spoke first.

"Nothing else need be said," David replied.

David held up his fist, and she touched it with hers.

"That was very clear," Kelly said softly. "Was it for you too?"

"Clear and quick, very efficient, we haven't been here more than a couple of minutes. We went right into the light, and bang, the message pops in."

"Let's go be with the others."

They swung around and went outside.

It hadn't cleared up completely. There was a large patch of clear sky directly above, where the Red Sun was, and it was mostly clear to the west, which was where it was headed. There was a massive black cloud hanging on the mountain peak to the east of the meadow, and thick clouds to the south, where there was still some fluttering of lightning and mumbling of thunder.

This was their first chance to see the Red Sun and the Blue Sun together. At this point, they weren't that far apart. The Red Sun was practically in the middle of the sky. If it rose in the northeast, like Chris said, then it appeared to be following the same ecliptic path through the sky as the Sun, the Moon and the other planets. At its current rate it would be close to setting at the time of the rising of the Yellow Sun. The Blue Sun was in its customary perch in the northwest.

David stood still and watched, flowing with these energies. He noticed that if you looked at the space in between them, you could see them both at the same time, one in the upper periphery of each eye. These two new lights were so different, and yet it seemed so clear that they were relatives, from the same star family, here on a mission at this most critical time for Mother Earth. The red light was about as bright as the full moon on a clear night, bright enough to cast faint red shadows. Everything was now bathed in a delicate red hue. The light of the Blue Sun was so much softer and more subtle, less obtrusive. The faint blue hue was now eclipsed by the intensity of the red light, and if anything, just dulled it a little.

To David they felt like male and female energies, polarities that were complementary, a cosmic yin and yang that flowed back and forth into each other. The Blue Sun had always felt like a female deity to him. The community had discussed this, and they all felt the same way. And now her counterpart had arrived, and they took their places in the sky, radiating a completely different set of energies, energies that have never been experienced in this plane before. One was red. One was blue. One was male. One was female. One was moving. One was stationary. The piercing fiery light of the Red Sun and the soft blue water of the Blue Sun. The sky would never be the same again. David couldn't even imagine what it would be like in a few days when the Moon, which was beginning its new cycle, entered the picture. And to think in a few hours the Red Sun might be setting at the same time as the Yellow Sun rising. The Yellow Sun now had a new brother and sister, both physically and spiritually. The world had shifted to an entirely different dimension.

David and Kelly basked in these energies for a few moments, then headed for the community house.

Everybody was huddled together, waiting for them in the shadows of the new red hue. They had decided years ago to wait in a circle, holding hands, when there was an emergency, and the bell was rung. Then, one night when it was extremely cold they collapsed the circle into a huddle for warmth. It felt so good they've been doing it ever since, even when it was hot out.

"Starting to wonder about you," Red Hawk hailed, "Thought you might have been beamed out."

They arrived at the huddle, touching its periphery.

"We practically were," Kelly said in a hush.

"It spoke to us," David added.

He eyeballed them all, and nodded.

"He spoke to us," he said, pointing up. "The Red Sun, he spoke to us."

Kelly: "He told us to keep doing exactly what we're doing."

150

David: "His exact words were: "You are prepared. Nothing else need be said.""

Kelly: "Very brief and to the point."

David: "We both heard it, in kind of a trance, in reply to our prayer."

The group stirred. It was like a collective sigh of wonderment and awe. It really was overwhelming how blessed they were. And at this moment they were all fully aware of this. The prophesies were unfolding, before their eyes.

They waited as one. Nobody talked, not even Jack. They knew how colossal all this was. They knew who their Chief was. They were waiting for David.

David took a deep breath, and grumbled in his throat. The immensity was overwhelming, even for him.

"We need to be with it," he started. "We need to watch it and be with it, for as long as possible. Who Knows? It could start raining again any minute."

He looked to the west.

"It looks pretty clear right now, and that's the direction it's moving. But you know that can change in a second. I'm prepared to stay up all night with it, with him. What is that, another four or five hours? Let's have a small fire in the pit behind our house. There's plenty of chairs and stumps for those who need that. Not a ceremony, just a gathering to honor this new star being, this Red Sun, to reach out to him, and be with him, to begin to form a relationship with this new relative. And we can each do it in our own way. Bundles are optional. Everybody do what you need to do to make it through the night. Bring food if you like, blankets, whatever. But we do need to be together for this, as a community. That's essential."

He looked at them all and nodded.

"OK, let's go."

Everybody scurried off to prepare.

They gathered around the fire and watched as the Red Sun continued its journey through the sky toward the western horizon. The stormy weather continued everywhere else, all around them. It seemed like it was going to start raining any second. Drops were felt from time to time. Inexplicably the sky stayed clear to the west, forming a pathway through the clouds for the Red Sun to stay clearly visible to them. It continued to shine bright red, so bright only a few other stars could be distinguished faintly in the gap in the clouds.

Everybody felt the same way Chris had described. This vision on this stormy night was too fortuitous to be an accident. They felt like it was just for them, a gift, a blessing that was being shared with them by the higher powers of the universe, shared with them because they had stayed so true to the spiritual path, because they always believed, even in the darkest of hours. They understood this, and yet they didn't understand it at all. They simply acquiesced.

Everybody connected to the Red Sun in their own way. Everybody brought their bundles. They prayed quietly to themselves. Music was played softly. Songs were sung. Many candles were lit. Some of them burned white sage and others made other offerings in conch shells. Others simply sat in meditation and prayer, reaching out with their vibration to their new spiritual relative. At one point Chris gently played his didgeridoo, which resonated so perfectly with these energies that when he finished, Red Hawk asked that he please continue, and play as long as he wanted. There was applause at this suggestion.

David reached out to the Red Sun with some words of prayer but mostly with his meditative state of being, body, heart, mind and spirit. He breathed deeply, closed and opened his eyes, and allowed the red light to wash over him and through him. He was simply with this energy with his energy, a communion, a merging. Like before, he felt joyful and at peace with this union. He felt like he belonged and often lost himself entirely in the red light, having to consciously bring himself back. He no longer prayed for a message in words. This spirit had said that no more words were needed, and he took him at his word.

After two to three hours the clouds started to swirl above them, and it started to drizzle. Misty clouds started blowing through the gap to the west, with the Red Sun dancing in and out behind them. It rained harder. Soon the gap in the sky was covered with thick gray clouds. The Red Sun was gone, not even a glimmer. The thick grey clouds surrounded them now, with flickerings of lightning and murmurs of thunder everywhere.

It rained harder. They were getting wet and cold. Most of them had rain gear.

It was not uncommon for their ceremonies to be rained or snowed on. They would always wait it out, continuing for as long as they could. On some occasions they would stay out no matter what. If they wanted to move their ceremony undercover, they had a teepee they used for this purpose, with a fire pit in the middle.

David and Kelly huddled beneath a blanket.

In his mind it was very clear what to do.

"Let's go inside, wait in there."

They got up together, and David addressed the community.

"Kelly and I are going to go inside and wait in there. If it clears up, we'll be right back out. Please do whatever each of you needs to do. If you want to stay outside, around the fire, fine. If you want to go back to your homes, fine. But please remember to keep tracking this new Red Sun with your thoughts and prayers. This is an extraordinary time we're in. It's probably a couple of hours before sunrise, or perhaps I should say the Yellow Sunrise. That could be a very important moment too."

Chris agreed to keep the fire going, as long as possible, and to keep watch. If the Red Sun returned, he would ring the bell.

David and Kelly kept the salt crystal lamps and the candles going.

They went up into the loft, lied on the bed, and talked a little. They agreed that their experience with the Red Sun thus far felt complete. It felt finished. They had delved into this light and merged with it. They had also shared their energy in turn to the best of their abilities. They felt like they already knew this spirit, as he knew them. They also agreed that some sleep would probably be a wonderful thing.

It rained until an hour or so after sunrise. It stopped suddenly, and the sky started clearing just as suddenly. Before long it was totally clear, a bright blue day. And it started to heat up. This was how it had been for about the last month, clear and hot, over 102 degrees every day.

By the time it cleared up the Red Sun was no longer visible. It had either set or it wasn't visible in the bright yellow light. The decision was made to have a fire gathering at sunset to witness the rising of the Red Sun and the setting of the Yellow Sun, with the Blue Sun remaining a constant, of course.

Otherwise, this was just to be another day. It was peak summer, and there was loads of work to do.

Then, around midday, the clouds moved in again. But these were different. These were more typical of the clouds they had this time of year in the extremely hot weather when it grew unstable. They were thunderheads, and there were many, surrounding them in all directions, near and far. This was their first appearance of the summer. They were massive in size, and a pure white, which looked thick, like it had a cottony substance. And they were puffy and billowy. The bottoms were flat and slightly darker, and from there it was billow upon billow upon billow, bursting up into the sky. If you watched closely, you could actually see the force of this updraft, as one puff exploded into another, into another, in an upward swirl. They were reminiscent of the cloud formations above erupting volcanoes, or even the mushroom clouds of nuclear bombs.

They were so spectacular it was hard to take your eyes off them. All of the members of the community were present and doing a variety of jobs, both inside and out. But everybody was aware of the clouds. They all watched them as the day moved on.

As it got hotter, the clouds continued to build and grew darker, thicker. Pretty soon there were only patches of blue sky. Grumblings of thunder could be heard all around, and lightning bolts shooting from the bottoms of the clouds. Then, in the late afternoon, a thunderhead appeared atop the ridge to the east of the meadow. It seemed like it came from nowhere, but they knew from past experience that it was actually forming in this very spot. The meadow was already beneath its dark underbelly, as it swirled toward them. Only a small portion of its white billowy crown was still visible. These storms were always the most intense, when the atomic bomb cloud was perched right on top of them. This happened often.

David was in his cabin, reading, something he deeply regretted never taking the time to do. He was rereading, for the zillionth time, *The Story of the Blue & Red Kachinas* from Jack's book on Hopi prophesy. He too couldn't take his eyes off the storm. It was still very hot and all his windows were open. Gusts of wind blew through the cabin, curtains flapping, papers fluttering. The front door blew shut.

It was now totally overcast. And the thunder was doing the same thing it did yesterday. It had become continuous. Lightning was fluttering all around, and the thunder was the rumbling rolling kind, with each one lasting about 15 seconds, maybe longer. Some were close and some were very distant. Before one would finish one or two others would start. This had been going on for about 10 minutes now. Yesterday it lasted over an hour. David remembered this happening rarely, and never two days in a row.

He got up, opened the front door, and went out on the deck. The wind was alternating between gusts and calm. Now it was calm. It wasn't raining yet. David closed his eyes, took a deep breath, and focused his attention on the cascading thunder. He would pick one out when it started, follow as it rolled along, then dissipate and fade away. Then another, then another, and each against the backdrop of the others, they were like ripples in a stream. It was a wondrous symphony.

Then he discerned something different, a different sound. It was hard to distinguish because there were so many strands of thunder going off in so many different directions. The sky was full of sound. At first he thought it might be the echoing of the thunder, coming back as one sound, like 100 people singing in exactly the same tone. It was the same sound, but different. It was the sound of thunder, but a different thunder. And it was more of a constant, without the variations of each clap of thunder. And it was also farther away, high in the sky, high above these thunderheads. It sounded like a huge jet engine, very far away. But that wasn't it. This was far vaster. If this was the sound of a jet, then it was a fleet of them, rumbling the sky in unison. That wasn't it either. It was like nothing David had heard before. Whatever it was it was huge in scale.

He opened his eyes and saw Red Hawk standing in front of his teepee, also watching the storm. He started down the steps to talk to him. As he approached the teepee, he continued to focus on the sounds and continued to hear the same thing.

Red Hawk saw him coming. Their eyes met, and they nodded amiably.

David pointed at the sky.

"You hear something odd up there, not just thunder?"
Red Hawk nodded.

"Sounds like a large ship, or a fleet of ships, very high up.
Maybe jets, but I don't think so. This sounds more high tech."

They listened for about 15 minutes. The sound of the
thunder continued, as did the other sound. Spotted Deer came out
of the teepee. She was hearing the same thing, and she confirmed
it with them. They all agreed on a couple of things. Whatever it
was it was large, covering most of the sky, and high up. And if it
was jets, it was a massive fleet that was taking a long time to pass
over. And all of this just happened to be happening in accordance
with this huge billowy thunderhead that was perched upon
Rainbow Meadow, at the time of the coming of the Red Sun.
Many strange things were going on in their world.

Then it started to rain hard. They went inside the teepee,
but the sound of the rain was so loud that they could no longer hear
the jet-like sounds.

David ran back to his house in a downpour. The windows
were still up in the cabin, and it was the same thing. The rain was
so loud you couldn't hear the sound. And along with the rain the
thunder began to dissipate. Pretty soon all you could hear was the
rain.

It rained all night. They cancelled their ceremony to
witness the rising of the Red Sun. Everybody went their separate
ways. The young people kept vigil that night in the community
house in case the Red Sun made his appearance or the sounds
reappeared.

But the sounds were gone. Whatever it was it was gone.
And they did not see the Red Sun that night.
They would have to wait at least another day.

CHAPTER SEVEN- *The Ark*

Thirty-five days passed, thirty-five days in which it rained every day, almost constantly.

It was September 21, the Fall Equinox.

David and Kelly had finished dinner, and they were sitting on the couch in front of the wood stove, on yet another stormy, cold and windy night. The wind was blowing in gusts of 40 to 50 miles an hour. The rain and the wind slammed against the windows and against the roof, and the entire cabin was rumbling, as all of creation was blowing around outside. When it was like this, no matter how well you fastened things down, things always blew loose.

This weather was totally unseasonal, an aberration. Normally, the hot dry weather lasted into September, with only slight cooling, and with cool nights. And the rain and the snow didn't begin in earnest until mid-October. But it was never like this, even at its worst. This was unprecedented. Even on light days they received an inch or two of rain. On a few of the worst days, where it rained hard constantly, they got seven to eight inches. And it was cold. The temperature was in the low 40's to low 50's most of the time, night or day, a few times dipping into the 30's. And the constant thunder, which accompanied the beginning of this storm, continued. The thunder was now their daily companion, and it was often constant for several hours, reverberation overlapping reverberation, filling the sky.

But this was not all. Many other odd things were happening in the world, also unprecedented. They could only make educated guesses what these

things were because they had almost no contact with the outside at this time. The rain was creating a constant state of emergency for their farming, their animals, their buildings, their drainage and just about everything else in their world, which required their total effort. Annette and Josh still shuffled back and forth between homes, and his family was their only contact, which didn't amount to much because they didn't know anything either. Even Peter stayed put during the rain, putting all the finishing touches on his new house.

The strange sound continued in the sky, the thunder-like sound, or the sound of a huge squadron of jets flying very high. Like the thunder, they heard this now every day, and sometimes it too was constant, lasting for hours. The sound itself was not that unusual. If it had only lasted a minute or two, you'd think nothing of it. But this was something very different. Something was going on in the sky, and it felt very huge. And with the rain, this felt even more peculiar because they were hardly ever able to see the sky. It was like there was a wall around them, and this sound was beyond the wall.

There were other noises they had never heard before and other occurrences they had never experienced. There were frequent explosions, huge explosions. It sounded far away, but the sound was still monumental, colossal. And it was an unusual, peculiar sound. It was sharp, like an immense crackle that you could feel in your body. None of them had ever heard a meteor strike the Earth before, but they imagined this was what it sounded like. David and Kelly had been close to a volcanic eruption once, and that's what this sounded like. These explosions weren't as incessant as the thunder and the jet sound. They heard them a few times a week, and twice there were two in the same day.

In addition, there was also a strange trembling of the Earth that they had never felt before. With the wind and the rain and water flowing all around them, their world was now one of constant movement anyway. And noise too, peace and quiet were rare. The wind was often so strong it shook the windows and walls. But this trembling was something else. Like the explosions, it was infrequent, and it didn't last long, thirty seconds to a minute. Often it was hard to distinguish from all the other commotion in their environment. But it was unmistakable. The Earth was shaking. Earthquakes in this area were rare, though the mountain range was still active, and Mount Camille, a sleeping volcano, was just 40 miles away. But it wasn't that. This trembling didn't feel like the average earthquake. There was none of the swaying and rolling, and this was not as violent as even a small quake. It was just a rapid short-stroke shaking. And the more they felt it the more they could tune into what it was. At first, as soon they noticed it, it was gone. It is odd to call a shaking of Earth subtle, but that's kind of what it was.

As the storm raged outside, David and Kelly sat quietly and stared into the fire. He was drinking fruit juice and spring water on the rocks and she was having some tea. They were sharing a huge cookie that was like a Rice Crispi square, only healthy, one of their favorites. It was a rare moment of peace, despite the violence outside. The more it rained the more they were having these. At first, it was a total disruption and preoccupation, like any crisis that comes out of nowhere. But now, after 35 days of crisis, they were adjusting. Crisis had become the norm.

And it took some time for them to realize they were safe, at least as safe as you can be in such unsafe and uncertain circumstances. It's hard to rest and be at peace when you feel like you are in constant danger of being deluged by the creation. But they had prepared for this, like the spirit of the Red Sun had reminded them. Rainbow Village was filled with water. The adobe mud and the rock beneath it could only absorb so such, and they had reached that point a long time ago. That's the bad news.

The good news was this was high ground. The water was moving, and it was nowhere near as deep as it could have been. It was moving the way that they directed it, with an intricate system of ditches, canals and culverts. They were accustomed to heavy and potentially destructive rains. They received this every fall and spring. It was part of the normal weather pattern. They had worked for years with their heavy equipment to build a drainage system that would keep the village and everything in it safe. And they planned on extreme weather. They believed in the ancient prophesies that foretold of colossal Earth changes. So the drainage system was overbuilt, and now it was doing its job very well. With the new rain, they didn't need to change anything in the design of the system. They only needed to dig deeper or wider in certain places.

As David and Kelly lounged on the couch in front of the wood stove, with their drinks and their beautiful cookie, they felt safe. The rain, the wind, the strange sound in the sky, the distant explosions, the trembling of the Earth, all these things were now a constant. The rain wasn't getting any worse. They felt like they had already seen that, and they had persevered. The water was going where they wanted it too. Everybody had to wear boots all the time. And yes, you could expect to be walking in inches of water and mud much of the time. But that's as bad as it got.

They felt safe because they had prepared so well. And everything was working just as they had visualized it. They also felt safe because they stayed true to their spiritual path. It was like a protective shield with supernatural powers. David and Kelly had been using this as their primary compass through this world for over 15 years now, and it had never failed them. This is the power that guided them to the point of perfection they were feeling in front of the fire on this stormy night. As adverse as their current situation might look, this is what they lived for. The prophesies were coming true, and they were in the midst of them, living them. Their entire life was perfectly on track. This was like a shield of armor, keeping them safe. And the prophesies said one other thing that was echoed over and over. Those who stayed true to the path and who lived in harmony with nature and Mother Earth, they would survive the Earth changes and paradigm shifts, and they would be the ones to create the new world from the ashes of the old. Everything they did was based on this belief. And everything was right on course. Nobody said it would be easy.

David and Kelly were talking about how it didn't feel at all like Fall Equinox. The storm had also put a dent in their ceremonies and spiritual practices. With all the work there was less time to pray. That morning they did have a sunrise ceremony, with no sun, inside at Jack's house, followed by a lavish breakfast. Jack, Chris and Wanda had built a beautiful candlelight altar, around which they formed their circle. For most of them they hadn't activated their bundles in weeks. The storm had created a form of timelessness that was all its own. It was always dark. They rarely saw the Sun or the Moon or the stars. The Blue Sun continued to be a constant, but it provided little light. Because of the Equinox ceremony they had looked up the astrological phase of the Moon and the day in the Mayan Calendar. But prior to this, they had lost all track of it. There were too many other things going on. It was also increasingly difficult to keep track of the days of the week. Every day was truly the same, and without any contact with the outside, it had become irrelevant.

The Red Sun had been with them now as long as the storm, 35 days. David and Kelly had seen it a total of seven times. They were together each time. It was the same for most of them. Some of them had other brief sightings. Every time it stopped raining, they would all go outside to see if they could see it. Of the seven sightings David and Kelly had four were brief, lasting less than an hour. On two of those occasions the sky was misty, and the Red Sun moved in and out behind the clouds. On only three occasions was the break in the weather enough that they could really spend some time with the new sun.

The first was three days after the original sighting. It cleared up almost totally in the late afternoon. This gave them time to prepare. Before the setting of the Yellow Sun, they gathered at the ceremonial circle in the meadow. They faced northeast and watched as the Red Sun rose over the ridge. By the time they saw it, the Yellow Sun was gone, but it was still twilight. It did seem that the actual time of its rising was almost the same as the setting of the Yellow Sun. It stayed clear until well into the night, maybe 11 PM. Then the clouds and lightening swooped in, and it started raining again. They stayed with the Red Sun the entire time, watching as it rose into the nighttime sky, following the path of the ecliptic, as they had surmised. There was also a crescent moon in the west, but they hardly noticed it.

The other two sightings were very similar to each other. One was about two weeks later, and the other about a week after that. They were both in the middle of the night, at about the same time, maybe 2 AM. The rain stopped, the sky cleared, and David and Kelly first saw it in their skylight. Both times it was in the same place in the middle of the sky. And both times there was also a moon. On the first, the Moon was a couple days past full and slightly behind and above the Red Sun, as they followed the same path through the sky. The distance between them remained the same the entire time. The Red Sun was considerably smaller, but its red light was more brilliant and piercing. It blended with the silver moonlight, giving it a reddish hue that was other dimensional. The silver face of the moon now also had this reddish hue. In comparison, the light of the Blue Sun was so pale it didn't penetrate the red brilliance. With the two lights, this night was as bright as it was on these dark days, only red.

David and Kelly sat in the red light for a moment, then got up, put on their coats, and went outside. They made sure all the lights in the cabin were out. They stood on the front deck and connected with the Red Sun and all the other energies. The landscape before them was surreal. It was truly like another world. The wind was calm and with no rain, it was much quieter and more peaceful than what they had grown used to. The only sounds were the flowing and gurgling of water. They were surrounded by water that was sparkling and glowing in the light of the Red Sun. It was like the Earth had become a shiny red planet. Close to them, around the house, the water had collected in huge puddles, like little ponds, several inches deep. The stone walkway from their house to the community house was totally under water. Much of this land had been cleared to accommodate the building of the village and the building of their firewall. It was the cleared areas that tended to be filled with water. There were also numerous glades where they let the trees, the bushes and the grass grow. In these areas the water tended to be absorbed and drained and the earth poked through. But this water was not sitting still. It was slowly draining in little rivulets that you could hear trickling and gurgling all around them. And farther away, where the more serious drainage ditches were dug, you could hear the rushing of far greater amounts of water. The rain had stopped, but they were still enveloped in water sounds.

They heard a sloshing sound, and saw a silhouette in the red light marching up the driveway through the water, up to the ankles of his boots. It was young Erick.

"Hi Erick!" Kelly hailed.

"Do you want me to ring the bell?" Erick hailed back.

David and Kelly looked at each other.

"No!" David answered. "Let's let everybody experience this in their own way."

"OK, aho!" as he sloshed onward.

David and Kelly stood in the red light a little longer, breathing, reaching out with their energy.

They were of exactly the same mindset. The extreme weather and all the water and mud had killed everybody's desire to be outside. Plus, it was impossible. Their little rock fire circle was completely underwater, and sitting out there was unthinkable.

That was an area where one of rivulets had grown quite large, and the running water might just knock your chair over. When everything was wet and cold, staying dry and warm becomes the top priority.

They looked at each other again.

"Let's go inside," Kelly nodded. "Watch it from the bed."

"Wonderful idea, maybe even fall asleep with it."

After all, the Red Sun had been with them now for two and a half weeks. Even though they rarely saw it, they could feel its presence in their world. He was now a part of their world. They could feel his impact in the cleansing waters and in the fierce winds. They could feel his impact in the reshaping of their world. They didn't need to see him. Along with the Blue Sun, he was now a regular part of their prayers and ceremonies. In Hopi prophesy, the Red Star Kachina was called the Purifier. This was no wonder. They understood it perfectly. This was happening in their world.

They returned to their bed and prayed and meditated with the Red Sun until he moved outside the skylight. Then they swung around, lied down, closed their eyes, and let the red light wash over and through them, as they fell asleep. The rain started again shortly thereafter.

The other 2 AM sighting was almost identical. The only difference was it was a week later. The moon was now just past last quarter, and it was considerably farther behind the Red Sun. When the Red Sun was in the middle of the sky, the half moon was just above the ridge to the east. And this time David and Kelly didn't even get out of bed. David didn't even wake up. Kelly had to wake him. And they swung around again, and prayed and meditated with the Red Sun for about a half hour. Then they swung back and fell asleep again in the red light. And this time the sky was still clear when the light of the Yellow Sun started to dawn. They got up and saw out the window downstairs that the Red Sun was now just slightly above the western horizon. They put on their boots and warm clothes and went out to the meadow to get a better view of their first Red Sunset. They had dug drainage ditches so there was no standing water in the ceremonial circle. When they got outside they saw the twinkling of a fire in the circle. Chris and Wanda and the other youth were already there. David and Kelly joined, and they watched as the Red Sun sunk below the western horizon. Because of the ridge to the east it was still a little while before the Yellow Sun made his appearance. But again these two celestial bodies seemed to be rising and setting at almost the same moment.

Every time David saw the Red Sun he felt the same. He was definitely a kindred spirit. David felt an affinity for the red light, a natural attraction, like how you feel when you get into a warm bath. The Red Sun touched this warm place in his heart and made him feel like everything in the world was perfectly OK just the way it was. It was simply a question of trusting these energies and flowing with them. Everything was just the way the Divine Spirit of a living universe had designed it. And in spite of how impossible things seemed most of the time, everything was going to be just fine, no worries.

The storm raged on. The wind ripped through the branches of the juniper and oak outside. The walls of the cabin trembled and water splattered against the windows facing east.

David and Kelly finished their cookie and drinks.

They continued to sit on the couch in silence, their feet up on their old bench that was covered with a saddle blanket. They were snuggled up against each other, in the firelight, holding hands.

It felt so good to be doing nothing, resting their weary bodies. They had been working so incredibly hard since the rains started. They always worked incredibly hard, but this kicked it into a totally higher gear. It had been a constant state of emergency. If something needed to be fixed in the middle of the night, which was most nights at first, well, you just had to do it. No questions asked.

They were on the same wavelength.

"We haven't done this in a long time, have we?" Kelly mused. "It's been too long."

David nodded affirmatively.

"This is the most at peace I've felt since the rains started," she added. "It feels wonderful."

"I feel the same," he said in a hush. "I don't want to go to bed. Let's enjoy this for a while."

"Mmm," Kelly sighed in agreement.

He leaned forward, looking back at her.

"Let's have a little medicine ceremony," he said with a grin. "I'm really in the mood. We haven't done it in a long time. Let's celebrate this moment with some ganja and this sacred day."

"Excellent idea, Papu," she replied. Papu was her pet name for him. "That's why you da chief."

He got up and lit candles all around the cabin. He came back with his medicine bag and his little pipe that was carved out of wood. He put them down on the bench before them, along with another candle. He got out the ganja pouch and carefully filled his little pipe. This pipe had been his first ceremonial pipe, many pipes ago, some fifteen years. He then picked up the pipe, held it in both hands before him, and prayed.

"Sacred ganja, sacred medicine plant, sacred spirit guide, this is David Rhodes and Kelly Archer, your humble servants. We reach out with our energy at this time to connect with your energy, and we pray for you to be able to connect with us. We thank you for the blessing of the gift of the energy you share, the beautiful healing energy, the beautiful medicine, the guidance, your essence that you share, your lovely vibration, the feelings of lightness and joy and living fully in the moment. We pray to be worthy to receive the blessing of these gifts that you share. We pray to be able to receive this sacred energy. And we pray to share this energy in turn serving the creation according to our purpose, and raising the frequency of our vibration so we can live as close to the spirit as possible. Thank you for the blessing of this opportunity to serve. Aho."

"Aho," Kelly echoed softly.

There was a bowl of white sage on the bench. He took a piece and broke off a small stick from the bottom. He held the stick in the candle until it caught fire, and he lit the pipe with it. The ganja was ground fine, and it started right up. He took a puff and handed the pipe to her. They each took two puffs, and Kelly put the pipe back on the bench. They had a standard rule. If it took more than two puffs, it wasn't worth smoking.

David leaned back and kissed her passionately on the lips.

"I love you," he said softly, looking deeply into her big sparkly brown eyes.

"I love you, Papu," she replied, mirroring his gaze.

The moment stood still. The fire popped.

"The fire always agrees, doesn't it," he said.

She nodded, grinning.

He got up.

"I'm going to celebrate with one of those lagers," he declared. "Maybe two. Can I get you anything?"

She threw her head back against the couch and closed her eyes.

"Make me a Bloody Mary, please," she replied wistfully, surrendering to this beautiful urge.

Kelly rarely drank. She disliked the taste of beer, wine and most liquor. But every once in a while, she had this deep seeded love, planted deep in her past, for Bloody Mary's. She always drank two. One was just a tease.

David cackled with laughter, as he went into the kitchen.

"All right, guess I'm going to get lucky tonight, huh!" he bellowed.

"I'm going to fuck you silly, Papu. Right now, you look like a ripe fruit, ready to be plucked from the tree."

"Silly is good. I'll take that, unrestrained silly."

He spoke from the kitchen, as he made her drink. The storm raged on, and he had to speak loudly to be heard above all the noise outside.

"Remember when we used to ask questions like, will we have Bloody Mary's in the new paradigm? Will we have beer in the new paradigm? Well, here we are. I don't know how much more new paradigm this can get. We're living sustainably here in the wilderness, and we're experiencing the transformative energies and the purification of the coming of the Blue Sun and the Red Sun. I think we just might have made it to the new millennium. And here we are, celebrating with lagers and bloodies. Isn't life a blessing?"

He came back with their drinks. He handed hers to her and held out his for a toast.

"Here's to this sacred moment, this perfect time, with my beloved, on this sacred day of the Equinox, as we celebrate our entry into the darkness, and as we celebrate each other, our love."

She clinked and took a sip.

"Heavy on the Worcestershire," he said.

"Perfect, a work of art."

They both turned to face the fire.

He said something he'd said to her many times before.

"I always have this same feeling at first when I smoke this medicine. I know I've said this before, but it's one of the things I truly love about the marijuana. Everything is instantly turned into a celebration. I know we talk a lot about celebrating the moment and celebrating all of life, and we practice this, and we think we're doing it. And we are. We're doing a pretty good job. But then I smoke some of this, and I can clearly see I haven't been, at least not as much as I think. All of a sudden, everything is transformed into a celebration. This medicine is celebratory. That's part of its essence, its healing power. If somebody truly lives in this celebratory way, the chances of them getting sick are slim."

Their medicine ceremony was very informal and unstructured. There are many different types of ceremonies. This was one that emphasized rest, relaxation and reflection. It consisted of reaching out with a meditative vibration. It consisted of connecting with the spritely and joyous energies of the medicine and feeling these energies. And reflecting together and talking about these reflections was an important part of this. One of the benefits of the plant medicines is they help you to see things differently and think about things differently.

On this evening, David and Kelly both felt like they had reached a milestone in the relation to the storm and 35 days of rain. They felt at peace with it, and they felt safe. They felt like they had seen the worst that nature was going to hand out them, and they had handled it superbly. Yes, it was probably far worse in other places, but that wasn't really relevant to their situation at all. Maybe nature was taking it a little easier on them. Perhaps this was part of their protection. They had always heard and they believed that the divine spirit would spare those who remained true to nature's way. They would be the ones to build the next world from scratch. Their entire life was built upon this belief. And it certainly appeared to be manifesting in the physical world.

Taking the time to reflect upon, to celebrate and to appreciate their achievements in this world was the theme of this ceremony, with a strong emphasis on persevering in the face of the worst killer storm any of them had ever seen. They reflected upon these things, and they felt good about them. They took pride and felt joy. The garden was pretty much finished for the season. The storm had almost no impact on it. The growing season in the mountains was short, and everything was usually harvested by Equinox anyway. Due to the sophistication of their irrigation and drainage systems there was no flooding, and nothing was lost. They were forced to harvest many of the plants a week or two early, but that was about it. And the greenhouses continued to operate at full capacity all year round. And now they transitioned into the season of drying, canning and freezing their harvest. That was pretty much on schedule too.

As the ganja flowed through them, they reflected on things and celebrated the blessing of their life. And they celebrated nothing at all, just being in the moment, with each other, feeling good. They played classical music on the stereo, a CD of Tchaikovsky's greatest hits. The intensity of the music matched that of the storm. They simultaneously rubbed and tickled each other's feet. David played a new ceremonial song on his drum that he'd been practicing. She knew instantly she wanted to learn it. They finished their drinks and David got another round. They smoked another bowl of ganja, two puffs each. The cabin sparkled with the light of about ten candles. The cabin was warm. So they let the fire fade to coals and embers.

Kelly said something she always said.

"My favorite part of the fire."

David: "We haven't done this in a long time, get high, stay up late. I'm thoroughly enjoying myself. When I feel this way, I wonder why I don't do it more often."

Kelly: "I don't want to move. You realize I haven't moved from this spot for a couple hours, feels wonderful."

They sat quietly and finished their drinks, with Tchaikovsky harmonizing with the elements around them.

They both allowed themselves to become lost in the music, like dreaming.

Pretty soon they were dozing, half here, half there.

When the music stopped, they were both asleep, in the candlelight.

Knock, knock, knock.

The rain and the wind were still blowing hard. Whoever was knocking at the door had to do it pretty hard to be heard.

They both woke with a start.

David had no idea what time it was. The fire was out. The cabin had cooled. Kelly was nuzzled up against him. It felt late.

It was probably another middle of the night emergency.

Knock, knock, knock, could be heard at the front door again.

They didn't even bother to move. The thought never occurred to either of them that it was somebody from outside the community.

"Yea, who is it? Come on in!" David yelled.

The person did not enter.

"Just an old friend, paying a friendly visit," could be heard in a man's voice outside the door.

They both knew it instantly. This was not a knock or a voice they recognized. It was somebody from the outside, and in the middle of the night.

Suddenly wide awake, they got up in unison, sitting on the edge of the couch. David looked back at the door, then at her quizzically. He got up, walked to the door, turned on the outside light, and opened it.

He didn't recognize the man at first. He was wearing a full rain suit, with the hood pulled tightly around his face. Water was dripping from every part of this figure, as his suit flapped in the wind.

"Oh," the man bellowed, as he undid the knot, and pulled the hood back over his head.

It was him, the cop, the renegade cop. David didn't remember his name, the federal marshal, who visited the community on that bogus good will mission a few months ago.

"Frank Jacoby!" he bellowed again, over the wind and rain. "Formerly Lieutenant Frank Jacoby, but don't worry, this is not an official visit. There is none of that anymore."

He was looking deeply into David's eyes. It was a look of compassion, which David picked up on instantly.

David was shocked at his reaction. Yet he trusted it. The moment actually stood still for him, and he was able to step outside of himself and take note.

He had every reason to be suspicious, highly suspicious, or at least extremely cautious about the man standing before him. But he wasn't. He remembered over five years ago how this man had showed up for a meeting of subversives, including David and Kelly, and he sought them out to warn them of the agenda that was hatching against them at the highest levels of the law enforcement system.

As their eyes peered into each other, David's entire abdomen, from his waist to his shoulders swelled with joy at this visitor and with hospitality to welcome him into their home.

David opened the screen door with one hand and waved with the other.

"Frank, yes, of course, come in."

Frank clomped inside.

David motioned for him to stop on the large mat inside the door.

"Take your boots and your gear off here. We'll hang it up on the shower."

They busied themselves with his gear.

Kelly got up and came over. She too was completely trusting. It never occurred to her not to be.

"Frank Jacoby, it's wonderful to see you. Don't get me wrong, but what the fuck are you doing here?"

His boots and gear were off. He stepped off the mat in his socks.

"I'm here because this is the last safe place on Earth, or at least the last safe place I know of. And I would very much like to survive."

David returned from hanging up his gear, and took him by the arm.

"Come, sit down. Tell us everything. I'll get the fire going."

He sat at the end of the couch.

"Do you want something to drink?" Kelly offered. "Tea, coffee, beer, booze, make you a drink?"

He noticed David's empty beer bottle on the bench.

"Can I sleep here tonight?"

"Yes, of course, you can sleep on the couch, right where you are, no movement necessary."

"Do you have any brandy?"

She nodded.

"Let me have a little glass of brandy, please, and one of those beers."

He slouched back against the couch for a moment. Then he sprang up to his feet again.

"Nope, can't do it, can't sit down yet, too wired."

David already had the fire going with some kindling.

Kelly came back with his brandy and beer.

"Huh," he chuckled. "Just a little while ago, I thought I was going to die, swept away by the waters into the sea. And now here I am next to this fire, drinking brandy, with you fine people. Thank you."

He sniffed his brandy, took a small sip, sloshed it around in his mouth, then took a larger sip.

"Now I'll sit down, before I fall down."

David watched in astonishment. Nobody was in a hurry to make small talk. They hardly knew each other, and yet this felt like the closest of families. David had been with Frank now a total of four times in a little over ten years, and each time for less than an hour. He looked as he always did. He was wearing his signature jeans, with a crease, and long sleeve white shirt with a collar. Everything was significantly more wrinkled on this occasion. Missing were his cowboy boots and tweed jacket. Frank was not an attractive man, per se. His face was full, his cheeks rosy and pock marked, and his grayish brown hair was thinning and combed back. Yet he had an impish quality that was irresistible and gave him incredible charm. You could see it in the twinkle in his brown eyes and his mischievous grin.

He took another sip of his brandy, then a sip of his beer. He looked up at both of them. Kelly was sitting on the other end of the couch. David was standing next to the stove.

The wind and the rain continued to smash around outside.

"So I guess you want to know what I'm doing here."

David cackled with laughter.

"The suspense is killing us," Kelly replied.

"I almost didn't make it all, you know," he sighed. "It's a total mess out there. The world is a total mess. It took me about five hours to get here from Rushville. What's that, about a 25 minute trip normally? The road is almost totally flooded, washed out completely in a few places. I had to get pretty creative to get here. I was completely off road a couple of times, and I've got the greatest truck in the world, with great big off road tires. Water was up over the tops of my tires a few times. I was totally stuck once. I don't know how I got the hell out of there, god damn miracle. And then I get here, to your road. Your road was the safest part of the trip, just cruised on up. Like I said, the last safe place on Earth."

They looked at each other.

"Is that still the case?" Frank asked. "Are you guys doing OK, functioning OK?"

David and Kelly both nodded affirmatively.

"Yeah, we're doing fine."

There was still a pink elephant in the room. David needed to get rid of it.

"Are you still a cop?" he asked.

"Huh," he laughed. "There's no more of that. Everything you once knew out there is gone now, no titles, no rank. I'm just a human being like everybody else. Whatever authority the system once delegated to me is gone now because the system is gone now. Oh, there are still soldiers and cops trying to act in what was once their official capacity, but it's all just blowing hot air. So many have defected that it's all really meaningless, like World War I in Russia when the soldiers all just walked away. That military brass didn't have a whole lot of authority, did they? Most of the military that's still intact have just become marauders anyway, just trying to survive, like everybody else. They have no orders, no agenda, because there's nobody giving orders."

The fire was crackling.

David was putting the pieces together in his mind. There was one more pink elephant.

"Did you know we were here that day?" he asked. "Did you know Kelly and I were here?"

"No," Frank shook his head. "We knew about Jack. And we knew practically everything that was going on here. He wasn't exactly secretive in his books. And you've been spied on from satellite and helicopter and through emails for a long time. But no, I didn't know you guys were here. I recognized you right away, and I remembered you from those days in Johnsport. I remember you talking to that crowd that night, and I remember a lot of what you said. And now here you are, making it all happen."

He sipped his brandy and then a gulp of his beer.

"Those two special agents who were assigned to me sure did recognize you though. Man, they wanted to take you in on the spot. And there was no doubt, as in positive ID of public enemy number one. It's a good thing I had final authority, or they probably would have shot you on the spot. I never did quite understand that."

David and Kelly looked at each other as they had many times before.

"We saw them," Kelly said. "They were extraterrestrial hybrids, part human, part reptilian ET. We've never understood why, but we've been able to see behind this human façade or mask of theirs for a long time. We can see reptilian features, and as is always the case, they saw that we saw them. And in their world, this never happens. They are totally incognito. And this is the greatest of crimes. If everybody could see them, the gig would be up. The illusion would be smashed. Truth would prevail."

Frank nodded with his impish grin.

"Makes perfect sense."

He laughed and shook his head in astonishment.

"That explains a lot of things. I always knew there was something creepy like that going on, in the department, all around. I always thought it was some kind of mind control, maybe related to an implant of some kind, or maybe some kind of possession, spiritual possession or stealing the soul. I don't know. I don't know much about that stuff. I knew the ET's were behind it because they're behind everything."

David's head was swirling with questions. He asked the first one that popped out.

"Frank, what's happening out there? Since the rain started, 35 days ago, none of us have even been past the end of our road down there, hardly. The only people we are connected with, they don't know anything either. We have no Internet, no phones, no TV. We never use our radio. All we know is what's going on behind our four walls up here. We see things and we hear things, but we don't know."

"Huh!" Frank bellowed again with laughter. "You've come to the right man. I guess I came to you, but you know what I mean. I came here from an underground facility west of here in Sierra, about 100 miles past the border. A friend of mine in the department leaked the information to me years ago, and I always kept it in the back of my mind. I went there about a week and a half after the storm when things really started to fall apart. I was on an assignment down in Heatherton, kind of snooping around like I was here. I just went AWOL, took a government vehicle that didn't belong to me. And the main reason I went there was because I wanted to know what was going on. To tell you the truth I didn't care that much about living or dying. But if I was going to go out, I wanted to know why. And where better to learn that than in belly of the beast, with the absolute best technology and communications."

He sipped and took a deep breath.

"I left there a little over three days ago. Nothing was working anymore. The communications finally broke down completely.. I could have stayed there. There was plenty of food and water and power. But I didn't want to live the rest of my life in a bunker. So I drove here on one tank of gas without stopping. I only got out of the truck to piss and shit. I stole the greatest truck imaginable, a veritable tank, a chain saw too, which I did use by the way. I did stop to take a couple of naps. I didn't see much until I got to Rushville. I was mostly in the desert and the country. When I got to Coronado there were a few small towns. I couldn't see much because it was usually raining so hard. But there was tons of damage. Some of them were wiped out completely. There were abandoned cars and junk piled all over the place. There was also some signs of life, people like you, with smoke coming out of their chimneys, and lights on. When I got to Rushville it was pretty horrible. It was dark and there were few lights. It was like a ghost town. I did see lots of dead bodies, mostly floating in the water. I only saw the lights of three or four other cars. And nobody was stopping."

"When I first got there everything was still working. All the communications satellites were apparently up and running. The Internet was up. They had all the latest in television technology. There was a strong telephone signal. There was technology there nobody even understood, like satellite and aerospace technology. We just kept our hands off that. At first there was a fairly steady stream of information about what was happening in the world. And most of it we didn't get from the regular sources. Regular television was almost completely down. Most channels were just showing reruns of the propaganda broadcasts by the Guardians, none of which had been updated in weeks. And a lot of channels were just blank. There were some brave attempts at national news programs and the 24-hour news channel and the weather channel, but conditions in the major media centers on both the east and the west coasts were just too harsh, with this weather and all. They just couldn't pull it off. And that's one of the first things we learned. This weather, this storm is everywhere, everywhere in this country, everywhere in the world. It's not some local freak occurrence. It's a world-wide storm of the ages. And you know, it appears to be much worse in most other places. For some reason the mountains of south-central Coronado and eastern Sierra are being spared. In other places there are killer earthquakes, volcanoes and tsunamis. It's all happening all at once, and civilization as we knew it is getting buried, swept away."

"We knew that," Kelly said. "We could feel it. And all the prophesies said that. This would be worldwide, a worldwide purification."

"So where did you get your information?" David asked.

"The Internet mostly at first. News items were still getting posted in the usual way. It was never really clear who was doing it. The Guardians didn't lay any claim to it. But there they were, kind of like some alien wire service. Most of it just dealt with the weather and the destruction and it was all pretty hopeless. And there was a lot of scuttlebutt about the red star that appeared that freaked everybody out the same way the blue one did six months ago. But we searched around a lot, and we found some other sources. In this massive sea of darkness there were islands of life. Hell, we found a guy who was very big in alternative conspiracy news, and he was still up and running on his website out of his home down in Heatherton. He was like you, with alternative power and survival resources. Only problem was there were so many breakdowns in all the communications and things like power outages that would never get fixed that he had a hard time picking up any news, other than the storm, maybe because there wasn't any."

He finished his brandy.

"Shall I get the bottle," Kelly asked.

"Please, another beer while you're up too, please."

"The best source of our information turned out to be a different kind of television. We didn't even learn about it until we'd been there for several days. There are TV connections and signals between high-level government facilities. And we're talking very high level, like the Defense Department in the capital, military bases, army, navy, air force, aerospace centers, other underground installations like ours, places like that. Well, we were able to tap into this network and connect with lots of people who were in the same boat we were, stranded in the face of monumental Earth changes."

"And the next thing we learned was definitely the most important thing of all. I'm sure you've noticed that I've mentioned several times here that none of us at this facility knew how to operate the equipment, the technology. That's because everybody who was there was like me. They weren't necessary supposed to be there. All the people who were supposed to be there, the top brass, the top technicians, they were nowhere to be seen. They never showed up. Before we got there the place was staffed by a group of superintendants who were trained to keep the place operating until disaster struck and the real experts arrived. Hell, I didn't have any credentials to get in there. I simply identified myself as a federal marshal, showed them my ID, and they let me in."

"We assumed this was just a glitch of some kind. Certainly there was a lot of that going on in the world. But then we saw it was the same at all these other bases or facilities. All the top brass, the top officials, all the people with authority, and many of the top technical people, they were all AWOL, nowhere to be found. It was a mass defection. At the military bases, most of them were on site, and then they disappeared, without a word. At installations like ours, which were for protection, they never showed up at all. We saw the list of the people who'd been invited there. It was quite a who's who - bank presidents, CEO' of major companies, lawyers, medical doctors, intelligence agency members, people like that, even big-name entertainers and show business people. And it was supposed to be run by some high ranking Army officials. None of them showed up. And there wasn't one peep of information from any of them about what was going on. They all just vanished."

"It took us about another week to start to get a picture of what was going on. And this is probably something we won't ever know for certain. And some other things happened, which led to the same conclusion. We can talk about all that. We'll get to it. But the bottom line is there is only one explanation. There is only one thing it could be."

He looked at each of them.

"They left."

He nodded and looked back and forth between them.

"They left. They left this Earth. They left this physical dimension. They left to find another world to infest, a mass evacuation. They probably already had one lined up."

He kept nodding at them, his grin on his face.

"We could argue forever about who they are. Nobody knows for certain because at the highest levels none of us ever see them. Everything I've learned in my career leads me to the conclusion that they are the beings who have ruled this world from behind the scenes for a very long time, probably hundreds of thousands of years, maybe a lot longer. Eight months ago they came out from behind their curtain of secrecy and identified themselves as the Guardians. They never came out and said it, but it's clear to me that they are not of this world. They are extraterrestrial or at least partly extraterrestrial. They gained their foothold of power in this world by interbreeding with humans and acquiring human appearance and characteristics. And now you tell me you can see reptilian hybrids. It fits only too perfectly."

His eyes opened wide, the grin still on his face.

"And now they're gone," he said matter-of-factly.

Before David or Kelly could speak, Frank continued.

"I know this probably completely blows your mind. I understand. But let me say this in a slightly different way.

He paused. None of them heard the storm.

"You won."

He paused again, no need for clarification.

"They surrendered. They chose not to engage any longer in this battle for the hearts and spirits of humanity. The system they had created here was failing so drastically that they decided it was more trouble than it was worth. So they just let it go, a business decision. The appearance of the red star and this world-wide weather calamity, those were the last straws. That was two ancient prophesies that came to pass, and they knew about these prophesies. They knew what they meant, and they feared them. They knew enough about real history to know that there were precedents for these things, cyclical precedents. When the weather hit, it was pretty clear the end-times were upon us. So they packed up their gear, and they left this planet."

He stared off into space, gathering his thoughts.

"Let me say this one last way; sum everything up all at once, so there's no uncertainty about how huge this is. This alien force of evil that has cast its wicked spell on this sweet Planet Earth and contaminated it for so many thousands of years is gone. The Earth belongs to us again. We have exactly what we have always wanted. We have been left to our own devices."

He exhaled in a huff, and stared blankly straight ahead. He was done talking, for a while.

David and Kelly felt exactly the same way. They were both in a state of shock, a pleasant state of shock, but a state of shock none the less. What Frank was saying was so monumentally huge that it was impossible to have a reaction to it. They both felt a peculiar numbness. There was too much here to grasp all at once.

And it wasn't that they didn't believe him. Everything Frank said made complete sense. They had actually considered this as one of numerous possible outcomes to their apparently hopeless situation. In their world of supernatural miracles, what he was saying wasn't too far a stretch. But it was just too soon to take the leap into total belief. This would take some time to sink in.

But the process had started.

David was aware that his heart was pounding at the possibility this was true.

Kelly was aware that she was light headed and her hands were trembling at what she was hearing.

Here they were again on the precipice of the unimaginable. It was happening, again. And it was completely overwhelming. Everything they had done for the last 15 years flashed before their eyes. This was what they lived for. Thoughts of Celine, his mother, and Red Cloud flashed before David like a dream. They had both implored him with their dying breath to continue the work to set humanity free from the evil spell that imprisoned it. Now if that work was done, it was just too much.

Kelly got up from the couch and walked over to David next to the stove. She walked right up to him, her body touching his, her face close to his, and she took hold of his hands.

They looked deeply into each other. They were both looking for an answer.

"Your hands are trembling," he said.

"I know," she laughed.

They looked deeply into each other again.

"I believe him, I think," she whispered.

She tried to smile, but her lips twitched downward. Feelings were coming up, and she was fighting to hold them back.

David could feel her chest heaving.

This was contagious. He could feel himself starting to crack. Inexplicable feelings of happy weepiness were breaking through, like in a movie with a happy ending.

His eyes watered up, as looked deeply back at her.

"I believe him too, I think," he echoed. "We'll have plenty of time to test it against reality."

With this, they hugged and wept together, allowing the feelings to flow freely, laughing and crying at the same time. They indulged in this for a few moments. Then they snapped out of it. They hadn't forgotten Frank was there.

They turned to face Frank, breath sputtering, wiping away tears.

David spoke first.

"Sorry about this, Frank. Normally we don't behave like this with company. I'm afraid you really bowled us over with all this, a little too much to take for one night."

Frank had been watching them the entire time, sipping his brandy, drinking his beer. His grin had grown into a broad smile.

"Not at all, I understand completely. It is totally mind blowing. It took a while to soak in with me too. Plus, you'll be able to see this in the world out there. You'll see. The world's going to be different, starting now. If I understand these things, and I think I do, it's going to stop raining, and the world's going to be different. You'll see."

"That would be consistent with Hopi prophesy," Kelly said.

They were silent. The storm raged on, and all of creation was rumbling around outside.

David and Kelly's heads were still spinning. Yes, they believed him, they thought, but much of this was on faith. There were still many gaps in Frank's story. They wouldn't be able to sleep until the gaps were filled in. They probably wouldn't be able to sleep anyway.

They felt the same way.

Kelly spoke first.

"Frank, we have no reason not to believe what we're hearing here. But I think you said there was more to the story. Fill in the blanks for us please. How do you know this?

David enthusiastically nodded his approval.

"I don't know for certain. Nobody does. I mean, they didn't make an announcement. But there's no other explanation. I sat in front of those monitors, in front of those computer screens, for 22 days. And I watched as one part after another of this advanced communications system became unplugged. It was like they wanted to disable it step by step so that whatever was left of humanity wouldn't have a chance. Like I said, when I first got there everything was working. You might not pick anything up, but the technology was operative. The lines were open, but nobody was picking up. And then TV was the first to go. At first it was patchy and chaotic. And then it just went blank, no signal at all, like the satellites had all been turned off, which they probably had. And the Internet was next, same thing, blank, just went dead.

And one by one we lost our TV signals to the military bases we contacted, places like that. Pretty soon we had none of those, just dead signals. Oh yeah, and the telephone signals, they all went down too, after the Internet."

"When I left the only contacts we still had were with the other installations like ours. The TV transmissions stayed intact. We talked to these folks every day. Their experiences with the communications were identical to ours. And we were all in the same boat. Nobody knew what the fuck was going on. We were in touch with 20 of them in this country. And that's pretty much all there were. The ones on the east coast had hookups with two more in Great Britain and one in Belgium and one in Sweden. There were others in Europe and around the world. We just weren't in touch with them. They were all located in remote locations, as far from big cities as possible. And they were all built to accommodate about 5000 people. That's a total of 100,000 people in this country alone. That's a pretty fair sized city, wouldn't you say. And we were able to pull up all the lists of who was invited and compare them. It was all very important people, the cream of the crop, the elite, if you will. And not one person showed up from any of these lists, not one. That's a pretty good percentage, don't you think, a pretty good indication that something serious went wrong, or, more likely, that there was a change in the plan. That's where the possibility of a mass evacuation of some kind must come into consideration. If the plan was to move these important people to these installations, don't you think a few of them would have showed up, somewhere? Hell, I got through, and I wasn't even invited, formally."

"Like me, most of the people who made it to these installations believed in the extraterrestrial aspect of everything that was happening on planet Earth. It's pretty hard to ignore at this point. It started becoming clear that pretty soon we would be the only ones left, at least the only ones who were still part of this communication network. Everything else had been unplugged. And you could survive a long time at one of those places, decades, at least. It's strange that they let them be, at least up until a few days ago, unless they wanted to leave open the possibility that they would return at some point. I doubt seriously it was a mistake. Whoever set these places up knew about long-term survival. There was an abundance of food, all with very long shelf life. And if ever that ran out, there were tablets and capsules and vials of liquids that they kept frozen, which were sufficient to keep a person alive. They were also totally off the grid, generating their own power with solar and wind. And they had giant diesel generators you would not believe. Yup, when the storm stops, and we're ready to go out and find what's left of humanity, this would be a good place to start."

"There were about 100 of us at each facility, and we had plenty of time on our hands, time that we used to brainstorm and try figure out what was happening. Most of us agreed to the theory of mass evacuation. We also agreed that it was happening step by step and that it was a complicated process. That's why it was taking time. Hell, if you just wanted to beam out the Guardians or some other other-dimensional beings, it would be a simple matter. You gather them in one spot and beam them to the other dimension or world. As a matter of fact, that is probably exactly what happened. The Guardians were probably beamed out at the beginning of the storm, maybe even before. There hasn't been any evidence of them in a while. As I'm sure you can recall, things weren't looking so good for the civilized world even before it started raining."

"But this was more complicated than that. This was like the evacuation of an entire civilization and all of its energy. It involved a lot of people, or hybrids as you say, who were widely spread out in the fabric of the civilized world, 100,000 people in this country, and probably a million world-wide. Most of us agreed since none of these people showed up at the installations that there must have been some kind of communication they all received about a change in plan. A majority of them probably had the chip, and could be located and tracked by satellite that way. But many of them probably also didn't. Remember these were the most intelligent people, the cream of the crop, people smart enough to know the dangers of the chip and the nefarious uses that were planned for it."

"Anyway, rounding all these people up, or beings or hybrids, and transporting them across the universe turns out to be a big job. We figured that this one million we're talking about were probably a second tier of the elite, not the top of the pyramid where the Guardians were, but the next rung down. And the plan was not to transport them directly to the final destination, wherever that was. That was reserved for the hot shots on top. Instead they would be beamed to a mothership, or motherships, parked out in space outside the Earth's atmosphere, and from there they would be transported to the final destination, by whatever means. Maybe there is no destination. Maybe they will all just live on those ships for a while, until they figure out where to go."

He stopped and looked into the embers of the fire. He took another sip of brandy.

"Did you guys hear the noise?" he asked, pointing his finger into the air. "There was a noise in the sky. It sounded like a massive squadron of high-tech jets flying very high. It was big and pervasive. It filled the entire sky. We heard it at all the installations, here and abroad. So it was everywhere. That's the clincher. It was not an isolated phenomenon. It started soon after the storm hit. It came and it went, with no definite pattern. On some days it was constant for hours. On others it was more sporadic. But it was every day."

David and Kelly looked at each other, nodded, and replied almost in unison.

"Yeah, we heard it."

"Haven't heard it in a few days though, have you?" Frank asked.

They looked at each other again, quizzically.

"Come to think of it, no," David answered. "I guess we got so used to it we stopped paying attention. There's a lot of other stuff to pay attention to, a lot of other noise."

"Yeah, it stopped about five days ago," Frank nodded. "That was when I decided to leave the installation. It stopped because the evacuation was complete. That's what we figured. It was the mothership, or more likely mothershps in different locations around the Earth. It had to be. It didn't sound like any normal aircraft, did it? It was so high and so vast. Plus, most of the usual aircraft weren't flying anyway. Commercial jets were all grounded with the storm and the uncertainty of the technological infrastructure both on the ground and in the air with the satellites. It was even risky for the most high-tech military aircraft. No, conventional aircraft was minimal, at a standstill. It had to be something else. It had to be a ship or something that was immune to our troubles here on Earth."

Frank yawned deeply, his eyes watering up. He leaned back against the couch, tilted his head back, and closed his eyes.

"That's pretty much the whole story. It's speculation, but it's darn good speculation. I'd bet my life they're gone. I did. That's why I came here."

As he was speaking, Kelly had resumed her spot on the other end of the couch.

Silence. The storm raged outside. The fire was almost out, but the cabin was warm.

It was late, not too long until Sunrise. Everybody was tired.

The story may have been complete, but David and Kelly weren't. Their heads were still spinning and their bodies were still numb at the enormity of it all.

Kelly got up, walked over to him and put her arms around him.

"A lot for one night, isn't it, Papu," she whispered.

"There's one thing we can always rest assured on," he nodded. "If it's true, or not, it doesn't change much for us. We're going to keep doing exactly what we're doing regardless. Except now we know that some entity's not going to fuck with us. And when the storm stops, we're going to have to decide about reconnecting with the world out there that has been reshaped."

They both looked at Frank.

His head was still back and his eyes closed. His mouth was now open. He was breathing heavily and starting to snore.

CHAPTER EIGHT – *The Dawning of the Fifth Sun*

On the 40th day, the rain stopped.

It was early evening, about an hour before the setting of the Yellow Sun. And it was dramatic. The rain had stopped often during the 40 days, but this was different. Everybody felt it. It not only cleared up, but it cleared up rapidly, overcast and raining one moment, clear the next. And it cleared up totally. There was not a cloud anywhere. The sky was a deep blue in the twilight. It even warmed up to about 60 degrees. And there wasn't even a puff of wind. It felt like a pleasant summer evening. Birds were chirping, a sound they hadn't heard in 40 days. It was like the world was coming back to life.

David and Kelly were inside getting ready to start dinner. They were drawn immediately outside, where they stood on their deck to experience this moment, and where they saw many of the others also outside, doing the same. Red Hawk and his family were standing outside their teepee. Several of the youth were in the driveway, outside the community house, where they had been canning vegetables. Several others were outside the garage, where they were finishing up their daily work.

David and Kelly went inside to get their boots. They immediately knew they wanted to spend more time in the energies outside, with the others. They made their way down the steps into the water, which was about three inches deep at the bottom. Their house was in a large puddle of water. They headed in the direction of Red Hawk's teepee. Annette, Adelle and Josh were also coming from the community house and Chris and Wanda from the garage. They arrived at the teepee together and decided to walk through the gardens in the meadow to the ceremonial circle.

They walked in silence, breathing in the magnificence of the moment. The path was through the tomato patch. They brushed against the lush gigantic plants as they made their way through. The plants were taller than them, and it was like a jungle. All the plants had been harvested, and only a few tiny green tomatoes remained.

They arrived at the opening of the circle in the middle of the gardens, and went inside.

"David, shall I ring the bell?" Erick asked officially.

David looked up the hillside and saw Jack hobbling down on his crutch, along with Peter.

He looked in the other direction and saw Don and Sandy sloshing through the water, along with Ian and Claudia.

"No need to, everybody's accounted for."

He instantly realized he had forgotten Frank, force of habit. Frank was now a full fledged member of Rainbow Village.

"Where's Frank?" he blurted. "Anybody know?"

"He's coming, taking a bath," Annette answered.

As soon as she said this, Frank could be heard bellowing excitedly. He was at the gate entering the meadow.

"Hey! Any of you guys see this yet?"

He was pointing in the air, at the Blue Sun.

None of them had. It was funny how they had learned to take the Blue Sun for granted. Maybe that was partly her job. She was a constant never-changing companion. You never had to think about where she was or what phase she was in. She was always the same, very low maintenance.

They turned to look at her as one.

The Blue Sun was dissipating. She had grown significantly fainter. Her pale blue light was not even noticeable anymore in the bright sunshine. Her strange speckled membrane-like surface was fading away. She appeared lighter and more transparent.

She had also grown smaller. She had shrunk by about one fourth of her previous size.

"Oh!" David gasped.

The entire group murmured in awe. A collective chill passed through them. Yes, they had grown tired of cataclysmic omens in their world. This only goes to show they were human beings with real feelings. Here they were again on the brink of an abyss they did not understand. But this was all part of their journey. Though they were weary, this is what they signed up for. And they knew exactly what to do. They were also excited to take this next leap.

It was crystal clear to David what needed to be said and done. None of them had brought their bundles, and he felt there might not be enough time for any kind of formal ceremony.

"My relations, this is obviously very important. We need to watch and experience this moment and reach out to the Blue Sun with our prayers, connect with this energy. We can talk later."

Inside the rock circle there was a circle of stumps for sitting. Everybody sat down and faced the Blue Sun. Jack, Peter, Don, Sandy and Frank joined them. They were also facing the setting of the Yellow Sun, which was just now touching the horizon. It was blindingly bright. They hadn't had a Yellow Sunset like this in 40 days. The Blue Sun was above this and to the north.

They sat in silence and watched for a few minutes as the Yellow Sun sank. It was imperceptible but obvious that the Blue Sun was dissipating and growing smaller. It was doing this at about the same rate as the Yellow Sun was setting. It was like she was dissolving back into herself. Pretty soon she was half her original size. Her fluid-like surface was now wispy. Traces of blue sky could be seen through. A few more minutes and she was a quarter her size. The Yellow Sun was almost submerged. The pale blue color of the Blue Sun had faded to almost white. It was difficult to see her in the brightness of the Yellow Sun. Her speckled and membrane-like features could no longer be made out. She was now a wispy circular cloud. Another moment or two and she shrunk to a singular point of pale white light. The instant the crown of the Yellow Sun disappeared below the horizon the Blue Sun vanished.

For the first time in over eight months, when the Blue Sun first appeared, the sky was profoundly empty, no Yellow Sun, no Moon, no Blue Sun, no stars, no clouds. It was a perfect vacuum. Because of the ridge to the east, the Red Sun wasn't due to rise for about another 45 minutes. None of them believed the Red Sun would rise on this night. His work felt done too. This spiritual vacuum felt like it should not be penetrated. But they would have to wait.

David knew what needed to be done, but he felt the need to say something.

"This isn't finished yet. We need to sit in silence a little longer and be with these energies. This is an incredibly important time. We wouldn't want to miss anything. Plus, the Red Sun is due to rise shortly. We need to be here for that. We need to know if the Red Sun is still with us. After that, we'll talk."

They sat in silence from twilight until the first stars started coming out, which was particularly early on this night because of the clarity of the sky and perhaps also the clarity of the spiritual vacuum that enveloped them. The Red Sun did not rise. He had also departed this dimension. After 8 months with one spiritual companion, and the last 40 days with both of them, a strange feeling of aloneness came over them. It was an existential aloneness, as in being alone in the universe. It was like the feeling of being in a deep dark cave and turning your flashlight out. It was like death from which new life will sprout.

Plus, the storm was over. They were all in the process of believing that. That was one of the things this glorious moment meant. It had cleared up before, but this was profoundly different. The Red Sun was yet another entity, a constant companion for 40 days, which had departed. The silence had awesome power. There was no thunder, no mothership performing an interstellar evacuation. There was no wind and no rain. The only sound was the gurgling of water around them and the rushing of water farther away. It was the sound of the waters of creation.

They were all getting accustomed to the idea of being alone in this world in a different way too. Frank had addressed them about his theory of the evacuation of the extraterrestrial hybrids who had been ruling the world behind the scenes for eons. Like with David and Kelly, it was a shock at first. But once it settled in, it became a very real possibility. The world certainly did feel different at this moment. For the last five days it had felt different. The rain continued to fall gently, but the wind and the thunder had stopped. And it warmed up a little bit. The rain became a more pleasant experience and the world a far more benign place.

Yes, this world felt different. She also looked different. The sky looked different. It was a deep dark blue, with none of the chemical haze. It was a darker blue than any of them could remember. It was like a different sky. And the view to the west also looked different. There was nothing blocking the horizon here, and the view was vast, covering three or four ranges of mountains and about 75 miles. But this looked different too. It looked even more vast, like it stretched even farther to the west. And some of the mountains looked rounder, like they'd been polished by the rain and wind. Red Hawk was the first to notice that Castle Rock, a large butte-like rock formation about 40 miles away, wasn't even there anymore. It had been obliterated. Not just the sky, but all the colors of this world looked more vivid and jumped out at you. The world was exuding bright colors. It was like a film had been removed.

It was getting dark and stars were coming out. They too were bigger and brighter than any of them had seen before. Among them, only Jack was here in the days before the chemical haze, when the sky was always ablaze with gigantic stars and the Milky Way was so frothy you couldn't see through it. This promised to be more spectacular than that, now that this film was gone. And there would be no Moon on this night. She was in her new phase and wouldn't be seen for a couple days.

As David sat with all this, it was crystal clear to him what it all meant. This was the most spectacularly colossal moment of his life, which had been full of them. His excitement and exhilaration were only tempered by his need to remain sober and clear. There was much yet to still happen. Events had closely been following the Hopi Prophesy. If this continued to hold true, then this was the dawn of a new era, a new world. And tomorrow's rising of the Yellow Sun would be the first of this new era. And this would be into a world that had been cleansed by nature and cleansed by the departure of the wicked beings who had befouled it so. Yes, this was an extraordinary time, a time they had all devoted their lives to.

He didn't want to talk. As Chief, he knew he needed to. They needed to have a plan. He would try to keep his words to minimum.

"My relations, this is as good a time as any to open things up a bit. Let's try and be brief. There's a lot going on around us right now, and we need to make preparations for tomorrow."

Chris broke in.

"Do you want some light, David? I can get some lamps."

"No, this is good. We're not going to be here long. This darkness is perfect."

He scanned them. It was too dark to distinguish most of them.

"I'll be brief. In the last hour we've received four of the most powerful omens imaginable. Most people live their entire lives and don't receive one such omen. The storm stopped. The Blue Sun is gone. The Red Sun is gone. And now we're here in the midst of this sea of incredible energies. Look at those star beings hovering up there now. It's like some kind of a veil has been pierced, and new energies are getting through for the first time."

An owl hooted loudly and distinctly in the trees to the south.

They murmured in awe as one.

David didn't need to mention the owl.

"As I see it the most important thing right now is tomorrow's Yellow Sunrise. We don't know any of this for certain, but if the prophesies continue to hold, this just might be the first sunrise of the era of the Fifth Sun. And we need to prepare ourselves for a ceremony to celebrate this unprecedented moment in the history of our world. We need to get out there very early, when it's still dark, so we can experience all the light. Let's plan on 4:30. And we'll have a wood fire. OK, Chris, can you and your band make sure we have lots of dry wood?"

"Now as far as the rest of tonight is concerned, everybody do what you feel called to do. I haven't decided yet. We need to eat, and Kelly and I need to discuss where we're going to sleep tonight. But for any of you who feel called to sleep out here, in this incredible field of energy, beneath these star beings, that would be wonderful. I recommend it. We might be joining you. The ground is soaked, so take precautions. Otherwise, I'll see you all at 4:30."

"Now, let's open the circle up for sharing. Does anybody have anything to share or questions? Please speak up because I can't see you."

Silence, just the gurgling and rushing of distant water, and the owl hooting at regular intervals, like it was part of the circle.

David allowed the silence. He waited about a minute, maybe more.

"Anybody? If nobody wants to share, let's disband and get ready for tomorrow."

Another moment of silence.

A voice came from the other side of the circle, in the darkness.

"David, over here, it's Jack."

David was surprised. Jack rarely shared, not like this.

"Yes, Jack."

"I won't take long. I promise. Nobody wants to share and nobody has any questions because everybody is so ready. We've talked about this over and over. We've been drilled in this for years. And now it's happening, and there's nothing more to say, no questions. Talk would be a waste of our time. It is simply time for each of us to take the spiritual action required."

As he continued, his voice started breaking up. His breath was sputtering, and it sounded like he was fighting back tears.

"I am definitely being touched by spirit. I can feel it throughout my body. Something is happening. My heart is pounding. I'm shaking all over. I'm dizzy. I feel like I might just float away. I can only imagine how the rest of you feel. You young people seem so clear and calm and resolute. I am truly in awe of you."

He was sobbing. He had to fight to get the words out, taking many labored deep breaths.

"It is such an honor to have lived long enough to experience this moment, these sacred times we're in. It truly is overwhelming. I don't know if I can take much more. But you are young and strong, and it's up to you to do the work that lies ahead, the most honorable work of all, building the new world. And what an honor it's been to serve along with you, this family of kindred spirits. I'm so blessed to have been drawn to you all. Now let's go and take that spiritual action. Aho."

It sounded like he was saying goodbye, like this was his last speech.

Everybody was deeply touched by his words and emotions. They said thank you to him together in low voices, most of them saying the same thing.

"Thank you, Jack, if not for you, none of this would be happening."

As soon as silence returned, David closed the meeting. Everybody went their own way.

David and Kelly sloshed through the water in the dark back to the house. They made a quick dinner and ate. Neither one of them was hungry, too much excitement, too much adrenaline. They forced themselves to eat to keep their tanks full for the journey ahead.

The decision about where to sleep turned out to be easy.

"We have to sleep outside," Kelly said plainly. "I really need to be out there all night. And it's going to take a little time to get ready."

"OK, you're right. I don't know what I was thinking earlier. I guess I get spiritually lazy sometimes. Do you think we should ring the bell, make it mandatory?"

"No, you said what you said. Let's let them decide for themselves. I have a feeling everybody will be out there. Just look at it."

She pointed out the window at the sky ablaze with colossal stars. It was irresistible.

They walked outside on the front deck and down to the bottom stair, just above the water. They held hands and soaked it all in. This was like no sky they had ever seen, here or anywhere else. The huge stars were also twinkling dramatically. The entire sky was dancing with light. There was also a multitude of ongoing shooting stars, of every size, some mere wisps, and others brilliant streaks covering large portions of the sky. The sky was alive. The cosmos was an organic being that moved and danced. The Milky Way passed directly overhead. It wasn't the wispy cloud-like mass it appears to be on the brightest of nights. On this night this cloud was thicker and more solid, and it glowed and pulsated like the coals in a fire. It also had shape and depth and shadow, like the nebulae it was. If you looked at one spot long enough, you could see the swirling movement of these energy clouds.

Out at the ceremonial circle headlamps could be seen darting around, as the youth did their work. Pretty soon they could see the fire starting up.

"Jack was right," David said. "The youth have been so awesome. They are so plugged into this thing."

"Let's go," Kelly said. "Let's get ready. I want to stare into this all night."

They went back inside and opened all the windows. It was getting cool, but they were going to be out all night, so what the heck. Besides they hadn't had their windows open for 40 days now, day or night.

It took them awhile to prepare. They both had to pack their bundles. They had a large rolled up pad and bedding that they used for this, but they hadn't used it in awhile. It was all put away, gathering dust. And they would have to use a tarp this time for dryness. They would need to use one of the quads to drive all of their gear out there.

With the windows open, they could hear and see the others milling around outside, preparing. It was a beehive of activity. There were headlamps and chatter. Firewood was being split at the community house. It sounded like two axes were going. And one of the quads headed up the driveway with a trailer for the wood. All of the lights were on in the community house. David and Kelly didn't know it at the time, but Kathy Spotted Dear was preparing bowls of berries and corn from the garden and venison from the most recent hunt, which was to be served at the end of the ceremony. This was a most sacred practice in many indigenous traditions, which was usually reserved for the most special all-night events.

It took a couple hours for everybody to get situated around the fire. It was probably around midnight, maybe a little before. It took several loads with the quads and trailers. Everybody was there, all 17 of them, including Josh and Frank. Even Jack, whose body was too brittle for the rugged ceremonies, was there. Everybody brought their bundles and everybody had the proper bedding. This was a group that knew how to sleep on the hard Earth on a cool damp autumn night. Frank was a newcomer to this kind of spirituality and didn't have a bundle yet. But he was well taken care of by the youth, who treated him like an elder, and made him a beautiful warm waterproof bed.

When the firewood and everything else was in place and everybody was ready, they walked clockwise together around the fire and vacated the circle out the east entrance. There they formed a line to come back in. Chris smudged everyone one by one with an eagle feather and sage that was smoking in a conch shell. They took their places around the fire. The night was breathlessly still. The smoke from the sage and the fire was going straight up in perfect straight lines.

The ceremony was now officially begun. Everybody was silent. David didn't need to say anything here either. This ceremony was running itself. David took note of this. It may not seem like much, but this had never happened before. Either he or Red Hawk or Kelly was always in charge of the ceremonies, which ran according to their instructions. They often told everyone what to do even though everyone already knew. They were the spiritual leaders, the elders even at such young ages, and that's how it worked. And the group always deferred to this. They would wait for David to speak, for his guidance. But this new development was wonderful. David was thrilled. He didn't want to talk and or decide what to do. He simply wanted to go with the flow of the energies swirling around them on this most magical of nights. And that's what he wanted for them all. And that's what was happening. Maybe he wouldn't say anything all night. Maybe this entire ceremony would run itself. Maybe this is how ceremonies will be in the new millennium.

Everybody seemed to be of the same mind. It was late and they had been working hard. This had already been such an incredibly intense day. Everybody lied down to watch the sky. Besides, their comforters and blankets and pads and pillows were all in place. Before long most of them had stripped down, and gotten under the covers.

With fire ceremonies, the centerpiece was always the fire. This was what they paid attention to. This was the focus. The fire was a grandfather. He was a great spirit guide. All of their prayers and songs and offerings went to the fire and through the fire. But on this night the fire was in the sky. They were all guided to this meadow, to this circle, to watch this sky and to be with this sky. That was the reason they were sleeping outside. Chris, the Fire Keeper, didn't need to be told this either. He kept the wood fire very low, usually two small pieces of wood on a bed of coals. David thought about asking him to let it go out, but he didn't want to say anything about this either. Let Chris decide.

This sky was different. It was a different world. And it was still changing. It was like the veil that was being lifted still had a ways to go. The curtain was not all the way up. There was more of this scene to be seen. The stars were even bigger and brighter and flashier. Several of the stars were moving slowly, and their paths were often curved. The Milky Way was even frothier, with swirls of energy everywhere. Shooting stars were a constant. There was so much movement it was difficult to discern if any of these were extraterrestrial ships. In all probability some were.

On five occasions orb-like bodies appeared. They came from different directions, but each time they passed directly overhead. They were about one third the size of a full moon. Their light was much duller than the stars, and they appeared to be gelatinous in nature. The last of these actually stopped directly overhead, where it began to slowly swell and transform into a bright purplish color. When it got to be about three times its size, it suddenly popped in bright flash of purple, like the flash of a huge cosmic camera. Then it resumed its original shape and color and continued its journey across the sky until it was out of sight.

After an hour or so, other light phenomena began to manifest. The first was a patch that consisted of vertical bands of shimmering light. This looked very similar to the Aurora Borealis, which was rarely seen here, except this was on the eastern horizon, over the ridge. The bands were yellow, a very light blue and very light red, and they pulsated slightly, like they were breathing. Some faded and dissolved, to be replaced by new ones. And after a few minutes the whole thing flickered, faded and disappeared. These patches continued to appear and disappear at various points in the sky, with no discernible pattern.

And finally there were mysterious clouds of swirling energy, which were very different from the swirls that could be seen in the Milky Way. They were much larger, and they were separate entities. They looked like thin cirrus clouds, except lit up, and they were swirling in both clockwise and counterclockwise directions. In a peculiar way they seemed like they weren't even a part of the sky, and probably weren't. Sometimes they seemed far away, like in the sky with the stars. And sometimes they seemed to hover in real close, like at the tops of the trees. Sometimes it seemed like you could reach out and touch them. And sometimes, if you closed your eyes, they would continue to swirl around inside your head.

Nobody said a word for hours, until deep into the night. There was no singing, no playing of instruments, no praying out loud. Nobody made any offerings to the fire. Except for Chris keeping the fire going and a few who felt the need to relieve themselves, nobody moved. Everyone was under their covers, watching the sky.

Everyone was mesmerized. Everyone was transformed. Everyone was touched by the magic, touched by the forces of the spirit that drove this magnificence. Everyone reached out with their energy, as they had been taught, to connect with the energy in the sky. Once connected with their totality, body, mind, heart and spirit, the energy in its various forms, would possess them and take them places outside their body. It was like none of them were there anymore. They had moved, or been moved, to higher dimensions of light.

Watching the light was not something they did only with their eyes or with their perception. The light entered them. They could feel it inside their physical bodies, in every part of their physical bodies. It made them feel lighter (forgive the pun), less corporeal, less dense. It made them feel like they could move at will with these light beams and travel outside their bodies to anywhere they wanted in the universe or to any dimension in the space-time continuum. And yes, the volitional or free-will aspect of this was very important. This was not being possessed by energy against your will. This was a sacred union of energy fields and moving together by mutual consent. This is the kind of supernatural power that is possessed by the most adept shamans. And at this moment, all 17 of the members of Rainbow Village had this power.

And they all had it at the same time, which multiplies this power exponentially. This is a fundamental spiritual principle of the universe. If an individual being experiences spiritual energy, this is one thing. If this same being experiences this same energy in communion with many other beings who are experiencing the same energy, the total energy of the group is multiplied exponentially. This is one of the reasons group ceremonies have so much power. Each person's experience with the forces of the light was intensified greatly because everybody around them was having the same, or very similar, experiences. They became like a huge battery or receptor that receives the charge from above, and then sends it back out by moving into the light.

They were all in this together, and they were doing this together. They were a unit, a union. As they journeyed into the light individually, they could feel the presence of the others there with them, which was a new experience for most of them. Several of them had light traveled or had journeys to other dimensions together. But this had always been in pairs. Never had all 17 of them left the planet together like this.

After an hour or two, David snapped out of his trance. As Chief, he had trained himself to do this. It was still his job to lead this ceremony, even if it meant doing nothing. And he needed to keep in touch with the here and now in the 3rd Dimension.

It was still completely dark, no sign of the Yellow Sun yet. Everybody was still, including the wind. The only sounds were the water and a few birds who were singing to celebrate the night. Chris was lying on his back next to fire, staring into the sky. He had a little stack of wood next to him, so he wouldn't have to move too far. He could hear Kelly breathing. She had been by his side the entire time, like always, in this dimension and all the others. He leaned his head back on the pillow and returned to the sky.

In about another hour, he snapped out of it again. The light from the Yellow Sun was just beginning to make its appearance on the eastern horizon. The ridge that was directly east dipped toward the north, making the horizon quite a bit lower. This was where the first light appeared. The light show in the sky was still on, and the others remained on their backs, under the covers, continuing their astral travels. David hated to break this up, but he felt called to bring everyone's attention to the new Yellow Sun. They still had lots of time before Sunrise, but they needed to start thinking about coming back. It would not be long before the lights in the sky would start to dim and then go out in the light of the Yellow Sun.

He got up, put on his pants, his shoes and his jacket, and took his position, sitting cross-legged on his mat, in front of his mesa, facing east.

He blew his flute in one even and very low tone to announce to coming of the light. He did this two more times. Then he prayed in a very soft voice, but loud enough to be heard by the others.

"Divine Spirit, Council of the Grandfathers, Spirit of the Yellow Sun rising in the east, we reach out to you as one at this time from this ceremonial circle at Rainbow Meadow. We say good morning to you, Grandfather Sun, and we reach out with the energy of our ceremony to connect with the energy of your sacred light. And we say thank you, Divine Spirit, for the incredible blessing of the sacred energy and the star beings we have witnessed on this night, and the astral traveling we have done together. We have never done this before, not like this. Everything that is happening now is new. Everything we are doing is new. I hardly know the words to say to even talk about it. But we pray for guidance to experience what we are called to experience on this sacred day, at this sacred time, and to flow with these energies of creation always. Aho."

He leaned forward and lit a candle on his mesa, which he had forgotten to do.

Nobody was sleeping. Everybody was experiencing the lights in the sky. As soon as David finished, everybody got up, put their clothes on, and took their positions in the circle, around the fire. They acted in perfect unison, like one body. Nobody talked. They were in ceremony now. Many of them lit candles on their mesas or burned sage in conch shells. Everybody was awake and alert and ready to flow with the energies of whatever was next.

Normally in ceremony all eyes are on the fire. This time all eyes were still on the sky. It was still mostly dark, and the sky was still ablaze with light phenomena. The orbs were gone, as were the swirling energy clouds. The stars were still huge and twinkly. There were still a few of the Aurora Borealis-like patches and the Milky Way was still dancing and swirling.

But even with the tiny glow of Sunlight in the east, the night had become day, and everything was different. The sky was still alluring, but it was losing the power it had in total darkness. As they watched, everybody remained in their physical bodies. Everybody was anchored to the Earth. That phase of this journey was completed.

As the sky grew brighter, the light phenomena quickly faded. Pretty soon there were only a few big stars and the Milky Way was just a trace. The sky was turning blue.

As the light show faded, the attention of the ceremony returned to the fire and to the dawning of the new day. Chris felt called to keep the fire as low as possible. Usually David would tell him or Chris would ask what kind of a fire to make. This time nobody said anything. Everyone remained silent. They were in a group meditative state, awaiting whatever was next. As one, they knew they were not finished. They knew they were in the middle of something. They knew there was more to come. And again, David didn't need to say anything. Nobody needed to say anything. This ceremony continued to run itself.

The ridge to the east was imposing, and for most of the year it delayed the rising of the sun considerably. During this time of year the difference between when they actually saw the sun and the time of what was considered to be its actual rising was about 45 minutes. They usually accounted for this in their sunrise ceremonies. Even though they were in the shade of the ridge, it was easy to discern when the sun was up because they could see the light in every other direction, in the trees at the top of the ridge to the south, and in the valleys that extended to the west and north.

When this time came, David blew his flute again. This time he did it the way he always did it at Sunrise. It was louder, beginning with a low even tone, then rising to a higher tone, then back to the same lower tone. Again, he did this three times, and followed with the simplest of prayers.

"Grandfather Sun, we welcome the dawning of your light that we can see all around us. And we await your rising on the ridge to the east. Aho."

That's all that David felt called to say. Normally during Sunrise ceremonies they would be praying at this time or smoking their pipes or making offerings to the fire or playing music, singing or chanting. This time they were silent, in a group meditative state. And there was no confusion. Everybody understood that this was what was needed at this moment.

The instant David finished his prayer, the entire ceremonial circle, from the large lava rocks on its circumference to the fire in the middle, was lit up with a faint golden light. It started on the ground and went up into the air in a cone. It was like a switch had been flipped, and there it was. It was a hue, with transparency. David could still see people and objects on the other side of the circle, but they were bleary and indistinct, like they were in a golden fog. Outside the circle David couldn't see anything. It was like this cone of light formed a wall around them.

Again they acted as one. Everybody looked up in unison. There, in the sky directly above them, was a solid disc of brighter gold. Obviously the cone of light that enveloped the circle emanated from this disc. It was impossible to say how big it was or how far away. Bathed in light as they were, they had lost all sense of proportion and all their frame of reference. This golden disc also made no sound. In this light, there were no sounds, total silence. They couldn't hear the water. They couldn't hear the birds.

And then they heard the voice. David, Kelly and Red Hawk recognized it right away. The voice sounded like it was in each of their heads, like it was talking to each of them individually. It was the voice of a man. The tone was even and gentle and soothing. The sound was melodious and pleasantly paternal, like a benevolent father.

> Greetings Rainbow Village on this glorious day.
> Greetings to you David, Kelly and Red Hawk, who
> I have spoken to before. And greetings to each and
> every one of you, who we already know well.
> Greetings to you Grandfather Jack, Grandmother
> Spotted Deer, to you Don, Sandy, Peter, Frank, Ian,
> Claudia, Chris, Wanda, Annette, Adelle, Erick, Josh
> and to you Wanda's unborn baby. The name I have
> given myself in your language is Kaleen. I
> represent the council of intergalactic beings who
> have been your ally in this great challenge. I am
> here with 16 other beings from this council. We
> have come to meet with you at this unprecedented
> time of the dawning of the Fifth Sun.
>
> But let me start with showering you with our loving
> congratulations. You have persevered in the

greatest challenge to face this Mother Earth in 13,000 years. You have not only survived, but you participated in the wave of energy that drove out the malevolent forces that have infected this world for millennia. Mother Earth has been saved. She has lived to see the dawning of this new day. And you who love her so deeply are now blessed with the task of being her primary caretakers. You are now the builders and the creators of the new world in harmony with Mother Earth. Few honors surpass this. Congratulations again on doing your work so perfectly and staying true to the path of the Divine Spirit despite all the odds against you. This is a time of great celebration and we have come to celebrate our future together with you. The cosmos is filled with radiant beings who are cheering for you now, and saying thank you for restoring balance to our universe in the eternal battle against evil.

Yes, this is the dawning of a new world, the world of the Fifth Sun. And the upcoming rising of the Yellow Sun will be the first. We have come to join you to celebrate this and to celebrate the purity of the new Earth, which is the soil for the next generations of life to come. We have waited a long time for this special day to come. We have never known the precise date. We have only known that the time would come. Like you, this is the manifestation of a vision that is of titanic proportions, not only for this Mother Earth but for the entire universe. We have always known the prophesies would come true, as they have. We have known that if the Earth was to be remade, she would first need to unmade. This is precisely what has happened. The world has been reshaped, with catastrophic tragedy and death to humanity that was not prepared, as you were. Remember we've been through this before. This is the fourth time this has happened, and each time a tiny percentage of humanity survived to be the ones to start over again, and get it right this time. This is what the prophesies tell us.

As you have already experienced on this night, the world is going to be very different now. Yes, an energetic veil had been lifted, and new energies are flooding in and will continue to flood in. It may be difficult for you for awhile. You will be like children again, having to learn everything all over again. Another of the things that's going to be different is your relationship with us, not only those of us who are visiting today, but all benevolent extraterrestrial life. We are only the first wave. There are many more of us, in all shapes, sizes and energy configurations. This is another reason why today is so special for us. The malevolent beings with their malevolent energy tricked most of humanity into giving their consent to their rule over them. This prevented us from getting involved directly, according to intergalactic law. With them gone, we are now free to communicate with you more directly and work with you more directly, as we are now, with your consent of course. If you want us to go away, all you have to do is say so. We cannot be here without your consent. That's the law.

Yes, we will be able to communicate with you now directly, as we are now. And you will be able to communicate with us. You can right now. All you have to do is call out, kind of like with your obsolete phones. We will respond. And it is our job to work with you. There is much to do. We understand that the work of your sustainable community is more than a full-time job. There are many others like you, surrounding the globe, not as many as we had hoped, but enough. The time will

soon come when you must reach out to connect
with them. The long-term goal must be for you to
form a network for the stewardship of the Earth.
You can share ideas and technology. There are also
many survivors out there who are in desperate
straits and who need help. We can help you with
these things. We can help you to develop new
forms of technology, new forms of communication.
Your reserves of gasoline and oil will not last
forever. Your solar system too will wear out and
must be replaced. Circumstances will force you to
develop alternative fuels and even new kinds of
machinery. We understand Don is already doing
that with his motor that extracts energy from the air.
We can help you with these things too. And we are
going to help to clean up the mess that now exists
on this beautiful planet. This will be highly
complicated, not impossible. There are extremely
high levels of radioactivity in many places, and in
the water, and things like ships and warehouses full
of nuclear and biological weapons. We can clean
much of this up and set the weapons off in deep
space where they won't hurt anything. There is
much to do. Our goal is the same as yours: to create
a world in which humanity is free to fulfill their
destiny as servants of the Earth.

But enough business. The Yellow Sun will be
rising soon, and we are going to come down now to
join you and to celebrate. We no longer have
physical bodies. So we must embrace you the only
way we can, with our energy fields. It's necessary
for you to lighten up a little too. We will help with
that also.

The perfect silence remained.
The instant he finished they all felt the same thing. It was
like a beam of energy possessed each of them and took over their
physical bodies. They felt tingly and light and blissful. Then their

bodies started to glow. Pretty soon their physical features weren't distinguishable anymore. Their humanoid shape remained, but now it was pure golden light that glowed. After this transformation, their energy bodies were also smaller than before, by about one quarter. They all shrunk. This energy apparently didn't take up as much space.

When this transformation was complete, the celestial beings started to descend from the light of the golden disc above them. They emerged together from one mass of light and separated as they slowly drifted down through the misty light in the cone.. They too were composed of light with humanoid shape. But as they floated down, this light was wispy and transparent, like wraiths. One of these humanoid shapes landed softly in front of each of them, on their feet. Then they too made the gradual transformation to solid gold with a glow. They too were smaller, and in each case their size matched the size of who they were paired with.

In each case, the celestial beings were standing over their partners, most of whom were sitting cross-legged before their mesas. A few were sitting in folding chairs. The celestial beings then rose slightly off ground and rotated slowly, like they were weightless, toward their partners. They continued to float slowly toward them, and when they touched, they slowly disappeared into them. They entered them, one energy field merging with another. One moment there were two energy bodies and the next there was only one.

David knew that Kaleen was the energy body before him. He didn't know how. He just knew. Kaleen had said they could speak out now. David couldn't resist the urge to try.

"Hello Kaleen."

He said these words, but he didn't know how. He could feel no mouth in this light body. He willed the words, and they emanated from him, in a calm, soothing, sublime tone. He knew that his words could be heard by Kaleen alone. He couldn't feel his eyes either, but he looked at Kaleen's face in front of his, which was just a ball of golden light, no eyes, mouth, ears, nose.

"Hello David, my cosmic brother" was the soft reply.

Like before, the sound was in David's head.

Kaleen continued to float weightlessly toward him. When their heads touched, all David could see was golden light. This lasted a moment or two. It was hard to tell because everything was so timeless. He also had an odd feeling of giving his permission, of saying yes to being entered in this way. When his sight returned, he could see the other luminous bodies, all 17 of them, sitting in a circle around the fire. Those on the other side of the circle had turned around to see the sunrise. They were still enveloped in the cone of misty light from the ship above, with solid walls of light that couldn't be seen through.

With Kaleen inside him, David was having feelings he'd never had before. He'd have to learn a new language to describe it. He could feel Kaleen inside him. He could feel his essence, body, mind, heart and spirit. And he felt it throughout the totality of his current luminous form. The new energy felt warm, like a warm bath, in every cell of his body. And it felt loving, and yes, sensuous. David could feel Kaleen's field intermingling with his in a way that was pleasurable. It was like their luminous bodies were gently fondling and stroking each other, which they might have been. And David could feel Kaleen's power, as a far more advanced light being from a higher dimension. This power was so far beyond David's at his current stage of development that it could have been humiliating. But David's reaction was just the opposite. Kaleen's power empowered him. He felt the potential of this power within himself, just waiting to be tapped, just waiting to be learned. And now he had a teacher. Kaleen's power made him feel that anything was possible.

And then, they all saw it as one.

On the eastern wall of the cone of light the crown of the Yellow Sun was breaking the horizon. Nothing else could be seen through wall of light. But this light had no problem shining through. At first it was just a point of very bright light. It slowly grew into its circular shape. It was so bright that normally you would squint or look away. These luminous bodies couldn't squint, so they just took the bright light in. They watched in a perfect meditative state as he took his full circular shape and broke free from the horizon, which they couldn't see.

They sat with this for awhile. Who knows how long, maybe 15 minutes? Then Kaleen made the announcement that they all could hear.

"We will be leaving you now. Thank you, Grandfather Sun, for the blessing of your rising on this the first day of the Era of the Fifth Sun. Thank you, Rainbow Village, for the blessing of this sacred union of our energies. And we look forward to developing our relationship with you on into the future and working together to build the new Earth."

And then he said something only David could hear.

"Until we meet again, David. You are a true cosmic brother. This council and the universe thank you for your generous service."

David willed his words.

"Thank you, and thank you for all your help, brother Kaleen."

The luminous beings pulled out and away from the bodies of humans, just as they had entered. Their brightness faded, and they rose like wraiths, just like before, back up into the mass of golden light on the bottom of the disc. The cone of light and the field of light within it were then flicked off. At that same instant, the bodies of those sitting around the fire returned to their physical form, same size, shape and color, with all their normal sensations. And then the golden ship whisked off and disappeared into the blue sky, without making a sound, just as it had come.

There they were, sitting around the fire. Everything had returned to normal. It had been awhile. Though what usually passed as normal would never be again.

Everybody in the circle felt precisely the same thing. There was a sense of finality in this moment. It was over. What had started yesterday when it cleared up and they spontaneously gathered, and then extended into a night of astral travelling with the lights in the sky, and then culminated with their sacred union with the benevolent ET's, was now over. The ceremony was complete.

They looked at each other, back and forth. Everybody was placidly grinning.

They had returned to the material 3rd Dimension, though none of them knew if those rules still applied. After all the transformation they'd been through, maybe this was a higher dimension. There was no way to know. They would figure it out as they went along.

There was one thing each of them knew for certain. Things weren't the way they were before, even as recently as yesterday. The entire world looked different. As they looked at each other and around at the mountains, the sky, the trees, all the colors were brighter and more vivid. Again, it was like a film had been removed from over their world. And the way that they felt was different too. They felt lighter and this world felt lighter. And all of their senses seemed to have come more to life. The whole world was more sensuous. The morning air caressed their skin with coolness. The crackling of the fire sounded resonant and vibrant. The gurgling and flowing of the water was a song for their souls. And the mood of the group was ebullient, ecstatic. They were like children who couldn't wait to see what was going to happen next. Yes, this mood could change. After all, they just came off this amazing experience. But who knows? Maybe the rules would be different now. Only one way to find out.

David smiled at them. He didn't want to talk. Words really didn't seem necessary. Maybe this would be another new feature of the new world, less talk. Everybody knew what they personally experienced. And everybody knew that everybody experienced the same thing and experienced it together. And everybody knew that the experience was over. So what was there to talk about?

David knew it was time to speak and he knew instantly where he wanted to go.

"Spotted Deer, I see you've brought a cooler and some bowls. May I ask what that is?"

"Yes, berries, corn and venison."

"Awe! That's so perfect," he exclaimed. "Can you get some of the young people to help you and can you serve that, please?"

Then he spoke to all of them.

"Then we will conclude this ceremony with the eating of the berries, the corn and the meat. And then let's gather at the community house and make a ceremonial breakfast that befits this incredible occasion."

That was it. He would say no more.

Small wooden bowls were passed around, then larger bowls with the berries, corn and meat. Everybody served themselves a small portion and ate with their fingers.

This practice was purely ceremonial. It had nothing to do with eating breakfast. And it was reserved for the most special ceremonies. They only did it a couple times a year.

After they cleaned up and everybody was back in their place, David got up to close the ceremony.

They closed their ceremonies the same way many indigenous and spiritual groups do, with the circle uncoiling in a clockwise direction and with everybody hugging everybody. It starts with the person on the immediate left of the eastern entrance, who hugs the person to their left. Then they continue around the circle until they've hugged everybody and they leave out the eastern entrance. That person is followed by the first person they hugged, and this continues until the circle is empty. They had a rule that there was no talking during this.

Since David and Kelly were on the western side of the circle, they were about in the middle of this whole process.

When they departed the circle, Chris was waiting for them. He looked troubled, holding his mouth stiff, breathing heavily.

"It's Jack. He wants to talk to you, both of you."

During the uncoiling they both noticed that Jack didn't join in. He was still in his folding chair, in front of his mesa, tilted back, with his feet slightly up. This was unusual, but there were a lot of weird things going on. They both intended to check in with him.

Jack was in the southern part of the circle, which was unoccupied.

David and Kelly reentered and walked over to him.

His eyes were closed. He was smiling and his face was beatific. His head was resting on his favorite Mayan pillow and his long silver hair was bunched up around his head and shoulders like the lion he often saw himself to be. They both noticed he wasn't wearing his glasses, which he was totally blind without.

They stood over him for a moment.

Jack's eyes opened slightly. They were very glassy. He spoke in a whisper.

"Come, come down, close to me. I haven't much strength.

They kneeled down, one on either side of him, and leaned over so their faces were close to his.

Jack's hands were in his lap.

"Please take one of my hands, each of you."

They did this.

"Thank you."

He looked intently at David, then at Kelly. He looked back and forth at them while he whispered.

"My son, my daughter, I thank the divine spirit everyday for bringing you to me. I couldn't love you any more if you were my flesh and blood."

He closed his eyes, then opened them again.

"We did it. I have lived to see the dawning of the 5th Sun. I have lived to see the defeat of the evil ones. I have lived to see our union with the ET's. I feel so incredibly complete. This is how my book ended."

He smiled as he said this. They could feel him gently squeezing their hands. There was almost no strength left.

"I'm going to be leaving now. The next time I close my eyes I won't be coming back. There's almost nothing left of me. I can't even feel my body anymore. And it feels wonderful, no more pain. And I'm so ready, so willing. Wherever I'm going is where I'm meant to be now. Please say goodbye to everybody. Tell them I love them and thank them for this miraculous achievement, Rainbow Village, the last outpost of the old world and the first outpost of the new. I don't want to say goodbye to them. I'm afraid I might snap out of it. And I really want to fall asleep now."

He smiled again.

"There's a will up at the house. I left it where you can easily find it. Please bury me in the site I have selected in the woods behind the house. No more government, so we don't need to worry about being told what to do with our bodies. Go now. Come back in a few hours and I will be gone."

He looked at each of them.

"Goodbye David, Goodbye Kelly."

He closed his eyes, never to open them again, and began his journey to the next world.

Jack Allis

APPENDIX

THE STORY OF THE BLUE KACHINA
& THE RED KACHINA
As Passed on to Robert Ghost Wolf
By Chief Dan Evehema,
Hopi Traditional Caretaker

The story of the Blue Kachina is a very old story, very old. I have been aware of the story of the Blue Kachina since I was very young. I was told this story by grandfathers who are now between 80 and 108 years of age. Frank Waters also wrote about Saquasohuh, the Blue Star Kachina, in "The Book of the Hopi." The story came from Grandfather Dan, oldest Hopi.

It was told to me that first the Blue Kachina would start of be seen at the dances, and would make his appearance known to the children in the plaza during the night dance. This event would tell us that end times are very near. Then, the Blue Star Kachina would physically appear in our heavens, which would mean that we were in the end times.

In the final days, we will look up in our heavens, and we will witness the return of the two brothers, who helped create this world in the birthing time. Poganghoya is the guardian of our North Pole, and his brother, Palongawhoya, is the guardian of the South Pole. In the final days, the Blue Star Kachina will come to be with his nephews, and they will return the Earth to its natural rotation, which is counter-clockwise.

This fact is evidenced in many petroglyphs that speak of the Zodiac, and within the Mayan and Egyptian pyramids. The rotation of the Earth has been manipulated by not so benevolent star beings. The twins will be seen in our northwestern skies. They will come and visit to see who still remembered the original teachings, flying in their Patuwvotas, or flying shields. They will bring many of their star family with them in the final days.

The return of the Blue Star Kachina, who is also known as Nan ga sohu, will be the alarm clock that tells us of the new day and the new way of life, a new world that is coming. This is where the changes will begin. They will start as fires that burn within us, and we will burn up with desires and conflict if we do not remember the original teachings, and return to the peaceful way of life.

Not far behind the twins will come the Purifier, the Red Star Kachina, who will bring the day of purification. On this day the Earth, her creatures, and all life as we know it will change forever. There will be messengers that will precede this coming of the Purifier. They will leave messages to those on Earth who remember the old ways.

The messages will be found written in the living stone, through the sacred grains, and even the waters. (Crop circles have been found in ice) From the Purifier will issue forth a great Red Light. All things will change in their manner of being. Every living thing will be offered the opportunity to change from the largest to the smallest thing.

Those who return to the ways given to us in the original teachings, and live a natural way of life will not be touched by the coming of the Purifier. They will survive and build the new world. Only in the ancient teachings will the ability to understand the messages be found.

It is important to understand that these messages will be found upon every living thing, even within our bodies, even within a drop of our blood. All life forms will receive the messages from the twins, those that fly, the plants, even the rabbit. The appearance of the twins begins a period of seven years, which will be our final opportunity to change our ways. Everything we experience is all a matter of choice.

Many will appear to have lost their souls in these final days. So intense will the nature of the changes be that those who are weak in spiritual awareness will go insane, for we are nothing without spirit. They will disappear, for they are just hollow vessels for anything to use. Life will be so bad in the cities that many will choose to leave this plane, some in whole groups.

Only those who return to the values of the old ways will be able to find peace of mind. For in the Earth we shall find relief from the madness that will be all around us. It will be a very hard time for women with children for they will be shunned, and many of the children in these times will be unnatural. Some being from the stars, some from past worlds, some will even be created by man in an unnatural manner, and will be soulless. Many of the people in this time will be empty in Spirit. They will have Sampacu, no life-force in their eyes.

As we get close to the time of the arrival of the Purifier, there will be those who walk as ghosts through the cities, through canyons they will have constructed in their man-made mountains. Those that walk through these places will be very heavy in their walk. It will appear almost painful as they take each step for they will be disconnected from their spirit and the Earth.

After the arrival of the twins, they will begin to vanish before your eyes like so much smoke. Others will have great deformities, both in the mind and upon their bodies. There will be those who would walk in the body that are not from this reality, for many of the gateways that once protected us will be opened. There will be much confusion, confusion between sexes, and children and their elders.

Life will get very perverted, and there will be little social order in these times. Many will ask for the mountains themselves to fall upon them just to end their misery. Still others will appear as if untouched by what is occurring - the ones who remember the original teachings and have reconnected their hearts and spirit - those who remember who their mother and father is – the Pahana who have left to live in the Mountains and forest.

When the purifier comes we will see him first as a small Red Star which will come very close, and sit in our heavens watching us. Watching us to see how well we have remembered the sacred teachings.

This Purifier will show us many miraculous signs in our heavens. In this way, we will know Creator is not a dream. Even those who do not feel their connection to spirit will see the face of Creator across the sky. Things unseen will be felt very strongly.

Many things will begin to occur that will not make sense, for reality will be shifting back in and out of the dream state. There will be many doorways to the lower world that will open at this time. Things long forgotten will come back to remind us of our past creations. All living things will want to be present for this day when time ends, and we enter the forever cycle of the Fifth World.

We will receive many warnings allowing us to change our ways from below the Earth as well as above. Then one morning, in a moment, we will awaken to the Red Dawn. The sky will be the color of blood. Many things will then begin to happen that right now we are not sure of their exact nature, for much of reality will not be as it is now.

There will be many strange beasts upon the Earth in those days, some from the past and some that we have never seen. The nature of mankind will appear strange in these times when we walk between worlds, and we will house many spirits, even within our bodies. After a time we will again walk with our brothers from the stars, and rebuild this Earth, but not until the Purifier has left his mark upon the universe.

No living thing will go untouched, here or in the heavens. The way through this time, it is said, is to be found in our hearts, and reuniting with our spiritual self. Getting simple and returning to living with and upon the Earth and in harmony with her creatures, remembering that we are the caretakers, the fire keepers of the Spirit. Our relatives from the stars are coming home to see how well we have fared on our journey.

ABOUT JACK ALLIS

Jack Allis is an author and spiritual teacher, who practices what he preaches, living a life that embodies the messages he transmits in his books and DVD's. His most recent novel, *Blue Sun, Red Sun,* tells the epic story that follows ancient Hopi prophesy about a small sustainable community in the remote mountains, which survives the devastation of the Earth caused by the dual catastrophes of the crash of the world economy and the worst world-wide storm in history, to see the dawning of a new world, the world of the Fifth Sun. Jack's personal life mirrors this. In December 2012 he took a hiatus from his writing and public appearances, and moved to the remote mountains north of sacred Mount Shasta, where he lives off the grid and in harmony with nature, preparing as much as possible, both practically and spiritually, for the monumental paradigm shifts that are still to come. Now he is back, sharing this epic story about how we, humanity, can reassume our responsibility as caretakers of Mother Earth and play our part in creating a new world.

His previous three books and two DVD's dealt with 2012 and the shift and how to take the necessary spiritual action to be able to flow with the transformative energies of these unprecedented times. Two other themes are recurrent in Jack's work and essential to understanding the truth about our world. One is the extraterrestrial presence and the fact that ET's have tinkered in human affairs for hundreds of thousands of years. The other is the conspiracy in which a small elite group of humans or beings have ruled the world from behind the scenes through deceit and manipulation for millennia and created the illusion that people are free, when in fact they are slaves. Yet, it means nothing to know these things without knowing how we can get ourselves out of this mess, both individually and collectively. This is the focus of all of Jack's work. He also shows people how to take spiritual action in their lives through the use of ceremony. This includes prayer, fire ceremonies, drumming and music, and singing and chanting. Get in the loop now by subscribing to his popular monthly newsletter, or check out his books, DVD's, videos, photos, audios and articles at www.jackallis.com.

Made in the USA
San Bernardino, CA
08 August 2017